The Overland Kid

MAX BRAND™

The Overland Kid
A Western Trio

Five Star
Unity, Maine

Five Star Western
Published in conjunction with Golden West Literary Agency

Cover photograph by Robert Darby

March 2000

First Edition

Five Star Standard Print Western Series.

The text of this edition is unabridged.

Set in 11 pt. Plantin by Al Chase.

Printed in the United States on permanent paper.

Library of Congress Cataloging-in-Publication Data
Brand, Max, 1892–1944.
    The overland kid : a western trio / by Max Brand. — 1st ed.
      p.   cm.
    Stories originally published between 1922 and 1934 in
Western story magazine under the author's other names,
John Frederick and George Owen Baxter.
    "Published in conjunction with the Golden West Literary
Agency" — T.p. verso.
    "Five Star western."
    Contents: The cabin in the pines — Joe White's brand —
The overland kid.
    ISBN 0-7862-1846-0 (hc : alk. paper)
    1. Frontier and pioneer life — West (U.S.) — Fiction.
2. Western stories.   I. Title.
PS3511.A87 A6 2000
  812´.54—dc21
                                     99-055131

TABLE OF CONTENTS

The Cabin in the Pines

Although still early in his career, 1922 saw forty-one Frederick Faust stories published in magazines under various of his many pen-names. Of these forty-one stories, eleven were serials. This short novel, "The Cabin in the Pines," appeared toward the end of the year in the issue of Street and Smith's *Western Story Magazine* dated December 9, 1922. It is the story of Babe Rourke and Angus Cairn, two giants among men whose similarly large reputations make them adversaries before they actually meet. Their enmity goes through several permutations after a chance encounter occurs in a cabin in the pines.

I

"Wolf and Mastiff"

He was marked three ways at his birth. His hair was red, his name was Rourke, and his weight was thirteen pounds. When he was thirteen years old he stood five feet and eight inches, weighed a hundred and fifty pounds of wildcat fighting strength, dared the whole world to battle with his pale blue eyes, and was known as Babe. It was such a misnomer as the West delights in. Moreover, Babe had been homeless, fatherless, motherless since infancy. His parent was Chance, and he looked the proper child of such a parent.

At fifteen he had topped six feet and put out his arms and declared himself a man. It was the golden age for Babe. His fame had not yet filled the mountains. He could find districts where he was unknown. Neither did he seem particularly imposing until he was in a rage. The result was by industrious hunting he averaged pretty close to a fight a day. Knife, gun, fists—it mattered not to Babe. He had the sensitive nose of a bloodhound and could scent trouble miles away.

He was not always victorious, but he could say that he had never been beaten in fair fight by any single man. And that was what saved him and his pride. To be sure two French-Canadians cornered him one day and beat him almost to death, with loaded blacksnakes. On another occasion, he was tied in his bed and thrashed with a horsewhip until he bled from a thousand slashes. Twice he was knocked down from behind with the blow of a club and left for dead. Once he was

9

ambushed and shot from his horse with a bullet through his thigh. Once he was stabbed through the throat by an irate Mexican.

But the main thing was that he lived; also, he never forgot. He found the men who had ambushed him. One by one they went down. It was said that he trailed the French-Canadians clear to Hudson Bay and then west and north into Alaska. He was two whole years on that trail. When he came back he was twenty-one—and hard!

Why he should have made the wretched village of Krugerville home, nobody could tell. But, because he had been born there, a relentless instinct, as strong as the instinct of the carrier pigeon, drove him back after every exploit. The sheriff used to say that, if Babe Rourke broke the law, he would not be hard to capture. A short process of time would bring him inevitably back to Krugerville and the waiting arms of the law.

The sheriff was a patient man. He had waited for the time when Babe should break the law. And when Babe came in from that long Canadian trail, the sheriff knew that, if he could find the true story of what had happened among the snows, Babe would, indeed, be ready for the gallows.

For, as has been said, Babe returned from the Northland as hard as nails. There was a hawk look in his eyes that was new; there was a shifting uneasiness in his glance; there was a fondness for the corner of the room with the wall at his back; there was a strange ability to step soft and soundless in spite of his bulk. In a word he had become one whom other men shunned because he carried the sign of his might in his face.

Only in Krugerville men looked upon him with less fear and more admiration. For it was known that in Krugerville he put on his gentler manner. He relaxed and unbent and smiled in the home port after many batterings of storm at sea. And so

Krugerville surveyed her most famous son. It found him towering up some four inches above six feet. It found him vast of shoulder and tapering to lean hips and thighs. It marked the floors bending and moaning under his two hundred and thirty pounds, from which all fat had been burned away. He would put on ten pounds more when he reached the very crest and bloom of manhood, they declared.

But in the mountains he was man enough for any. He looked five years older than his age. Women declared that he would have been very handsome if it were not that one side of his face was marked by a scar. The same scar drew the cheek muscles a little, so that he seemed to be perpetually smiling in mockery and contempt of the rest of the world.

Perhaps in spite of the scar and the sneer people would have found him good to look on, if it had not been for the intolerable steadiness of his eyes that were never contented until they had forced another pair of eyes to meet them, until they had bored into the other and forced his glance to the floor. It was bad enough to use such tactics with men, but Babe Rourke used them with women, also. Men said that he had been poisoned by a lady whose admirer he had removed from this vale of tears. But whether he had been poisoned or not, Babe looked upon a woman as a serpent. The entrance of a woman made him more nervous than the entrance of a man with a drawn gun.

When Babe came back from his long trail into Canada, he found that the flower and the sunshine of his life had faded. There was no more fighting. Men avoided him as they might avoid a pest. The only way he could draw action on his head was to hunt out groups. One man, even a brave man, thought it no shame to flee from him. Even two would retreat, but three determined characters would stand their ground.

But law-abiding men do not gather in groups of three and

prepare for battle. It is the outlaw who seeks shelter in numbers. So Babe enlisted on the side of the law and went out in quest of adventure as a sworn deputy to the sheriff. Now the list of his exploits grew. He made his district in the mountains so safe that a man could hang a gold watch on a bush and come back at the end of a month and find it still there. He was like a pestilence that decimated the ranks of the wrong-doers.

Not that people gave him credit as a loyal upholder of the law. They recognized the truth—that he fought for the mere love of battle which was the light deep within his blue eyes. They did not love him for his valor; they dreaded him on account of it. They looked upon him as upon a natural prodigy. It was not until another wielder of terror came out of the North to challenge the supremacy of Babe that the men of Krugerville awakened to the discovery that they were proud of their man-killing giant.

First they would not believe that another such man could exist. They did not know the old law that Mother Earth produces her strange births in clusters and not singly. When finally Angus Cairn came in person into the town of Krugerville, the town saw, wondered, and believed.

Cairn was as large as Babe. Yes, by actual measurement he was larger. The door of the entrance to the hotel dining room, under which Babe could barely stand erect, was low enough for Angus Cairn to bump his head on and curse prodigiously as he did so. He was not only a half inch taller than Babe, but he was bulkier as well—not wider of shoulder, but built solidly from head to foot. He must outweigh Babe by a full twenty pounds. But granting all this, the townsfolk said that mere size was the least of Babe's acquirements. What was Angus Cairn without that magic of hand that had made Babe great—that uncanny deftness with weapons?

They had not long to wait for a demonstration. The

Christy brothers and their followers, who had long lived soberly in dread of the terrible Rourke, had chosen this occasion of his absence to come down out of the mountains and harry the home town of the giant. But, although they found Babe gone, they found an awful substitute in his place.

It all happened in the hotel. They came in with a rush. With the flash of their weapons they scattered the men who were there—all save one, and that one was Angus Cairn. Truthful men swore that Angus lifted a two-hundred-pound table from the floor, as though it were a stool, and cast it at the invaders. Three of them went down under the shock. He finished three more with his revolver. One man escaped to his horse and was dropped from the saddle with a snap shot.

When the tumult and the shouting died away, the men of Krugerville came stealing back to look and listen, and they saw three dead men and three living men tied in a bundle like so many sacks, and Angus Cairn was seated in a corner, quietly smoking a cigarette.

Then it was that, with bitterness of spirit, the men of Krugerville admitted that a man as great as Rourke had come out of the North. They stared upon him more particularly. In every respect, except in size, he was the exact opposite of Babe. He was about thirty in the first place, a full eight years older than Rourke. In the second place, Babe was pale, with a pallor that no sun could change to a tan, but Cairn was swarthy as evening. Babe was red-headed; Cairn's hair was as black as ink, and it was rather long, curling hair, and he wore a square-trimmed, short, curling black beard that gave his fierce face a Biblical air of gravity. Like Babe he was handsome in a way, but whereas actual scars marred the features of Babe, it was an expression of dour malignity that clouded the good looks of Angus Cairn.

Such was the monster the men of Krugerville found after

his victory on the scene of the battle. Presently he reared himself from his chair. Their murmurs of praise and of wonder died away. As he stood up, they noted him in closer detail. If Rourke was like a great wolf, this fellow was like a giant mastiff. Unquestionably he was the stronger man.

"Are there any friends of Rourke around these parts?" asked the big man.

A faint chorus of affirmation followed.

"Well, then," said Angus Cairn, "you can tell him that I been hearing a pile of talk about him. Some folks goes as far as to say that he's quite a man. You tell this Rourke that I sure hate to leave so sudden. But I got business on hand. I'm sorry that I ain't found him home, but I'm coming back a week from today, which is Tuesday. I'm coming riding into town about sunset time, and, if I find him here, I'll be mighty glad to look him over. Tell him that from Angus Cairn!"

Then the man of the black beard strode from the room, went to the stables, saddled and mounted a horse hardly less than a monster among his kind than Cairn was among men, and so thundered down the street of Krugerville and away into the dark of the night.

II

"A Mongrel Dog"

Bad news travels on a buzzard's wing. In a day it seemed that the story had been broadcast by men who had spurred relays of swift horses through the mountains. Before nightfall out-of-town people began to drop into Krugerville. They were like the early comers at a prize fight, eager for seats beside the ring. Moreover, who could tell if the fight would not come off before the scheduled date?

Babe Rourke came in two days after Cairn had left. He had heard the story on his way back. When the townsfolk stared anxiously upon him, as though to ask in what sort of fighting condition he found himself, he merely grinned upon them. Nevertheless, he was impressed. The strongest lion that ever lived alone in the desert is impressed when he sees across the wastes the shadow of one of his own kind approaching. Babe Rourke cast back in his mind to his fights with other men. But since he was a youngster the only equal fights he had fought had been against odds. Three to one—that was about the right proportion to make an interesting brawl. A lesser number did not interest him. He had only to get to close quarters and smash the ribs of the two with one grizzly hug. But here was a man who had ridden into his home town and delivered a challenge to meet him at a definite date, at an appointed hour. To say the least, it was very, very strange.

The next day he rode out of town and kept going until he felt that he was alone. Here, in the solitude, he practiced almost daily with rifle and revolver. He tried all manner of shots. He tossed up stones with one hand and shot them with the other. He tossed up two stones at a time. He threw up three stones at a time, and, two times out of three, he had nicked them all with bullets before they struck the dirt. Yes, his skill with guns was in no wise impaired. A barbed-wire fence was at a great distance. The strands of the wire were a mere twinkling, disappearing edges of light. He cut four strands with four rifle shots.

But mere precision was a small thing. If the fight should turn out to be with guns, it was speed of hand—lightning speed of hand that would count. So he practiced the art of the draw. Before he had drawn the heavy Colt twice, his whole arm, his whole body was trembling with nervous eagerness. It was not a gesture—that convulsion of wrist and fingers that conjured the gun forth. It was an explosion of energy, the leap of an electric spark.

How could a human hand move more swiftly? But what one man can do, another can do. To be sure, he had never met his master, but, for that matter, Angus Cairn had doubtless never met his. Otherwise that challenge would never have been sent. No matter how many hours he had practiced, Angus Cairn might have practiced as many.

Babe Rourke rode back into Krugerville a nervous man. And he found a nervous frown awaiting his coming. For, of course, he had been followed. His performance had been observed. And, although it was a marvelous exhibition, the fact that Babe was so unsure of himself that he had to practice put a dent in the faith of Krugerville. Men like to feel a mystery about their heroes. It is not enough that a man conquer—he must conquer with a consummate ease. He must be invincible. His vulnerable spot, if he has one, must be no more than the heel.

Some of the aroma of invincibility in that instant evaporated from Babe in his home town. No matter that the cunning spy, who had followed and seen all, related the wonder of the severed strands of wire. No matter that he told of the little stones that winked in the sunshine one moment and were knocked into dust the next. What really mattered was that Babe should require practice. It was most disheartening. It was as disheartening as the knowledge that the poet does not sit down and dash off a masterpiece in five careless minutes. When it is known that he must work, men shrug their shoulders. Anyone can work.

So it was in Krugerville. In spite of the size and the prowess of Cairn, there had not been a stir of doubt as to the outcome of the Homeric conflict that was to take place. They were eager to see the fight, of course; but it was like another battle between Achilles and Hector. The gods were against Cairn. He was brave in a lost cause.

That feeling passed in a twinkling, and a profound concern took its place. Men muttered in corners with scowling brows. Gamblers began to place odds—one to five that Cairn would win—one to four that he would win—one to three that he would win. On the morning of the last fatal day reasonable men were betting even money that Angus Cairn would be the conqueror. Even in so short a space had the faith of Krugerville vanished!

Worst of all, Rourke had breathed that poisonous air of doubt. The passing of time, while he waited for sunset on Tuesday, was like the dropping of water upon the stone of his courage, and it wore him away. It was a test for which his nerves were not keyed. He was not equipped to meet this trial. He could fight against any odds on the spur of the moment, but to wait a stretch of five days among dubious companions was too much.

His sleep was broken. He wakened with a start in the middle of the night and found that his body was covered with perspiration. Dark purple shadows began to appear under his eyes. Even in broad daylight small noises made him start violently.

Tuesday was an unforgettable day. He sat in at a game of poker in the morning and managed to waste time until noon. But the afternoon was an eternity. When the sun at last dropped into the west and rested its rim on a hilltop, Rourke was at the breaking point. The street was clear, but every front porch up and down its length was occupied. Men and women and children sat at upper windows watching the porch of the hotel, where Rourke was waiting for the foe. But down the street came no giant horseman on a giant horse. Amazement began to grow. The orb of the sun dipped slowly down and disappeared. But still the red was in the west, and so long as the color lasted, no matter how dim, it might be called sunset time.

Eventually the past particle of color was gone, and the dimmest of twilight settled over the town, and the stars came out in bright hosts and burned low in the sky. But still Angus Cairn did not come. A murmur of disgust was growing through the town.

Then it was that Rourke stood up and stamped into the hotel. His face was the face of an old man. He went straight to a back room, kicked open the door, and sat down in a chair. It was the center from which moonshine of potent powers and dubious quality was dispersed through the town when the sheriff was away. And the sheriff was away now.

"Hello!" roared the voice of Rourke. "Everybody liquor. Trot out the stuff, Andy. I'm dry!"

Babe was dry, indeed, and he was dry to the bone with a consuming thirst. Not that he was a drinking man. Leading such a life as he led he dared not be under the influence of alcohol often, but now he yearned for the burn of it in his throat, the burn of it in his brain until the nerve strain was loosened, relaxed, forgotten.

A hundred other men were of his mind at this moment. They packed into the back room of the hotel, and there was a swift filling of glasses. Everyone wanted to get as close as possible to Rourke. He had been reëstablished as an invincible. The mere weight of his name had kept Angus Cairn away. It was all easy enough to explain, now that it had happened. In the interim Cairn had heard tales of the exploits of Rourke. He had heard far more than he had stomach for, and the result was that he had absented himself from the appointed meeting, thinking that a shamed life was better than no life at all.

So the red-eye flowed in the back room, and the only argument left was whether or not those who had wagered on Angus Cairn should not lose their money because their champion had not appeared. And those who had made the bets were almost willing to forfeit the sums rather than let Rourke know that they had ventured their money against his chances.

No one, however, pressed his claims very far. There was a general spirit of good nature, an enlarging of the heart, an open-handed carelessness. In the midst of that good feeling no one paid any heed when a little gray-and-brown mongrel cur sneaked through the open door and wandered into the room.

It was a spiritless sneak of a dog. When a man walking in thumped his heavy toe against the little beast and knocked it a dozen feet across the room, it was too frightened even to squeal. It only crouched and whimpered silently and raised its head and watched the man with its haunting eyes.

After a time it gathered courage to proceed again with investigations. Although it was trembling with fear, something made it go around from man to man, stand on its hind legs, and plant its forepaws on knee after knee.

There was only one answer to this maneuver—an oath and a heavy open-handed blow that knocked the dog headlong. Yet the stupid creature went on until it came to the last person in the circle, the formidable bulk of Rourke himself. When he raised and put his paws on Rourke's knee, the half-drunk giant scooped him up with a monster hand.

"Sit down, captain!" he said to the dog, patting the little fellow on his knee. "Sit down and tell me about yourself."

But the dog wriggled away and jumped to the floor. He ran halfway to the door and turned his head to look back. Rourke was already oblivious of his existence, talking loudly with a companion. The mongrel came back and jumped into the lap of the giant. This time he caught the projecting stem of a pipe in Rourke's pocket, jerked it out, and jumped down to the floor, trotting slowly toward the door and always looking back to wait.

Rourke rose with an oath. "By guns," he exclaimed, "there's something in that pup's fool head, or I'm a liar!"

III

"The Prostrate Figure"

As Babe walked forward, the mongrel fled through the door, but there he turned and looked back, his head cocked to one side, with the pipe thrust out at a foolish angle from his mouth and his little flop-ended ears pricked up.

Rourke walked down the hall, and still the dog trotted ahead, looking back. Through the main door, across the verandah, and into the street it led. Babe Rourke paused at the head of the steps and looked down on the tiny vagrant. He was irritated at the thought of his best pipe being worried in those sharp teeth. But even in his sober moments he was a gentle man with animals, however fierce with men. Besides, the fiery moonshine had mellowed his humor.

He followed down the steps and mounted a broad-backed roan gelding tethered at the rack, a brute made for endurance and carrying power. Even under the bulk of Rourke the gelding had done eighty miles over happy country in a single day. Now it jogged forward down the street.

At the sight of the man on horseback the little dog went into a frenzy of pleasure. It came back on the run, leaped up to touch noses with the horse, and, yelping for delight, lost the pipe in the dust. Before it could pick up the pipe again, Rourke had swung to the side deftly and scooped his pipe from the dust. But when the cur saw that the rider was still willing to follow, even though the pipe was in his pocket again, he loped off contentedly down the street.

Rourke followed, grumbling his wonder. The dog was plainly leading him to something. He had heard stories of such guidance before, but it seemed a wonderful thing to watch now. Doubtless the trail would be to a buried bone or some such other treasure. Yet Rourke followed, laughing at himself and at the absurd and joyous antics of the little dog.

In another moment, they were climbing a hill outside the town, reached the crest, and then began the descent. By this time Babe Rourke was sobering. Following a stray dog as leader through the night was a little outside his ordinary habits. And suppose that Angus Cairn arrived in town late, but ready for battle? What interpretation would be used to explain the retreat of Rourke?

However, he dismissed Cairn with a heavy curse and rode on. There was something more than humanly appealing in the way the little animal ahead of him led on, turning now and again to watch the lumbering creatures he was guiding, and even coming back, now and again, to jump up at the nose of the horse and yelp his pleasure.

They were an hour on the way and a full ten miles from the town before Rourke at last made a halt. But no sooner had he halted than the little dog began to show the most frenzied anxiety. It came back and fawned in the path before the path of the rider. It whined pitifully. It turned and repeated a few steps, looking back over its shoulder.

Rourke could not resist. He went down the path, shaking his head in wonder at his own folly. Another hour and another ten miles passed; now the little dog darted away into the darkness and was lost. Rourke checked his horse and swore at the universe, from the stars to the ground. Had the infernal little beast led him all that distance as a practical jest and left him here at the end of nowhere?

Presently he heard the shrill yelping of the dog out of the

dark ahead of him. Plainly, that was the end of the trail. So Rourke put the gelding into a canter, and they swept down the narrow gorge until he made out by starlight a saddled horse standing at one side. When he came a little closer he could see that the dog was yelping and wailing at the side of a prostrate figure—a woman's figure, something told him.

He threw himself out of the saddle, and his heart went cold. Had some brute waylaid and murdered a woman? She lay on her back, her arms thrown out wide, her face white under the stars. When he touched her, Rourke knew that, if she were dead, it was a recent death—the body was still warm. He felt for her pulse and found it beating faintly.

What was wrong with her? He turned to the horse. It was a finely made animal, a dainty-limbed mare with a noble head. There she had been waiting hour upon hour, perhaps, for the mistress to rise and take the saddle again. Not even thirst had driven the patient creature away.

The first clue to an explanation was offered by the fact that one side of the saddle was badly scratched, and the hair and skin on the same side of the mare were rubbed off in small patches. There had manifestly been a stumble, a slide, and fall. Another thought came to Rourke—concussion of the brain. Perhaps the woman would never waken from the trance that held her? He lighted a match and looked at her face. It was covered with dust, flushed with sunburn. Wisps of dark hair trailed across her forehead. The hat was crushed to one side. Rourke stared until the match burned his fingers. And even when the match went out, he could see the face, half womanly, half childish, half sleepy, and half anguished.

Babe raised her head, and she moaned faintly in her trance. He took her by the shoulders and lifted her to a sitting posture. There was no complaint, and he let her sink back, sighing with relief. At least the injury was not to the spine. He took her legs at the ankles and bent the left leg up and let it come straight again. But when he touched the right leg, it sagged in, just halfway between ankle and knee, and there was a shrill scream of pain from the girl.

Rourke jerked upright and struck his hand across his face. It seemed to him that her shriek of pain had sent a thousand burning arrows of pain shooting through him, and still his body and brain tingled in an agony. The leg was broken, and she lay there twenty miles from a doctor. Not even in Krugerville was there a doctor capable of treating anything other than a horse or a steer. The greatness of the disaster appalled Rourke. He spread out his great hands. If he tried to care for her with those huge and clumsy instruments, what would be the result? It seemed that she must break under his touch.

Where there was no other help, he must do what he could. Had it been a man, he would have had no doubt at all. Not for nothing had he spent a winter in a Canadian lumber camp and, when the doctor was killed in a brawl, had doctored the wounds in the camp. He had set three broken legs that winter. Now in the case of a man he would have to set to work without misgiving. But a woman was quite another matter— and such a woman. But first he must have light, then water, then that leg must be put in splints. The girl began to rave feebly, and the sound of her voice tugged at the heartstrings of Rourke. He listened for an instant; then he started to work in a wild haste.

He tore up some dead shrubs. The firelight leaped quivering through the narrow gorge. After that he threw himself into the saddle on the gelding and raced around the next turn of the ravine to a spring of which he knew. There he filled his canteen and returned.

The little dog was sitting in the hollow of its mistress's

arm, whining into her face. But the little beast jumped away and whined with pleasure, wagging a stump of a tail vigorously, as Rourke raised the girl's head and put the canteen to her lips.

She drank deep, but, when the canteen was lowered, she began to rave again. He took her pulse once more. It seemed to have doubled in speed, and her face was flaming hot.

There followed the most cruel hour in the life of Rourke, as he cut straight strong branches from shrubs and fashioned his splints. Then he cut away her stocking and began the real ordeal. Mercifully, the first touch on her foot brought a shriek of agony from her and then silence. She had swooned deeply.

Perspiration streamed down the face of Rourke as he worked. It seemed to him that every touch of his huge fingers must be torturing that white, soft flesh. The splints were laid, and now his shirt was torn into strips and made part of the bandage. From a kit of clothes behind the girl's saddle he found more cloth and completed the bandage.

At last he stood back, shaking and weak, and looked down into her face. She had passed from the swoon and was begging for water. He gave it to her, and she looked up into his face as she drank with great, pain-ridden, blank eyes, searching and seeing nothing.

This half of the labor was done. What remained seemed the least part to Rourke. In the hollow of the ravine he cut two saplings, with the small axe without which he never traveled. He cleared away the branches, cut them of a length, and stretched his slicker over the two and made it fast. Eventually he had a rude stretcher. One end of it he tied to the saddle of his gelding, the other end to the saddle of the mare, and then into the stretcher he lifted the body of the delirious girl. The little dog had leaped up and sat at her head, overseeing everything, and taking heed that no harm came to the mistress.

It was sufficiently safe to move her for a short distance with such a conveyance. It would be hopeless to try to move her far. However, he knew this section of the mountains well, and he recalled that there was a small shack, rapidly going to pieces, but still offering a fairly whole roof. It was half a mile or a mile up the ravine and on a small tableland beside it. It had been built near a spring, so that the main essential water would be accounted for.

In this direction, therefore, he proceeded, leading the horses carefully on, and groaning when one of their stumbles brought a cry from the victim.

IV

"Angus Cairn"

All that night he waited for the voice of the girl to cease its ravings, and all night he waited in vain. She murmured constantly, or cried out—sharp shrill cries that made Rourke wince and brought out the sweat on his forehead. How, he wondered, could she endure it—that slender body and this long torture?

In the meantime, he worked. In the heavy pack behind the girl's saddle there was a supply of flour and coffee and bacon and salt enough to last them for several days. He could shoot the meat. But there was much to do to bring the cabin into a habitable condition. The roof was as he had remembered it—in fairly good repair. But there was the rust-eaten ruin of a cast-iron stove to be cleared out. There were a dozen kinds of débris to be cleared away, and he worked as silently as possible. For it seemed to Rourke that, when the girl awakened, the ugly interior of the hut would be like a weight on her spirit. Finally, he went out among the pines that stood in a pleasant cluster around the spring and lopped off branches and cut down saplings. He brought back a great load of them and filled the corners of the shack and strung sprays of the green stuff here and there.

It might have been the rising of a cool breeze with the dawn of the day, or it might have been the change of the light itself that affected the girl. Or it might have been that the first strength of the fever had simply wasted itself. But, when she fell into a sound sleep, Rourke vowed to himself that it was the sweet breath of the pines that had made her slumber.

For a time he sat beside her, watching and wondering, as the daylight grew, at the way her face was formed. He had never before wasted time or observation on women. And instinctively, as he looked down at the girl, he lifted his hand and touched the scar that furrowed his cheek and the ragged lump on the side of his throat, where the Mexican had driven the knife to the hilt. Again he studied the crystal clearness of the girl's features, smooth as cut stone and delicate beyond belief. And he stretched out his great hand and moved it just a fraction of an inch from her skin. It seemed to Rourke that a faint current passed from her body to his, a strange thrill like nothing he had ever known before.

At last he forced himself to stand up, and went out into the fresh clear air of the morning, with rosy light sweeping over the mountains. His life had been too full of battles for him to have spent much time in the contemplation of nature. But now he stood at the door of the little shack, and his eye lingered over the sweeping lines and over the shadow of trees that filled the hollows and over the rock faces of the cliffs, softened and brightened by the morning. And Rourke felt that to the end of time, when he saw a clear sunrise, he would see the girl's face.

His labors of the night put an ache of weariness in his head. So, in the seclusion of the grove around the spring, he stripped off his clothes and plunged into the pool that formed a little distance from the spring itself, and from the brim of which a trickle of icy water ran down the hillside. It was a deep pool, but he forced himself down to the bottom of it, then sprang up to the top.

He dried and clothed himself as fresh as though he had newly risen from a long slumber. He went back to the cabin for his rifle, glanced at the girl, saw her still lost in sleep, and then started out to hunt. The chase led him farther from her than he cared to go. It was an hour before he sighted a rabbit and dropped it with a snap shot, as it sprang across his path. Two ground squirrels were killed near their holes. Another rabbit was his victim a moment later, and he started back with enough provisions for the day.

Once started on the home trip, he swung into a run. He was not like most cowpunchers, who are lost away from the saddle. Many a time he had had to make trips when there were no horses around him strong enough to carry the burden of his weight with any speed. Long trips through the mountains had made him as strong below the waist as above. So he raced like an Indian back to the hut, and he had come within fifty feet of it when something like a feel of a cloud shadow, dropping across his path, made him glance up.

Just outside the door of the cabin where the girl lay, resting with one hand against the wall of logs, stood the biggest man he had ever laid eyes on—the first man in his mature life who was taller and heavier than himself. He knew by the first glance that it was Angus Cairn. There was the short, black beard of which the villagers had spoken. There was the crop of curly black hair, worn long in a thick shock. There were those mighty shoulders, almost too broad to let him walk squarely into the cabin door.

Instinctively Rourke dropped a hand to his revolver, but the giant at the door merely smiled on him, a disdainful smile. Slowly he straightened and then strode to Rourke. At his near approach Rourke caught his breath. The man was a monster—a very Hercules. He had only to glance at one detail— the long-fingered, heavy-veined hands—to realize that here was his master in physical strength. Here, perhaps, was his master in indomitable fighting spirit, also. There was no scar upon his face or upon his hands, but, nevertheless, an aroma of battle dwelt about him. The fact that he was unscathed to all appearances made him all the more dreadful.

Cairn hooked a thumb over his shoulder. "Nobody ain't told me that you had a wife," he said.

"And I ain't," said Rourke.

"You ain't?" A frown gathered like a thunder storm on the brow of the giant. "Is she," he said slowly, "is she in there . . . your woman?"

Rourke crimsoned, and his right hand doubled. He even balanced his weight on his toes to strike such a blow as he had never struck before. "Why, curse your heart," he said, "have you seen *her* . . . and then ask me a thing like that?"

The big man smiled, and that smile came from his heart. "I'm sure glad to hear you say that. I been in there looking at her, but I wasn't quite sure. There wasn't no sign that I could see. There wasn't no calluses on her hands, or no wear on her face. I thought that she might be another man's woman."

Rourke set his teeth. The thought of the monster leaning above the girl was strangely repulsive to him. "Has she been talking to you?" he asked, savage at the thought that she might have roused from sleep and spoken to the big man.

"She's sleeping sound," said Cairn. "But how come?" He explained himself by a sweeping gesture toward the house.

"How come?" repeated Rourke. "When you didn't show up last. . . ."

"I'm sure sorry about that," said Cairn. "I'll tell you how it came about. My good-for-nothing hoss went lame. I had to leave him behind and go along on foot. And that made me late. But, now that I've come, maybe I can make up to you for what you missed." His lips parted in a mirthless grin, and the teeth flashed white, deep in his beard.

A quiver of cold ran through Rourke, as he watched.

"And about the rest of this?" inquired Cairn.

"Her dog came into town and led me out here," said Rourke.

"What the hell?" roared Cairn. "Her dog? How come?"

Rourke shrugged his shoulders. "I didn't figure you to understand," he said.

"You followed her dog out, then?" asked Cairn, gloomy with anger again.

"I found her lying senseless beside her hoss," said Rourke. "She'd been lying there several hours. Her leg was broke."

"You don't say," breathed Cairn with a softness that made Rourke open his eyes and stare.

"I fixed up a splint and set that there leg," said Rourke.

"Are you a doc, maybe?" asked the man of the black beard with a touch of awe.

"I picked up a little doctoring," said Rourke. "I can set a bone, all things being equal to giving me a chance."

"And she won't heal with a crippled leg?"

"Not if she don't die of the fever."

Cairn winced. "D'you think that there might be a chance of anything like that, partner?"

Rourke scowled at him. "How long you been here?" asked Rourke.

"About an hour, pretty close."

With that Rourke understood. The same quiet magic that had stolen over him had stolen over even this rough giant. The same queer ache of pain and of happiness, that was in his heart, was in the heart of Cairn. It drove Rourke wild with rage, and a haze swam across his eyes.

"We got to get her down to a doc," said Cairn eagerly.

"There ain't none but a hoss doctor in Krugerville," said Rourke. "Old Doc Smith died last spring."

"No doc?" growled Cairn. "Whoever hear of a town that ain't got a doc in it? I could tell by the looks of Krugerville that it wasn't no good. It ain't got half the makings of a place where white folks would live."

"It's good enough for me," said Rourke with a quiet malice.

Color rushed into the face of the other, but he controlled his passion. "What's going to be done with the girl?"

"There ain't nothing that nobody can do but keep her here and treat her as good as I can."

Cairn dropped his head and sighed. He seemed to be buried in thought for a time. At length he said: "I see there ain't anything else to do."

"But what?" asked Rourke.

"Son," said the other, although he had no such advantage of years as his speech seemed to pretend, "son, I got to stay here and take charge of things."

"You!" gasped Rourke, too furious to find words and gripping his gun.

Angus Cairn waved violence aside.

"This ain't no time for a gun play," he said. "If you wasn't a plumb fool, you'd see that. I come down here looking plumb eager for you. I'd heard too much chatter about Babe Rourke. I come down to see how much of a man he was. And," he added, sweeping his eyes over Babe Rourke from head to feet, "I can't see that there's much cause for any holler about him. He looks sort of small to me."

"I'm big enough," said Rourke. "But I ain't handy at making myself big with words and puffing up like a toad with a lot of hot air."

The other grinned a deadly smile again. "What you aim to do," he said, "is to get me out of the way and then get the girl well."

"That's tolerable straight talk," admitted Rourke.

"But suppose that I dropped you . . . instead of you . . .

me?" asked the big man. "Who'd be left to take care of the girl? I ain't got no doctoring skill."

"Then get out of here and leave me alone to finish the job that I begun without you," said Rourke tersely.

Cairn shrugged his heavy shoulders. "Short and sweet," he said. "And I'll tell you plain that I'm damned if I get out. I'm going to see that girl when she wakes up!"

"Not unless I'm mud first," snapped Rourke, the fighting devil bright in his pale-blue eyes.

They drew back a little. The hand of each rested on the butt of a gun. Death was not the quiver of an eyelash away from them.

V

"Gertrude Talks"

"Look at this little game another way," Cairn said. "There ain't nothing that I'd like better than to cut the liver out of you, Rourke, but there's another thing to be counted in. Suppose that we was to have this out and only one of us be left. How can he take care of the girl?"

"Ain't I been doing it?" asked Rourke, savagely ready to fight, but held back by the thoughtfulness of the big man.

"You been doing it, sure," said Cairn. "But, while you was away this morning, wolves might have come and eat her up."

"That's fool talk!" sneered Rourke. "Wolves ain't to bother people this time of year."

"Would you take a chance with her?" asked Cairn.

Rourke blanched at the thought.

"And some gents that might come along," said Cairn, "are a whole sight worse than wolves."

Perspiration poured out on the face of Rourke. "I didn't think about that."

"There ain't a chance in twenty," said the other, "but ain't that one chance more'n we want to take with *her?*"

It angered Rourke to hear that *we,* but there was sufficient point in the other's remark to make him nod.

"You're sort of talking sense," he admitted.

"You're sort of young," said Cairn, "or it wouldn't have took all this time to show you that I was right. Rourke, this is a two-man job! I'd rather that my partner was anybody in the world but you, but beggars can't be choosers. Suppose that one of us had to go to town for something one of these days. That would be a five-hour trip. We sure couldn't leave her alone all that time."

"We sure couldn't," admitted Rourke gloomily. "Cairn, as soon as she gets able to travel, you and me'll have our little party. I hear that you've been telling folks that all you needed was a chance to dig the gizzard right out of me."

"Talking by and large," admitted Cairn, "that's my main idea, right enough."

"You ain't seen the day," said Rourke, "when you was man enough to beat me with a knife, or gun, or bare hands." And he showed his teeth, his muscles tensed, his whole body swaying a little in a passion of battle.

"Talk don't mean nothing," sneered Cairn. "When the time comes, I'll show you more things happening inside of ten seconds than you ever seen in the rest of your life. But until that time comes, we got to work together. A broke leg is a broke leg. She's got to be cared for."

The mention of the girl made Rourke start. "If you want to be useful," he said, "fix these rabbits and squirrels and get a fire going to roast 'em. I got to take a look at her and see how she's coming."

Cairn raised his hand. "How come you get all the cream?" he asked. "Why can't *I* find out how she's doing?"

"Can you take care of a broke leg?" snapped Rourke.

"I can ask her how she feels," said Cairn. "Besides, if you got that leg in a splint, there ain't nothing much that *you'd* do to change her now. I'll tell you what . . . we'll toss a coin to see who goes in to see her."

There was a rough justice in this proposal that appealed to Rourke. All the way through their conversation he began to feel that Angus had shown the more foresight, the greater justice.

"Call it," he said, and brought out a broad silver dollar.

"Heads!" called Angus.

The coin spun up, glittered, hung in the air for a moment, as though suspended on an invisible wire, and then dropped with a light *clang* on a stone. Rourke leaned over it, breathless with a feeling that the outcome of this first small contest would be the symbol of the whole struggle between him and Cairn for the supremacy in fame—and in the eyes of the girl. Who could tell to what far-reaching results the spinning of that coin might extend? And his gaze grew dull, a blow was struck against his heart, as he saw that a broad head was lying uppermost.

"What is it?" asked Cairn, striding up.

Rourke snatched the dollar from the ground, flung it into the air, and with a lightning draw smashed a bullet through the center of it. He turned to face Cairn and found the latter smiling.

"I guess it was tails that was turned up," Cairn said.

"It was heads," admitted Rourke with something like a groan, "and be damned to you!"

A sweet voice called from the inside of the hut: "Where am I? Oh!"

It raised to a sharp cry of fear and pain and bewilderment. Rourke sprang forward. A hand of iron caught him by the shoulder. That grip was beyond all dreams of Herculean power. It bit through his flesh, grinding against the bones of his shoulder. Babe was stopped short in his stride. With a clubbed fist he beat away the arm of Cairn.

"We tossed a coin," said Cairn.

"Go on, then," muttered Rourke. "Go talk baby talk to her . . . you got the face for it."

Cairn had already turned his back. In a moment more he had disappeared through the door of the cabin, stooping as he entered. Rourke followed hastily and remained just outside, peering through a crack that gave him a clear view of them both. He saw the giant throw his hat on the floor. He saw the girl, who had raised herself on one elbow, shrink back from the monster. The sight of her face gave Rourke a bitter satisfaction.

"Lady," said Angus Cairn, in a voice so soft that Rourke marveled at it, "there ain't no call to be scared. I ain't going to do you no harm."

"I . . . ," murmured the girl, "I thought it was the end. I thought it was death."

"I ain't the devil, ma'am," said Cairn, "if that's what you mean."

A faint smile came on her lips. A twinge of pain erased it. "How did I come here?" she asked.

"You was found lying by your hoss with a broken leg, nearby here."

"A broken leg?" She laid her hand over the leg that was stiff with splints, as though she had discovered the change for the first time in her bewilderment. "Did you find me?" she asked.

Rourke waited, holding his breath. If the other lied, he vowed to have his life.

"No," said Cairn, "I didn't find you. A . . . a friend of mine found you."

Rourke smiled in spite of himself.

"A doctor?" asked the girl.

"A gent that knows something about doctoring. He can set bones sure fine."

Again Rourke smiled.

"You'd been lying there in the sun and dark after the hoss throwed you."

"I remember the slide of the stone, and how poor Nell fell

with me." Her voice trailed away into words that Cairn could not understand.

"Lie down," said Cairn. "You're tuckered out. It don't take no doctor to tell that."

She collapsed on the bed and lay with her eyes closed for a moment.

"You jest lie here and rest," went on Cairn. "There's nothing for you to worry about."

"God bless you," breathed the girl. "I . . . I didn't know that there were men like you in this horrible world."

"What sort of hounds have you knowed that called themselves men," asked Cairn, "and wouldn't bust themselves wide open to take care of a woman that was hurt?"

She shook her head as a mute sign that she could not or would not answer that question.

"Tell me your name," said Cairn.

"Gertrude," she answered, opening her eyes again.

"And your last name, so's we can get word to your folks."

But she raised a hand in protest. "No, no!" she pleaded.

Rourke was thunderstruck.

"For pity's sake," she said, "don't let them know. They'd take me back."

"You run away from 'em?" asked Cairn.

"Yes."

"Your father and mother?"

"No, they're dead. And the others . . . in the name of mercy, don't let them know."

"Not a word, then," said Cairn. "They ain't going to hear a word." He dropped to one knee and took her hand. How childishly small it was in his great palm. His other hand covered hers.

"You've done talk enough," he said. "Lie here and get your mind fixed on forgetting your trouble. We ain't going to ask what's happened to you. Questions ain't in our line. We'll keep you here till you're fit as a fiddle, and then you can go where you want to go."

"But the other people in the town . . . ," she began.

"It ain't a town. It's just a lone shack in the hills."

"Then I don't mind the pain," she said with deep relief. "The pain is half heaven to me. It tells me that I'm free from them all . . . it tells me that they'll never find me." Her voice changed. "And if they do, you won't let them have me?"

"Not in a thousand years," declared Cairn fervently. "Now sleep again. You ain't strong enough to talk."

VI

" 'A Few Kind Words' "

He came out to Rourke with a half-foolish, half-frightened face.

"She's run away from her folks," he said to Rourke. "Can you think of white men treating her bad . . . a girl like her?"

"More'n likely," said Rourke, "it's just a fool notion of hers."

"Are you calling her a fool?" asked Cairn.

"Women got a failing in that direction," said Rourke wisely. "Ever know any with sense, Cairn?"

Angus Cairn glowered upon him. "D'you have a mother . . . and yet you talk like this?" he asked.

Rourke sighed. "You're full of talk that don't lead to nowhere," he said. "Let's get a fire going. That girl's got to be fed. Or, maybe, you're up here just for noise and entertainment."

There was no answer from Angus Cairn. He started to build the fire as obediently as though he were a hired man. Not only was the fire to be made and the wood brought in, but the fireplace itself had to be constructed. And Rourke, as he cleaned the rabbits and the squirrels and made other preparation for the meal, watched Cairn out of the corner of his eye. The man was a marvel of physical prowess.

Cairn's rage at Rourke found an outlet in his work. Rourke heard the rending of wood among the shrubbery down the slope. Presently Cairn appeared under a load of fuel. He deposited it and began clearing a place for the fire among the boulders at the very door of the cabin.

It was a task that Rourke himself would never have attempted, for all his power. But Cairn laid hold on deep-rooted stones and heaved them up lightly. They landed with a weight and force that made the ground quiver. Yet, when the place had been cleared and the smaller stones neatly laid for the fireplace, the giant was not even breathing hard. He kindled his fire, and, when it was burning briskly, he stood back and looked around him with his hands half-clenched, as though he were still looking for a place to vent his unused forces.

Babe Rourke watched and saw much and said nothing. But all the time he was thinking more vividly than he had ever thought before. Every rock on which the big man set his hands seemed to be a part of Rourke's body. Would he, too, when the time came for the battle, be uprooted and cast down on the earth, a dead, crushed weight? Assuredly he must try to make his fight with something other than brute might of hands. Possibly when the great moment came there would be no chance to choose or, perhaps, Cairn would directly challenge him to battle with bared fists. Rourke shrugged his shoulders at the thought. He could only pray that the girl would not be near to witness his ruin.

But there was a thing which impressed him even more than the handwork of Angus Cairn, and that was his ability to control his emotions—his talent for silence. It was not so with Rourke. Whatever he felt, he coined instantly in words and spoke—spoke even more than he felt. Many a time he had lashed himself to a fury over some small matter by the very violence of his language. But with Cairn it was otherwise. He thought before he spoke, and, when the words came, they were a great distance beneath the power of the emotion out of which they were born.

Rourke went on with the cooking, while Angus Cairn brought up his horse from the hollow and removed the pack. He was busy for a time undoing it. Then he sat down on the shady side of the house, and the strumming of a guitar amazed the ear of Rourke. Next a mellow bass voice, with the volume of a roaring mountain torrent that crowds a ravine with echoes, and the smoothness of smoothest silk—a voice whose strength was delicately controlled and modulated—began to sing to the guitar.

A sense of doom took hold of Rourke as he listened. The man whom she had seen first when she wakened in pain and bewilderment, the man who could sing and play to her in this matchless style—was there any doubt in what direction the affections of the girl would turn? He could only hope that she would look at neither of them, decided Rourke gloomily, as he turned the rabbit on the spit. But when the first song died away, a voice from within called: "Oh, won't you sing again? It made me forget that there was such a thing as pain in the world. It was beautiful!"

Angus Cairn raised his head and cast a glance dark with exultation at Rourke. As for Rourke, he dropped his head and listened in a daze to the next song. It was very good singing. The knowledge made his misery more perfect. Had they been common cowpuncher songs, Rourke could have joined in them. For so melodious was that voice, and so strange and pleasant were the songs he sang, that Rourke felt in spite of himself a certain pleasure in listening.

When dinner was cooked, he laid out her portion in tin dishes that he had scoured with sand until they shone like mirrors. Then he carried in his offering.

The scent of food brought a faint flush of color into her pale cheeks, and she smiled up to him. Her smile had a strange effect on Rourke. He had not minded being near her when she was raving in a delirium. But now that her sound senses were with her, that smile shook him to the ground and made him want to drop the dishes and flee headlong through the door.

But he summoned up his courage and, the better to fortify himself against fear, gathered a terrific frown and peered down on her from beneath it. The scowl had immediate effect. It banished her smile and wiped out her color, as though he had struck her. Rourke, groaning inwardly, decided that he had dealt his chances their own death blow. He had played the part of the hopeless boor—the stupid idiot. Ah, for one moment of the matchless grace with which Cairn had dropped upon one knee and taken the hand of the girl! But no, he could not find in his nature the ability to invent such postures.

"Raise your head," he grumbled at her.

She raised her head. He slipped his broad hand down her back beneath the shoulders, raised her, and heaped blankets until she was sitting at a sharply inclined angle. Ah, for the ability to say three gracious words. But his tongue was tied. He could not speak. And, outside the shack, Angus Cairn— might he be doubly damned—was singing a new song softly. Rourke spread the food before her.

"I don't think I can eat," she said faintly.

"You got to eat," said Rourke, as he winced at the sound of his own voice. It came roughly from his throat. There was a brutal threat in it. "What chance have you got to get well if you don't eat?" he went on.

She raised a frightened glance to his face, and her eyes dropped hastily as they met his scowl. They were blue eyes, he had seen, and they were extraordinarily wide. Never before had he looked so deeply into the eyes of a human being. Had it been Angus Cairn he would have found something to say about them. But he, dolt and fool that he was, could not frame a syllable. He turned on his heel, as her hand obediently raised knife and fork.

"You. . . ." The faint voice was trying to speak.

He wheeled back to face her. To his utter amazement she was smiling on him.

"You are the doctor," she was saying, and looking at him straight in the face, as though there were nothing in the world to fear.

"Me? I ain't a doctor," said Rourke.

"You're the one who found me," she insisted. "I remember how in the middle of that horrible dream and the torture someone raised my head and gave me water. I . . . I thought that death had come, and that I had reached heaven."

Gently she drew in her breath, as though she drank again. "And you spoke . . . I remember the voice," she said.

Again she smiled, and the panic grew more welled up in the heart of Rourke. The mongrel dog came fearlessly to him, stood up, planted both paws on his knee, and wagged its stump of a tail furiously.

"How did you find me in the dark?" she asked.

"It was the dog," said Rourke. "It was him that done it. He come into town and got me."

"Dear old Jerry," said the girl.

The dog sprang to her, and she fondled its head. "But how could you guess . . . and how far away is the town?" she asked.

"Not so far . . . about twenty miles," said Rourke, still scowling to beat the panic out of his heart.

"You followed Jerry for twenty miles?" breathed the girl, her smile going out and then coming again like sunshine. "Oh, how did he lead you?"

"He come in acting sort of queer," said Rourke. "He

44

swiped my pipe to make me foller him, dog-gone his eyes! And so I come along and seen that he wanted to take me some place."

"I wonder how many men would have followed a dog twenty miles?" she asked.

"Oh," grunted Rourke, "if it hadn't been me, it would have been somebody else."

She shook her head, then grew grave. For the beat of horses' hoofs came over the rocky plateau.

"They've come for me," said the girl, breathless with fear.

"Who's they?" asked Rourke.

"The men who . . . but I can't tell you!"

"Have they got a right to take you with 'em?"

"Yes, yes, but. . . ."

"But you don't want to go?"

"No!"

"Lady," said Rourke, and his lower jaw thrust out, and the scar on his cheek drew his lips into an ugly sneer, "we're a tolerable distance up in the hills, and I sort of figure that we can get along without the law, if it comes to a pinch. If it's the ones you think, I'll go out and tell 'em a few kind words!"

He went to the door of the cabin and drew it shut behind him, a staggering wreck of a door that a child could have beaten down with a stroke of his fist.

VII

"Callers"

It was a whole cavalcade of five riders that was approaching the cabin, five well-mounted men who had paused for a moment near Gertrude's horse, Nell, and now came on again at a round canter. Instinctively Rourke looked to Angus Cairn, and Angus Cairn rose and stretched to the full of his height. The riders reined their horses close by, knocking up a cloud of dust that blew across the two big men.

Rourke wiped a grain of sand from his eye and grinned evilly upon the newcomers. But this nearer view of them increased his respect for them tremendously. They were as hardy a crew as he had ever seen. If ten thousand had been searched for five big, grim-faced men, a better five could not have been found. They were dressed like cowpunchers, but obviously they did not belong in that rôle. No common cowpuncher could afford to buy such blooded horses as these fellows were riding. As for their ages, they ranged from twenty-five to forty-five, which was the apparent number of years of the leader of the party, a stocky man with a pair of long, sandy mustaches. He paused a moment before he spoke. Then he appeared to select Cairn as spokesman.

"I see you got my girl here," he said cheerfully. "She stopped over from yesterday, maybe?"

"Girl?" said Angus Cairn with admirably feigned wonder. "I was over at a dance at Krugerville last month. I ain't seen a girl since then. What might a girl be doing wandering around the hills alone?"

Before answering, the man of the long mustaches turned in the saddle and deliberately looked to the other members of his party.

"The little fool has been talking," he said, "and here's the result of it. Just scatter out a bit, boys, will you?"

Like the sticks of a fan the "boys" spread out, focusing on Rourke and his ally. Angus Cairn picked up the eight-pound rock and began to juggle it idly from hand to hand, while he whistled a dainty tune and regarded the newcomers wearily.

"About her being here," said the man of the mustaches, "there ain't no doubt. We seen her hoss over there. I bred and raised Nell. I'd ought to know her."

"That hoss over there?" asked Cairn. "Tell 'em about it, Babe."

"You go find my hoss," said Rourke, "and you can have that spindle-legged mare. I sure ain't got any use for her. We was off hunting yesterday, and, when we come back, we found Tom, my hoss that I paid three hundred bucks for, gone, and this skinny runt of a mare left in his place all dripping with sweat."

"The devil you say!" exclaimed the spokesman of the others. "I thought we had her at last. Confound the little imp! She's got clear of us again!"

A big fellow urged his horse to the front. He was a handsome chap, the youngest of the party, and with a spread of shoulder almost as formidable as that of Angus Cairn or Rourke themselves.

"We might take a peek into the cabin to make sure," he suggested.

"Meaning that I might be lying to you?" exclaimed Rourke, simulating wrath, as he saw that he must find some sort of an excuse for not letting them into the interior of the cabin.

47

"Now, hold on a minute," said Angus Cairn. "What sort of talk is this? You come up here, and we tell you a straight yarn, and you call us liars and say you're going to bust into our house. D'you know what busting into a house without the will of the owner is?"

"Tell me," said the other quietly.

"Burglary," said Cairn. "That gets a man about fourteen years."

"Fourteen years?" asked the youth. "Well, well . . . that's quite a time." Now he smiled up at the other members of his party who responded with uproarious laughter. Even the man of the sandy mustaches grinned broadly, although the point of the jest remained obscure to Rourke.

"So we'll take a chance on the fourteen years," said he of the black eyes, "and have a peek at the insides of your shack."

"Don't hurry this, Larry," said the leader.

"I'm tired of waiting," said Larry. "We've wasted a good deal of time on this trail already."

"And I'll see you damned before I let you open that door," said Rourke.

Larry turned and looked down upon him with a fearless smile, a smile of such utter contempt as Rourke had never faced before.

"My, my," murmured Larry. "This naughty boy talks right out in meeting. Can you beat it?" His hand dropped to the butt of his gun, and there were similar gestures made by the rest of the party.

"Hold on, Babe," said big Angus. "There ain't no use making a fight over it . . . no use at all. We're two, and they're five on hosses."

Rourke turned in wonder to his companion. No matter what he thought of the other, he had not expected such talk as this. Surrender—while the girl lay yonder in the hut? He

48

would have taken up fire in his bare hands sooner.

"That's sense," said Larry. "I'm sorry to do this, friend. But we've come a long way, and we don't want to leave any stones unturned. Come on, boys!"

"All right," said Angus Cairn, and he pitched the eight-pound stone with the force of a cannon shot.

Too late Larry saw the flying danger and threw up his hands to ward it off. But his arms were useless against that crushing force. It beat through his hands, struck him on the shoulder, and knocked him flying from his saddle, while the horse with a snort fled to a distance.

So much Rourke saw from the corner of his eye. But, the instant the hand of Cairn stirred to raise the stone, Rourke himself had charged. The man of the sandy mustaches was nearest to him, and at him he drove. Swiftly he came, the revolver was naked in the hand of the leader of the horsemen, but, before he could swing it across his body to fire, Rourke had leaped into the air and struck. He missed the temple at which the blow was aimed and struck the jaw instead. Otherwise, his victim would never have spoken again. As it was, the blow lifted the smaller man out of the saddle and shot him to the ground.

Rourke wheeled with a wild yell of exultation and with a sweep of his arm caught another man out of the saddle and crushed him to limpness. With one arm he hugged this man to his breast, a shield against bullets that might be flying soon. With the other hand he poised his revolver. By that time, however, the struggle was over. For Cairn had torn a second man from his horse and left a twisted, crumpled figure on the ground, and the last member of the party to sit the saddle, bewildered by this hurricane attack, sat with a gun in either hand and no target to shoot at. For Cairn was shielded by a horse, and Rourke could only be got at through the body of one of his companions.

"Stick up those hands and drop them guns!" called Rourke.

With an oath the fellow obeyed.

"Pick up the guns, Angus," said Rourke. "We got to have some souvenirs of this little party, I guess."

He cast his own second victim to the ground, where the wretched fellow lay groaning and writhing to get air back in his lungs. In another moment the weapons of the party had been gathered, and the stricken men began to pick themselves up, one by one. There were apparently no serious hurts. Larry had gashed his head on a rock in his fall from the horse, and the side of the sandy-whiskered man's face was a rapidly swelling and purpled bruise. But, otherwise, there were no marks of the battle visible. It had all passed in a flash, without the discharge of a single bullet. Never were there five faces more surprised than the faces that now confronted Babe Rourke and Angus Cairn.

"Where you make a mistake," said Cairn, addressing himself to Larry, "is talking sassy to your elders. It don't never pay, son. You get spanked for it, and there's the end to the business. You boys just trot along on your way now. We'll keep your guns for you in case you should forget yourselves and get nasty."

The leader remounted and caressed his swollen face with diffident fingertips.

"Boys," he said, speaking with difficulty from one side of his mouth, "I sure hate to tell you all the bad luck you're going to have on account of this one little party. But, before I get through with you, you'll both wish you'd raised the devil sooner'n crossed me."

"Thanks," said Angus Cairn. "Thanks for the fun you've just give us, and thanks for the promise of what more's coming. I might add something by way of encouraging you, too. A rattler bit me once when I was a kid, and, whenever I see a snake these days, I aim to knock its head off with a chunk of lead. If I see any of you gents crawling around these parts again, I ain't going to look twice. You can put the name of Angus Cairn under what you write."

The other started.

"Are you Cairn?" he asked.

"Guilty," said Angus.

The leader turned on Rourke. "And by guns, you're Babe Rourke!"

"I am," said Rourke.

The eyes of the other opened. "Well . . . I'm damned," he breathed. But he added with a savage heat: "I've seen you now, and I know what to expect. I'm coming calling again. And when I do, I ain't going to send in my card first! Boys, here's where we beat it!"

He gathered his followers with a single gesture around him, and they cantered away to the place where Larry was still striving, and striving in vain, to capture his horse.

VIII

"The Interlude"

A moment passed, and then the whole group swept over the edge of the plateau and was gone from view. Now it was that Rourke turned to face Angus Cairn and found that Angus Cairn was already turned toward him.

"That might be a lesson to you, son," said Angus. "The next time you get into a pinch, wait till you throw 'em off guard before you hit."

"Thanks," said Rourke dryly. "I knew before all this that you needed watching. When you throw me off my guard, you're welcome to everything you can get out of me."

"But you didn't waste no time after I'd made the opening," said Cairn.

"D'you call throwing a stone making an opening?" exclaimed Rourke, savage at the patronizing manner of his companion. "Why, even a kid would call that fool stuff."

"That stone knocked their best fighting man out of the saddle," said Cairn complacently. "After he was down, the rest was easy. They didn't have any gimp in 'em when they seen that Larry was down. But if you had kept on the way you started and made a show of fighting from the first, we'd have had five guns salting us down with lead. But, as I was saying a while back, you ain't too old to start in learning."

It occurred to Rourke that every word they spoke was audible to the girl in the shack. In his rage he desired only to tear the life out of the bull throat of Angus Cairn. The latter's content seemed to grow, as the fury of Rourke increased to a white heat. A laugh was bubbling back in his throat. But now he shrugged his shoulders and forced himself to be grave again.

"Son," he went on, "no matter what we think about each other, the fact remains that the two of us cleaned up the five of them. They ain't going to hurry back to see us."

"You're wrong," answered Rourke. "That gent with the whiskers has got a memory as long as an elephant's. And he'll come again."

"You think so?" asked Angus, entirely serious at once.

"I know so," said Rourke. "What's more, he's got some sort of a right over the girl. He might come back with a sheriff, for all I know."

"A sheriff?" asked Cairn. "That gent hates the sight of a sheriff. You can lay to that!"

"You thing he's crooked?"

"Crooked as a snake. Did you see the sort of hosses they was riding?"

Rourke shook his head.

"They're made for speed, every one of 'em," remarked Cairn. "They blowed a pile of money on those nags . . . if they bought 'em."

"You think they're hoss thieves?" asked Rourke.

"They were all bays, weren't they?" asked Cairn.

"Every one."

"Well, about five months back the Peterson Ranch up in Idaho, that's been raising a brand of hoss that's pretty close to pure Thoroughbred and that has been running straight bays for ten years . . . this Peterson Ranch, as I was saying, was raided one night. Old Hal Peterson and his two boys heard a pile of noise in their corrals. When they get out there, they seen some gents making away with a gang of hosses. They tried to foller, but lost 'em. When the morning come, they found that their herd had been hand-picked. Fifteen of their best hosses were gone! Well, as I was saying, all them Peterson hosses was bays!"

"Hoss thieves!" snapped Rourke, and his lip curled. "Well, whiskers and the rest will get strung up, one of these days. Hoss thieves!"

His disgust was complete.

"Only hoss thieves on the side," said Cairn. "They got bigger game than that in their hands. They swiped them hosses because they needed to have some speed under 'em . . . that's all, Babe. And they needed the speed, because in their line of business they got to strike quick and get away fast."

"Longriders?" murmured Rourke.

"You've guessed it, son. But what would a gang like that worry over a gal for?"

"Because she means money to 'em," suggested Rourke.

"Aye, maybe that's it. Rourke, we got to get her to tell us her story."

"We got to get help first of all," said Rourke.

"If one of us goes for help, their watchers will spread the news around, and they will come down to scoop up the one that's left. Not five of 'em, but a dozen, maybe."

Rourke nodded. "They've got us jailed here."

"It looks that way. I'm going to try to get some information out of Gertrude, and you go out scouting and see if them skunks are around."

It was an assignment of labor the distribution of which Rourke would gladly have reversed. But he did not try to dodge the more dangerous task, even if it gave Cairn a better opportunity to entrench himself in the esteem of the girl.

Babe started at once and made a two-hour detour with his horse. At the end of that time he came back with a bullet through the crown of his sombrero and a staggering mustang under him to tell Cairn how he had been jumped by four hard-riding men, and how he had barely come off alive. He found Cairn equally disconsolate; for, when Cairn had striven to gain information from the girl about herself and the hold that these men held over her, she had shaken her head, and, when he insisted, tears welled into her eyes, and he was silenced.

"Under the whole thing," he said, "there's something damned black. And how long is it going to be before that leg of hers is healed?"

"Weeks," said Rourke, and they groaned in unison at the thought of the long trail.

Now, after the first day or two, they reduced things to a system. They had to have fresh meat, and to get it they had to leave the cabin and hunt. They alternated in these excursions. When one went out, the other stood guard in the cabin with a gun ready to repel a rush. And the man who went out to face the brunt of danger and hunt game slipped out onto the plateau that extended around the cabin. They went out at odd times—in the early gray of the morning, in the dull time of the twilight, or when the moon was shining, or at high noon—anything to take the watchers at a relaxed moment. It was a season of plentiful game, and they never had to go far afield. Each time they came home safely.

For seven days there was no sight or sound of Larry or his men. On the eighth day Angus Cairn was fired on from behind, as he rode toward the cabin, with a deer behind his saddle. But the shot sang past his ear, and, when he brought his horse into a labored gallop, the attempt was not repeated. From that day on, however, they were made aware that they were being watched. They decided that, during the seven-day interval, the outlaws might have withdrawn entirely to attend to other and more vital business. But now they were back, and the two besieged men could only curse their fate for not having made the attempt to get to town for help during the period of quiet.

Only one thing made their existence possible, now that there was always a watcher near the cabin. The sentinel could not come too close. There was only one shelter on the plateau, and that was the group of evergreens around the spring, but the trunks were too narrow and too scattered to afford a real protection. And lacking this, they had to keep under cover on the edge of the little plateau. But the circle of that plateau was too large to admit of a close guard. The result was that, night after night, one of the two besieged men slipped out, stole down across the edge of the plateau on foot, and slipped away into the hills. There he killed the required meat and came back before the dawn.

Not that all these excursions were scathless. Three times bad luck brought them close enough to the sentinel to be fired upon, but in every instance they were able to retreat back through the scattering rocks on the edge of the plateau, regain the cabin unharmed, and make the attempt in a different place, later on in the night. Angus Cairn carried away the only mark of these encounters, and that was when a bullet clipped him across the arm—a shallow flesh wound that was hardly more than a needle scratch—but it soaked his sleeve with crimson, and, when the girl saw him come, she shrieked at the sight.

After that it seemed to Rourke that she gave up even the effort to maintain a pretense of interest in him. All her talk, all her glances were for Angus Cairn. When they were not talking, Angus Cairn was sitting in a corner of the cabin on the floor, strumming his guitar and singing soft songs to her.

Rourke watched her smiling at the ceiling, with eyes half

closed, and he ate out his heart in a jealous frenzy. He had only one hold over her, and that was his rough skill in doctoring. But when at last the day came when she rose and could rest her weight on the leg and walk, he knew, with a sigh, that the end of his last claim upon her had come. After that she would have little, indeed, to do with him.

It was three days later, when strength was swiftly returning to Gertrude, that she at last gave them enough news of herself to strike confusion into their minds.

"What I wonder," said Angus Cairn, "is if they think that they can starve us out here?"

"They don't care," she said. "All they want to do is to keep me here for three days more."

IX

"The Mystery of the Lady"

It changed the atmosphere immediately. Where they had been contented to fight on the defensive before, it seemed that they must become the aggressors.

"Then," said Rourke, "we'll get you out if you have the nerve to come out with us."

She shook her head violently. "There's no hope of that," she said. "Oh, I understand that there's no hope. I know that one of you can get out at a time without so much trouble. But if the three of us went at once, they would be sure to see and hear us. If they did, what could keep them from catching us? I know how fast their horses run. If we tried to get out on horse-back, we couldn't get out at all, because, even if we were on horses, they'd run us down."

What she said was sound sense. There was no doubt of that. The only possible manner of escape was in sifting out across the edge of the plateau singly and then proceeding on foot. Rourke went to the door and stared into the darkness of the night to find a new thought. But there was none there. When the thought did come, it was like a flash of light. He whirled on the others.

"You're right," he said, "the three of us could never make it. The thing to do is to split up the party. One of us must try to sneak with you through the lines on foot. The other must stay here and do something to make those gents out yonder think that all three of us have stayed. That'd make 'em rest

58

easy. You can make sure that they're within hearing distance."

"Two go and leave one?" asked the girl. "One man against that crowd?"

"One man with guns in a fort, you might say," said Rourke. "That ain't so bad. And the two that get through, if they're lucky, can send back help the next day. Cairn, does it sound like sense to you?"

Cairn was grave. Plainly he did not like the thought, but he was ashamed to disagree.

"It sounds like sense," he agreed as heartily as he could.

"There wouldn't be no danger for the gent that was left behind to make the noise like we was having a party?" went on Rourke with a meaning glance.

"No danger at all," growled Cairn. He added: "But what's to be gained for you by getting out now before the three days is up?"

"It's her secret," said Rourke, pleased to have thrown Cairn in the wrong.

"She knows us now," said Cairn. "Maybe she'll tell us what she wouldn't tell us before. How about it? If the chance was taken, it *would* be a chance. Will you tell us what all the mystery is about, and why you have to get out of here before three days?"

She flushed and looked from one of them to the other.

She was obviously fighting a battle with herself before she could make herself speak. "If I tell you anything," she said faintly, "I have to tell you everything, and it's hard to tell."

Neither of them spoke, but looked down to the floor. After all, it was hard, indeed, if they should risk their lives blindly in a cause of which they knew nothing.

"To go back to the beginning," she said at last, "my father was the son of a prosperous rancher. When my grandfather died, he left quite a little to both my father and my Uncle Charles. But he left all of his business sense to Uncle Charles and none to my father. Poor Dad ran through his money in a few years, and at the same time Uncle Charles was doubling and redoubling his." She paused, very ill at ease and looking wistfully at them, as though to beg them to understand without the necessity of words. "Finally," she said, "poor Dad was in such a condition that he was unable to give my brother, Lawrence, and myself an education. All he could do was to shift from place to place and try to dodge his debts. Oh, those were terrible days."

They raised their eyes from the floor and watched her with keen glances.

"And about that time . . . I was ten . . . we came across Uncle Charles in the mountains. Dad and Uncle Charles had quarreled years before. Uncle Charles was disgusted at the way Dad had run through his patrimony. And Dad was disgusted with Uncle Charles because he could no longer get money from him. Dad had received a good many loans, and there was no prospect of returning them. But when he saw how much money Uncle Charles was making, and how that fortune grew and grew, he could not see how Charles could deny him. That was not Dad's nature. What he himself had belonged to all his friends. They had only to ask in order to receive. So he considered his brother parsimonious. You can understand how they both felt. There had been quarrels and accusations.

"But when Uncle Charles found us in the mountains on a hunting trip, his heart was a little softened by us kiddies. He took a fancy to us. You see, his own wife had died childless, and he was so fond of her that he would never marry again. There was no prospect of his having an heir. Lawrence and I were sure to step into his money when he died. Naturally that gave him an interest in us. He had an interview with Dad, and at the end of it they had agreed that Lawrence and I were to be sent East to school at the expense of Uncle Charles. In return Father agreed that he would not interfere. And, the year after we left him, poor Dad died. Loneliness and failure had broken his heart, I think. And he *was* a darling."

She paused a moment, breathing deeply, her eyes bright with tears. It seemed to Rourke that it would be a priceless privilege to take her in his arms and comfort her. All he could do was look upon her tenderly.

"I had a glorious time at school, though," she said, lifting her head at last and smiling suddenly on them. "It was all new to me, and it was all happy. I had no friends at first, except a riding horse, but that changed. In two years I was perfectly at home.

"Lawrence is two years older than I, and he had had too much freedom for too long a time. He couldn't settle down at his school. There was one long series of fights with his teachers and his schoolmates. Besides, he began to spend more than his allowance, and . . . it was a nasty mess from the start with poor Lawrence. Not that he was bad, you understand, but he simply drifted into the wrong habits. Can you understand?"

Both men nodded.

"Then he was expelled from the school he was attending. Uncle Charles sent a very cruel letter to him with a severe reprimand, warning him that it must never happen again. At the same time he arranged matters so that Lawrence could enter another school. But there was such a sting in the letter that Lawrence . . . he was only fourteen, you know, and very wild-headed . . . was terribly shamed and angered. And"—she blushed as she told it—"instead of taking the money to the new school, he went off to New York with it, and in a month men had taken every cent away from him. After that, he dropped out of sight for a whole year and finally turned up in the West again. There he got into trouble which was not all his fault, and he was . . . was put in jail!" She bowed her head and her interlaced fingers worked and struggled. "Uncle Charles heard about it and went down and cleared up the matter. But he told poor Lawrence that he was through with him and would never help him again, no matter what trouble he fell into . . . and Lawrence was thrown on the world when he was only sixteen."

She sighed, and her starry eyes looked out through the open door and into the past with a world of pity. "Of course, I helped him as much as I could," she went on, "by saving on my allowance. But all that I could send him was not a very great deal. He had to work . . . he had to do all sorts of work, and Lawrence didn't like work. He hadn't been raised in that way, you see. And he could not keep in the offices, where Uncle Charles put him to work up into a profession. The only thing he liked was something in the open air, where he had freedom . . . or what he thought was freedom, poor boy. He punched cows, worked in mines and lumber camps . . . he grew up in a rough school. And all the time he kept brooding on what he felt to be an injustice . . . that I should have so much, and he should have so little.

"You see, when I came West during vacations, I always went to see him, and though I dressed as simply as I could, I was always riding an expensive horse, or there was something about me to remind Lawrence that he was disinherited . . . for it had come to that by this time . . . and that I was the favorite and would get everything. It was hard on him, of course. I always promised him that, when I inherited the fortune, I would give him his half . . . but . . . but . . . he'd been among such rough men . . . and he'd had such a hard time . . . he'd naturally grown suspicious, you see. . . ." She paused and watched them with miserable eyes.

"The damned puppy!" exploded Rourke, wild with anger.

"You have no right to say that!" she cried, white with anger and pain. "I . . . if he were here you wouldn't dare to say that and. . . ." Suddenly she melted. "Oh, forgive me for saying that, but try to understand him. He isn't bad . . . only misled. At any rate, he stopped writing to me after a while, and, when I came out in the summer, it was harder and harder to find him. Then there came a time when he had trouble with his employer, and after that Larry lived with very bad men. There was more worry for Uncle Charles before he died. When I was eighteen, I met a handsome young Englishman, and my head was turned, don't you know?" She blushed and smiled a trembling smile. "I was engaged when I came out that summer," she murmured. "And when Uncle Charles heard about it, he was furious. He was a very absolute man, you see. He always would have his own way, or else smash things. Dad said he was that way when he was a boy, and he never grew out of the habit. When he saw the picture of my fiancé, he was very angry and ordered me to break the engagement. I refused."

"Good!" said Rourke.

"I was stubborn, too," she admitted. "We had a very sad quarrel. I went East again. By that time I admit that I was forgetting all about the handsome Englishman, but I wouldn't tell Uncle. And just after I left, he died and made a strange will. In it he declared that I should have an income until I was twenty-one. And on my twenty-first birthday, if I were unmarried and presented myself at the town of Truxton to see the executor of the estate, I should have the entire fortune. At noon on my twenty-first birthday, you see? But if I did not come at that time, or if I were married before . . . he wanted me to have three full years to drift apart from the Englishman . . . the entire fortune should go to Lawrence."

"By guns!" cried Rourke, springing up. "Lawrence is the one they called Larry in the gang that rode up here."

She made a sign of assent. "That was he. I heard his voice and knew it. Two months ago, he came to see me. That night he took me out riding and wouldn't let me turn back. We traveled for two days, and at the end of that time he brought me to a gang of rough men, and there he kept me ever since."

"The hound," muttered Cairn.

"Finally I managed to break away, get my horse and saddle, and ride off. I rode and rode like mad until there was that fall . . . and you know all the rest of the story."

X

The Battle of the Giants

For a time Rourke could only stare at her.

"This Lawrence," he said slowly, trying to control his emotions, "this brother of yours, has been holding you so that you can't show up to get the property that's due to come your way, if you show up on the day." He choked. The thought of such baseness and to such a girl overwhelmed him. He remembered the handsome, sneering face of Larry and wished profoundly that the stone of Cairn had struck him on the head, instead of on the breast. There would have been an end to their problems in a single stroke, if that had happened.

Cairn suddenly took charge. "Take a step across the floor."

She obeyed without question.

"Now run to the door and back as fast as you can."

Again she obeyed, with a faint laugh of embarrassment, and in her running she limped only slightly on the leg that had been broken. Luck and chance and some skill had made it a perfect recovery.

"There's only one thing that remains to be settled," said Cairn, "and that's which one of us goes out with you, and which one of us stays here." He turned to Rourke. "Suppose you and me go out and talk it over in the night? When there's a free sky over a gent's head, it sort of helps him to think sometimes."

Rourke gave his eyes one strong embrace of the girl. It

seemed to him that a glory had settled around her. Perhaps it would be the last time he ever saw her, and yet he could not bid her farewell. Then he turned and walked through the door behind the other. Cairn led the way straight to the circle of evergreens around the spring. There he paused. It was a dark, dark place for such an encounter. The starlight filtered vaguely through to them, and that uncertain light made the bulk of Cairn more terribly imposing than ever.

"Here's a place for us," said Cairn. "We'll have no talk, no shouting, no cussing. We'll fight silent, son. No gun work, either, because one of us has to be left enough alive to play a part in the game while the other two get away. Between you and me, I wish that I hated you more. I been trying hard to work myself up to it all these days, but somehow I sort of like you, Rourke. You've played tolerable square with me. We've worked together, and we've fought together. But the devil of it is that we love the same woman, and we're going to fight for her here. Am I right?"

"Right," said Rourke.

"We fight till one of us gives in. And the gent that gives in . . . if he's left living . . . stays here and starts doing something that'll make the gang out yonder in the rocks think that the whole three of us is still here."

"Right!" said Rourke huskily again.

"Then," said Cairn, "start in. I'm bigger. You make the first move."

"I can't do it," sighed Rourke. "Cairn, we've been through too much together. I . . . I can't."

"You fool!" snarled Cairn, and he struck like a flash and with all his might.

Rourke saw the danger in the last instant and strove to side-step. But the rock-hard fist grazed his head, and there was force enough to knock him stunned to his knees. He heard a gasp of joy from the other as though Cairn could not realize that such a great advantage had come to him in the first assault. Then Cairn closed with a rush.

Already Rourke was rising and strove to side-step the rush. But he moved too sluggishly from that awkward position. The great body struck him. They rolled in a heap to the ground. It was like battling with a bear. A great hand caught at his shirt, as though it were made of tissue paper. Rourke clubbed his fist and beat it into the face of the giant. It was like beating on granite. Cairn laughed, a horrible bubbling sound, and reached again for the throat.

Once he had that grip, the fight was ended before it was well begun, and Rourke knew it. Babe struck his left fist past the face of Cairn, missing purposely. Then he jerked back the elbow, and the elbow bone landed heavily, like a striking club, on the side of Cairn's head. There was a groan, a sudden relaxing of muscles in the great bulk that bore him down. It was only an instant of bewilderment. But in that instant Rourke rolled from under and leaped away. Cairn swung to his feet and followed.

He came slowly, silently, crouched, with his left arm crooked across his face to shield him from blows, and his right fist poised. He could either strike with bone-breaking force with that poised fist, or he could grapple if he came in close.

One more close grapple would be the last. Luck had favored Rourke in that first encounter, but he dreaded the power of those thick arms. His flesh burned where the fingers of Cairn had gripped him, and his ribs ached where the pressure of the arm had been around him.

In the meantime, dancing slowly back, watching his antagonist every instant, he took stock of his surroundings. Nothing except a closed room could have been better for

Cairn. The circle of trees closed them in like a fence, and the gloom was all in favor of close combat. In the open sunlight, with plenty of room and a firm footing, it would have been far otherwise. But here there was neither light nor room, and the mastiff had the advantage over the wolf. The very ground, covered with slippery pine needles, made swift footwork dangerous or impossible.

Yet, activity he must show to escape close combat. Suddenly, Cairn rushed. Rourke, instead of retreating, leaped to one side and struck with his left hand, as the monster went by. He had been in many a battle before but never since his boyhood had he ever struck with half his might. Now his whole force was behind the blow that landed squarely on the side of the giant's head. But Cairn neither halted nor staggered. He merely turned with a grunt of rage and rushed again.

Rourke stood his ground long enough to whip in two long-range blows. But he merely battered his fists against the head of Cairn, and still the latter came in. It was not a blind advance. The bearded man came in with a cunning, weaving motion that made him hard to strike solidly, and always he waited for a wide opening before he struck, hoping rather for that wished-for chance to set his hands a second time upon Rourke.

But it was not the same Rourke who had begun the battle, for the despair was leaving the heart of Babe, and in its place was the old fighting lust that had been born in him. He had felt the strength of his enemy, and knew that he was over-matched in sheer brawn. But he had also felt his own blows drive home with all his force. If he could only make that head go back—if he could drive home either right or left to the vulnerable jaw.

Watching like a hawk, he danced away. Once more Cairn came within range. Rourke bent and smashed up with a swinging uppercut. It flashed under the warding arm of Cairn, found the face, and crunched to the bone. Cairn jerked up his head, badly hurt, and struck savagely in return. The blow was short, and, while it was still swinging, Rourke stepped in and struck again, swaying forward all his weight behind his stiffened right arm. Now he found the target. It was not the point of the jaw, or the battle would have ended there. It was the side of the face, and Cairn drew back with a gasping curse of astonishment. Never before in his hundred battles had he felt such a blow. Never in a hundred battles had Rourke smote with such force. And he had the proof that he could, indeed, hurt the giant and stop him. If only fortune kept him away from the rib-smashing power of those arms.

An instant later, he was almost cornered among the trees. He escaped by a fraction of an inch from those clutching hands, wheeled away into the open, and met the next lunge with his former maneuver, a swinging blow from beneath, and then an overhand punch with all his might behind it. Once more the first blow went home, jerked up the giant's head, and, when the second blow crashed home, the fist of Rourke knocked out a spatter of crimson. Laughing in brutal satisfaction, he stepped back again, and that instant his foot slipped on the smooth needles. It was only a momentary stagger, but, before he could recover, the larger man had him.

Down they went again. The force of the rush tumbled them over and over. They became stationary, with Cairn on top, his crimson-stained face, his gasping breath close to Rourke. The man underneath saw the latter reach out, clutch a stone, and swing it up for the finishing blow.

Babe struggled with all his might. It was like struggling against a grizzly. The blow descended. He jerked his head up as far as he could, and the stone merely grazed his head. With an oath Cairn struck again. There was no question of fair play in his brain now. Cairn was fighting to kill, but terror gave Rourke Herculean force.

His legs, twined around the legs of Cairn, gave him leverage. He twisted, and the crushing bulk rolled away from him. They came to their feet. Cairn had retained the stone, and now he followed more actively. What his bare hands were not strong enough to accomplish, he could certainly succeed in with this weapon. Rourke danced back, feeling that the last moment had surely come. His heel struck the stalk of a fallen branch and knocked it behind him. Instantly he swerved, scooped it up, and, as Cairn came in, lurching after the weight of the stone with which he was striking Rourke, aimed for the head. The blow went home. The branch crunched like rotten cork and broke in two. But the giant halted, wavered, and then sank to his side. Instantly Rourke was on him. Babe caught up the fallen stone. He flattened the half-conscious Cairn and poised the stone above him.

"Cairn," he asked, "are you through, or do I bash your brain out?"

Cairn groaned: "You've won . . . you've won!"

XI

" 'Follow Me' "

The sense of his wounds did not come to Rourke until he stood up again. Then he felt the warm trickle of crimson from a wound on the side of his head. He was covered to the hips with bruises. His throat was swollen and bruised, and his head was singing with a thousand voices.

He stood back, fearless now, and saw Cairn stagger and reel to his feet. It mattered not now what strength there might be in the hands of the big man. His spirit was broken, and no broken-spirited man could stand for an instant before Rourke. He watched Cairn slump away into the night, going slowly, slowly toward the cabin.

Would the beaten man try to get at a gun now? He himself hurried on ahead. But outside the door of the cabin he paused. He dared not show himself in that guise to Gertrude. He could hear the tingle of her cry in anticipation. Instead of entering into the light of the shack, he called from without softly, and she came at once.

In the door she paused an instant, framed in a bright edging of light. It was as though she shone from within. The heart of Rourke leaped, and all the pains of the battle vanished from his limbs.

"We've talked it out," he said, when she was close to him. "We've talked it out, and then we tossed a coin to see who'd stay behind. Cairn lost the throw, so you go with me."

She hesitated a moment, and the hesitation was a bitter

thing for Rourke to witness. Plainly, he told himself, her heart was with Cairn. Now he wavered in his own mind. If she were truly fond of Cairn, would it not be more generous to change places with the big man, beaten though he were? After a moment he decided against that impulse. If Cairn kept a sharp look-out, there was no danger. They would not rush him in the face of his known skill with guns.

"Wait here," he said to the girl. "Get your eyes used to the night. I'll be out in a minute."

In the cabin, he buckled on a cartridge belt, slipped his Colt into the holster, and took his rifle. So equipped, he felt that his strength was doubled. Then he went back to the girl, to be greeted with a question about Cairn at once.

"But he hasn't come to say good bye," she said.

"It's a queer way there is about Cairn," said Rourke. "He sure hates to say good bye to anybody. Besides, he told me that he wanted to be scouting around on the far side of the plateau, when we started south over this edge here. We'll see him inside of three days, when we ride back from Truxton."

She nodded. "We'll see him then." Rourke could barely make out her gesture in the darkness. "And to think of leaving him here alone with all this danger. I think I could hardly say good bye to him, face to face. Oh, what a great-hearted man he is, don't you think so?"

The ache of Rourke's wounds returned. "Yes," he said, "he sure is." He pointed ahead, and, in anticipation of the danger to come, he lowered his voice to a murmur. "We're going to aim at that bunch of rocks yonder," he said. "I'm going first, in case we should scare up anything. I'm going slow. You follow close behind me, but far enough back so's you can watch the ground you're walking over. I'll take short steps. Try to step where I step. I'll keep clear of dead brush and things that might make a noise under our feet. Now get this one idea tight in your head and don't let it get out for a minute. If there comes any trouble . . . I mean, if we should have any bad luck and run into 'em . . . drop flat on the ground and stay there. Don't try to run. If you start running, they'll start shooting, and they ain't apt to miss even in this darkness. But if you lie still, the worst that can come is to have them take you, and that's better than being slugged with a chunk of lead. I'm talking straight to you. Will you remember?"

"Yes," she whispered, in imitation of his own voice.

"And you ain't afraid?"

"N-n-no!"

Presently he turned his back on her and started ahead, and he could hear the rustling of her clothes, as she followed. He made a careful way across the plateau, taking advantage of every little hollow, moving up behind every projecting rock that might shield them from the eyes of men looking for them. Halfway to the edge of the plateau he stopped short.

Out of the dark, far behind them, a mellow bass voice rose, rough and quavering on the first notes, and then swelling out into magnificent music and the metal twanging of the guitar hummed and beat around the indistinguishable words.

The small hand of the girl caught Rourke's shoulder. "Do you hear? Do you hear?" she whispered. "He's covering our retreat. Oh, it's the bravest thing I've ever heard. But . . . but it breaks my heart to think of him . . . so generous . . . so kind, and so alone . . . left behind us."

"Hush," said Rourke, his own throat swelling almost shut with emotion as he listened. For he had not dreamed that Cairn had it in him. It was a fineness of which he had never suspected the big fellow. After all, then, Cairn loved the girl as she deserved to be loved. He had put behind him all the humiliation of his defeat. He had risen like a hero to serve her in his own bitter hour. And Rourke was on the verge of turning and going back to him to clasp his hand. But he knew that this could not be. So, with another urgent whisper to the girl, he went on.

The rocks on the edge of the plateau loomed larger now. It seemed to him that here and there little bits of the quartz glistened in the starshine. There was ample covering for them, if they could ever attain those rocks, but there was ample covering, also, for a sentinel who might be lying in wait there to watch. What better place could a sentinel have chosen for a look-out position?

When there were not twenty feet between them and the rocks, he heard the crunching of walking feet beyond the edge of the plateau. Instantly he reached back and crushed the girl to the ground, as he himself dropped into a shallow hollow.

"Hello!" called a voice from the rock just before him.

Was that a hail meant for him? He set his teeth. Much could be done by a sudden attack on men taken half by surprise. He gathered his feet under him a little, prepared to leap up and spring forward. If he struck down that sentinel, even though the alarm were given, he might be able to place the girl on the sentinel's horse and send her shooting away swiftly through the night.

"Hello, Hal," called another voice, that of him who approached beyond the plateau rim.

"Here, Jim," answered another voice turned from Rourke, where he crouched in covert.

"Anything stirring?" asked he who had newly come up, and his feet were heard grinding on the rocks, as he climbed up.

"Not a thing," said Hal. "This is sure some job we got on our hands."

"Job is right," said the newcomer, "I'm plumb tired of the whole business."

"But there's a whole barrel of coin in it, if we can keep the girl here," said Hal.

"Maybe there is," said Jim, "but I sure don't hanker to put in a lot of work making the fortune of Larry. The looks of him makes me kind of tired, pal."

"Sure they do. They make all of us tired. He talks like he owned the golden key and could open the gates any time with 'em. But maybe he'll grow out of that foolishness. I was kind of a fool myself when I was a kid. Listen to that bull roar over there."

"That's because he knocked you off'n your horse, Hal, that day."

"If he's happy, let him sing. Four days from now, when everything is finished up, and Larry has the old man's stuff, we'll clean up on Rourke and Cairn. That's the word the chief passes along."

"The main thing is how do we know that Larry will split with the rest of us, fifty-fifty?"

"He'd better wish himself in hell if he don't make the split, and he knows it. Oh, he won't try to back down. He ain't got that much nerve."

"When we start that clean-up party, what'll become of the girl? There'll be a nice bunch of trouble raised when she gets loose and rides back to civilization with a yarn about what's happened to her, and how she's been held."

"The chief will tend to that. Maybe she'll be a pile older than she is before she gets back. Anyway, she sure won't get back till Larry has cleaned up the estate and given us our half. What he does with the other half is his own business."

"Say, that sounds like sense. But the clean-up of Rourke and Cairn . . . that'll be a job."

"Nope. As soon as Larry gets his business in his own hands, we'll just tighten up the lines and starve 'em till they're weak. They won't stand much starving. They ain't that kind. They'll come out with a bull rush, and we'll drop 'em!"

"But what if they should get in among us?"

"You keep that in your head to keep you awake. I got to be moving along." He strode off down the rocks, whistling softly. At the same instant Rourke touched the girl reassuringly and moved off to the side. There he flattened to the ground again. Not until the sound of the man who was going the rounds died out, did he rise up again, and this time he stood up to his full height.

"Oh, Hal . . . Hal!" he called, and walked swiftly toward the rocks.

"Hello! Who's that?" called Hal.

"Don't you know me?"

"Can't quite make you out, pal. Is it Larry?"

"Wrong. Do I look like that fool?" As he spoke, he came close and saw the sentinel, only the head of the man appearing above the rocks.

"But what the devil . . . ?" began Hal in bewilderment, as the giant figure loomed close before him. "Who are you?"

"A friend," said Rourke, and leaped over the ridge of rocks.

There was not even an outcry from Hal. A great hand had been clapped across his mouth, and the gun fell from his hand. In a trice he was helpless, hand and foot.

"Now," said Rourke, "I ought to wring your murderer's neck for you. But I ain't going to if you can buy your rotten life from me. Where's your boss?" Cautiously he removed his hand from the mouth of his victim.

"Yonder . . . below the rocks," stammered the sentinel. "My Lord, it's Rourke."

"That's right, it's me. Wait a minute."

He dragged his victim to the edge of the rocks. Below, in the hollow, he saw the horse. Without another word he bound and gagged his man and then hurried back to the girl.

"Quick!" he said, and sprang forward again with her at his side.

"And the man in the rocks?" she breathed. "He's still living?"

He wondered at her. How could she think of the welfare of the enemy at a time like this? A moment more and he had her in the saddle on the horse in the hollow.

"Follow me," he said, and struck forward swiftly across the hills.

XII

"On His Shoulder"

Never before had he put his full might into any work. Not even that brief and terrible battle with Cairn had drawn out all his powers. It had been too short truly to test him. But that night, throwing away his rifle, throwing away even his cartridge belt and revolver, trusting in the crisis only to the rifle that was slung by the saddle on the stolen horse, he matched his speed on foot against the speed of the horse. It was a fair contest. There were level stretches when the horse shot ahead of him. But in the rough going he easily worked up again—only to find the terrible strain of another open-country run behind him.

But when the dawn came, they had covered half the distance to Truxton. In that dawn for the first time the girl saw him with the crimson stains of the fight with Cairn dried on his face and all covered with dust, his flannel shirt rent open at the throat, his whole appearance terrible.

In bewilderment she gazed at him. It was a savage she saw, not Rourke. "Ah," she cried, as the truth came to her, "you fought him . . . you fought Cairn . . . and you won. Oh, that was it!"

He lay exhausted on the sand, dragging his breath in with a rattle. They had covered an incredible distance that night. Now he raised himself and stood reeling. "You'd rather that Cairn came with you?" he asked wearily. "Is that it?"

She only bowed her head. "All I wonder," she said at last, "is how two such men could be in one world at one time."

A moment later, they were on the way again. There was one hour to spare when they completed that long journey and came into Truxton, a bedraggled pair. But, weary as they were, there was something that remained to be done, and no time was spared.

It was Rourke who carried the word around. It was Rourke who banded together twenty good citizens eager for adventure and a fight. Then he went back to the meeting place in time to see Gertrude take into her hands the document that meant a fortune to her. Five minutes after noon the party struck back into the hills on the return journey.

She rode with them—for it was in vain that Rourke begged her to stay behind.

"I owe it all to you first and to him second," she said. "Oh, not the money only, but everything. What might they have done when they found that I was in the way of so much money? You can guess what they would have done. I can guess. It was my life you saved when you kept them from me."

And so she rode with them and set her teeth and fought away exhaustion.

That trip was made in record time across the hills. But when they swept over the last rise a day and a half away from Truxton, there was no sign of a siege. When they surged over the edge of the plateau, the first premonition of disaster was seen in a little smoking heap of ruins that marked the spot where the shanty had stood.

She screamed when she saw it, and the heart of Rourke stopped. If that house was down, was the body of big Angus Cairn—Black Cairn as so many thousands called him—lying charred in the midst?

No, they found him lying twenty feet from the door. He had been literally cut to pieces and died by inches. Neither had he died without exacting a toll from his slayers. There was a fresh heap of dirt nearby, and over the dirt was a rock, and on the rock had been hastily chipped an epitaph.

Here lies
Steve Sanders,
Hal Munroe,
Jim Banting.
They died fighting hard
and took their stuff from the front.

Such was the monument raised to the murderers. As for Angus Cairn, in death he seemed more formidable than in life. They had stabbed him in a dozen places. He carried enough bullet wounds to have stopped and killed five ordinary men. Yet, what he had done was plain enough.

The story could be read at a glance. When the bound man was found in the gray of the dawn, he told his story of how two had escaped, while the third of the party remained behind in the cabin and sang songs to put the sentinels off guard. That day there had been a vain pursuit of the girl and her escort, but the gap that lay between was insurmountable. And in the night they returned down-hearted, savage. And, perhaps, they heard from the cabin the ringing of the guitar and the mellow, golden voice of Cairn rising out of the darkness.

It must have driven them to madness. On horseback—the ground bore witness to that desperate charge—they had rushed the little cabin. And the defender had scorned to stay behind the walls. He had come out to meet his death like a man. He had come out from the door of the cabin. He had received those terrible wounds at a distance. Still, he had rushed in, and before he died he had dragged from their horses and finished three of the assailants. The others had killed him with their knives, where they dared not use revolvers.

Such was the death of Cairn. As they found it written on him and on the ground around him. They found beside him, laid in good order, his revolver and his rifle. Even the murderers, when their frenzy passed, must have realized that they had killed a hero. All of this was what the rescue party found and understood at a glance.

But what meant more to Rourke than the very picture of death was that the girl turned to him in her saddle and stretched out her arms to him. And, wondering, he drew her close to him and let her drop her head on his shoulder.

Yet even for her he would not stay behind. How he followed with the other men on the long ride north while only two men with worn-out horses turned back to escort Gertrude to Truxton again, how he and the others rode down the outlaws in the northern mountains, how they were shot down, one by one or in small groups as they were cornered, and how Rourke finally risked his life to take Larry alive and then escaped with him from the rest, got him to the sea, and sent him out of the country to try to find a new life elsewhere—all of these are things which happened and which were wonderful in the happening, but they formed another story and a long one.

But when all was ended, the trail finished, the vengeance exacted, there remained between Rourke and his wife, to the end of their lives, one place that was kept in a sacred silence.

Joe White's Brand

"Joe White's Brand" was first published in the October 14, 1922 issue of Street & Smith's *Western Story Magazine*. It appeared under Faust's George Owen Baxter byline. The heart of this story can be found in a line of its dialogue: "You can't judge a day by the middle of it. What makes it different comes in the beginning and the ending." So Joe White, a forty-five year old outlaw and long past his prime when he was named Young-Stallion-On-Fire by the Indians, learns once he meets up with Ted McKay, a young man with plans to be just like Joe.

I

"Six Against Six"

When he came out of the soft East, that is to say, from the Bowery of Manhattan, the Indians called him a strange combination of sounds that purported to mean: "Young-Stallion-On-Fire." Although that was thirty years ago, one could still find traces of the fire in his face. His eyes were, more often than not, dull and dead, but in the corners, at odd moments, one might catch a glimpse of something among the shadows, some glint and spark of danger.

At fifteen he had been a man in prowess. He had his full height of six feet and an inch. He weighed a hundred and seventy-five pounds. He was straight with the arrow straightness of a young poplar. He was strong as the toughest fir that wild winds ever cuffed back and forth vainly along a hillside. His nerve was chilled steel. And his strength was to the strength of other men as the muscle of a mule is to the muscle of a horse. With his hands he could smash or crush. With other weapons he was marvelously deadly. He was one of those marksmen, one of those rare experts with a gun, who miss only on the hundredth chance, when they grow careless. He seemed to carry in his head a range finder and a wind gauge combined. When he jerked his rifle butt against his shoulder, he was ready to kill as far as powder would drive the ball.

That was Young-Stallion-On-Fire. He had worn his hair long. His wild face had been handsome enough to strike home in many a girl's heart. His soul had been born full of joy. And in his mind was the profound belief that a life spent in danger was not a life spent in vain.

That was Young-Stallion-On-Fire thirty years ago. The thirty years had reduced his name to plain Joe White. They had worked other changes, also. To that original hundred and seventy-five pounds it had added forty pounds of massive, solid muscle. The erect head sank a little forward. The handsome face broadened at jaw and cheekbone. The laughing mouth was now a grim, straight line. The brows grew thick and beetling. And the eyes under those grizzled brows, as has been said, were habitually wearied and dull.

They were weary and dull because in every three years of the past thirty Joe White had packed away the contents of an ordinary life, or more. The danger that he had come courting had been his constant fellow. Now it had come to be his shadow, also, so that, no matter where he went, fear haunted him. What had happened to him was that which happens to hunting beasts that are trailed by men. Terror grows into an instinct. They are bred into the fear of man. So it was with Joe White. He could never escape from the chill apprehension of disaster about to overtake him.

Of course, it was something that he confided to no man. And no man in the wide universe would have dreamed of suggesting that there was anything timorous about Joe White. Yet, for a full twenty years, now, there never passed a night when he did not waken suddenly, as though a hand had fallen on his shoulder, a sinister voice had struck his ear. Then he would lie awake for an hour or more, his heart beating fast, his nerves quivering, and that sick feeling of impending disaster ever growing in him.

So it was that his face came to be marked. He grew more and more taciturn. Men felt the difference. Whereas he had been a famous boy hero twenty-five years ago, and still, although outlawed, a glorious and daring figure who had won the sympathies of men even ten years before, he was now, at forty-five, darker, more forbidding. The chill that possessed him could be communicated. Of late, men of all kinds had joined in the pursuit of Joe White, some because they hated him for injuries he had inflicted upon them or their friends or their relatives, and some for the glory that was to come to the man who struck down the great outlaw, and others hunting simply for the sake of the gold that was to be won by the successful killer.

When this last class appeared, Joe White knew in his deep heart of hearts that he was lost. For love of fame, love of beauty, will not lure men to such desperate ends as the love of money. The lucky bullet that brought him down would bring to the hunter a fair competence for life. Therefore, Joe White knew that this, in fact, must soon be his end.

These things were in his mind; they could never be out of his mind. They clung in his thoughts even while he was scanning the trail with his glass.

But, of course, those hardy followers of his who were grouped a little higher on the trail, standing beside the horses that the panting beasts might rest the more during this priceless breathing spell, could not dream what lay in the heart of the leader. To them he seemed what he had ever been—indomitable, invincible, filled with power and exhaustless luck. They would no more have dreamed of questioning a decision that he made than they would have dreamed of putting a conundrum to a sphinx. They would no more have questioned his wisdom than that of eternal providence.

"Step up here, Ike," said Joe White presently.

There strode forth, from among the group huddled under the trees on the mountainside, a tall, raw-boned man, one of those strange persons who are ever ravenous as vultures, and as famine-struck in appearance.

"There they come," said Joe White. "Look yonder, down that third hill."

Ike, changing color suddenly, snatched hurriedly at the glass and glued it to his eye. Having located what was pointed out to him, he began to curse with a swift and guttural ecstasy of rage. For it was Ike who had suggested that they come in this direction. Since this was a little farther north than Joe White usually ventured in his expeditions, he had for this one occasion departed from his usual habit of taking his own ideas alone. He had allowed the opinion of Ike to overrule his own on the vote of his men. So they had come by the north pass.

Of course, there was sure to be a hot pursuit, at any rate. The daylight robbery of the Justin bank had been too bold, and the sum with which they had escaped had been too large for him to get away without a violent struggle with justice. Yet, they had secured such an excellent start, they had so fooled the first rush of the pursuers, that they should have gained more ground than this. But this one party had apparently guessed their destination and had struck out blindly and had fallen upon the right trail. Now, a thousand yards away, or even less, they came toiling up the slopes, growing closer by the momemt.

Ike lowered the glass with a profound oath.

"Chief," he said to Joe White, "I sure was wrong to give you that advice. But I got a way of fixing it up, I think. You seen how many there were?"

"Yes," said Joe White. "I seen how many there were, Ike. There were six."

"Six?" said Ike, his face brightening as he caught the leader in an error, no matter how small. "Six, did you say? I guess there was only five, chief!"

"There's another one coming, though," said the leader. "He'll be around that corner of the hill in a minute."

The others had heard the small dispute. Now they looked to one another with faint smiles. It was as though they would say to one another that the great leader was drawing things a bit fine when he pretended that he could look through walls of solid rock. But now, to Ike's utter amazement, another form of a horseman rode into view on the winding trail so far beneath, trotting his nag briskly to catch up with the leaders. The general exclamation of wonder brought no reply from Joe White.

All the men saving one were too accustomed to similar feats to make a comment, but reckless young Cloudesley, in spite of his youth and riding his first trail with Joe White, broke out: "And how the devil did you know that, chief?"

The leader turned quietly toward him. "They were looking back over their shoulders, son," he said, "but they weren't looking back as though they were running away. So I figured that they had somebody coming after 'em."

Cloudesley pondered the simple answer a moment.

"But how'd you know that there was only one coming behind?" he asked.

"That trail ain't steep enough to make more'n one man fall behind," said Joe White. He turned again to Ike. "Got anything in your head now?" he asked.

It was a mild reproof for the bad advice that had put them in this trouble.

"I got one good idea," said Ike.

"Let's have it, son. We sure need good ideas, now."

"Well, there's six of them, and there's six of us. Suppose we wait for 'em right here. When they come nosing around the last turn, we'll let 'em have it! Each of us will pick out his man. And there . . . one puff . . . and the whole gang of 'em go to kingdom come."

His little eyes sparkled with delight at the thought. And there was a general silence as they waited for the opinion of the chief.

When he spoke, it was with a little more than his usual heat. "There you are again," he said. "That's the way with all you youngsters. You want to rush right in and take the bull by the horns, but you don't do no thinking! It's a pretty rare thing when six men die without even wounding one of them that are doing the killing. If one of us was wounded, it would slow up the riding of the whole gang of us so much, afterwards, that we'd most likely all get caught."

There was a breath of silence after this. Young Cloudesley struck in. "Seems to me," he said, "that we ain't in a grocery store. We're in a game where the chances are big to win and big to lose. If a gent ain't got the nerve, he oughtn't to take up the trail with us. And if he ain't ready to take his medicine, he ain't got a right to a share of the profits."

"You mean," translated Joe White, who was so painfully eager to reduce things to their lowest terms that strangers who did not know him were sometimes apt to think him a fool, "that, if any of the boys get shot, we ought to leave him lie? We ought to ride along and leave him behind to swallow his medicine?"

"Why, sure," said young Cloudesley. "That's what I'd expect. All I'd want would be some water and a few extra rounds of ammunition. Then I'd be ready to fight my own last fight."

"It'd sure be your last fight," said the other. "You killed that fat gent at Justin, and there was no call for him to be butchered any more'n for a calf to be shot in the pasture. They'll remember you for that, Cloudesley!"

The eye of young Cloudesley shot fire as he stared back at Joe White. But, bold as he was, he dared not answer the mild-spoken chief. He waited another moment, and then he said: "Still, what is there against what I want to do?"

"Nothing," said Joe White, "except that, if you dropped, I'd stay behind with you, through thick or thin."

"The devil," grunted Cloudesley. "I wouldn't be asking you to."

"I wouldn't be staying, mind you," said Joe White, "all because I wanted to pull you through, but partly because I wanted to stay on account of myself."

"I don't understand," said Cloudesley.

"I didn't figure that you would," said Joe White. "But, if one of my boys dropped on the trail fighting a fight for his own sake and the rest of us, his ghost would come on behind me if I was to leave him lying there. Nope, I'd turn back and take my chance with him."

The others muttered briefly and faintly in approval, for each in his mind's eye saw himself fall and saw this dauntless and invincible warrior coming to his aid with the power of a ghost in his brain and in his hand. But young Cloudesley still shrugged his shoulders and shook his head, unconvinced.

"Maybe you'd keep on running around the world to avoid having to knock over one of 'em that are following us?" he asked with a half sneer.

Joe White raised his burly head and looked fixedly at the youth. "Yep, son," he said quietly at length. "I'd run around the world, right enough, to get away from having to kill a man."

Cloudesley started to laugh, remembering the terrific record of this man-slayer. Then he found the laugh withering on his lips.

As they continued along the trail, he allowed his horse to

fall behind the rest. That was a sure sign that he was growing absent-minded with thought, for ordinarily he was ever up at the front, and at the front he seemed fretting that even Joe White should ride before him. Falling behind in this fashion, he took occasion to drop a whole lap behind the others. Loitering thus far in the rear, he used every opportunity to get a glimpse of those who followed, staring at them through his own glass.

He made out that there were five seasoned men of the mountains, with rifles and revolvers, all well-mounted. In addition, there was a mere youngster who rode a dancing horse at the head of the rest and was continually opening a gap between himself and the others in the eagerness of his pursuit. When he saw the youth, distinguished by that restless horse, by the solid crimson of his silk bandanna, and by the old, black felt hat whose wide brim flopped about his face, young Cloudesley sneered and involuntarily reached for his gun. When mere children took the trail of famous Joe White, it was a sign that the latter was growing old.

II

"The Kid Shows Fight"

He pondered one thought long in his head, but at length he determined to let tall Ike into his confidence. From the first, he and Ike had taken to each other, if not as boon companions, at least as men who liked each other better than they liked any of the others.

So he rode on until he could draw Ike back beside him. They were toiling up a mountainside scattered with a wild rubble of boulders. The gorge below was choked with huge stones and the naked stalks of trees that had been swept there by a landslide two winters before. And, still climbing toward the skyline that loomed white-hot above them, young Cloudesley on the way opened his heart to his companion.

"Ike," he said, "I'm for dropping back, the two of us, and waiting till we get a good chance, and then spraying lead into that posse. D'you figure in on that game with me?"

Ike seized on the offered chance. "You and me think alike," he said. "It sure has been riling me to ride along through the mountains, running like a parcel of quail from six ordinary gents like them that are coming behind us. I dunno but that Joe White. . . ." The criticism stuck in his throat.

"I know," said Cloudesley darkly. "I know just what you got in your head. Maybe you and me think the same about him, too. Well, rifles get rusty and hosses get old, and maybe the best of men get old, too." Here he winked broadly at Ike, and Ike grinned joyously in return.

"Old hosses and old guns get throwed away," said this natural philosopher, "and maybe the time ain't far off from Joe White, for all he thinks that he knows so much. But getting back to this little party, when d'you think, Cloudesley?"

"I think," said Cloudesley, "that the time for it is when it begins to get sort of darkish in the lower valleys, but there's still good light for shooting on the upper slopes. They'll be looking down, and, seeing all the shadows, they'll be thinking about getting ready to camp for the night when the full darkness comes, d'you see? So they won't be watching the trail ahead of 'em as hard as they might."

So it was agreed between them. Through the rest of the afternoon they said no word to their companions of what they intended. Before the night, they should have made themselves distinguished in the eyes of the others in the party, or else they would lie dead on the road. Therefore, it was that they looked far behind them and smiled sternly to themselves.

But when the shadows began to pool in the bottom of the gullies like blue smoke, heavier than air, Ike made an imperceptible sign to his fellow marauder, and they drew back from the others.

Joe White marked them falling behind, and he turned in his saddle as though to speak, but he changed his mind and merely watched them drop from sight around the next shoulder of a hill. Then he said, loud enough for those nearest to him to hear: "They sure learn hard, these young folks. That is . . . they learn if they live long enough. But them that has just fallen back . . . I dunno . . . I dunno."

So they went on, with the steam rising from their horses in the sudden evening chill of those lofty mountains, climbing and climbing, until, half an hour after Ike and Cloudesley had disappeared on the back trail, there was a brisk fusillade of rifle fire behind them.

It began and ended in the space of thirty seconds, but that time sufficed for Joe White to swing his horse about, sweep through the rear of his party, and thunder down the slope. But, as he did so, over the crest of a higher shoulder of ground just above him on the other side appeared Ike, riding at full speed, his right arm hanging helplessly at his side, and the reins in his teeth, while he urged his mustang forward with quirt and spurs.

Just as he came into view, a rifle clanged behind him, while poor Ike tossed up his arms and rolled out of the saddle. If the bullet had not killed him, it seemed that the fall certainly must. Yet Joe White was as good as his word. He raced his steed up the slope. He flung himself out of the saddle, and he sprawled at the side of Ike.

The latter was unspeakably crushed by his fall, but now he managed to open his eyes and gasp out a few words, while the other members of White's crew, in imitation of their leader, pushed up to the top of the hill-shoulder and prepared to drive back any rush of the pursuers.

"Chief," said Ike, "I'm sure ashamed."

"Ashamed of what, son?" said Joe White kindly. "The best of us got to be beat someday."

"But I turned around and run from what was coming to me," said the dying man.

"Your gun arm was busted. What else could you do but run?" asked the leader.

"Lord bless you for saying that, Joe White," said Ike solemnly. "I'll tell you what happened . . . Cloudesley and me thought that we could blow the life out of them that come after us. We figured that, after we'd wiped them off the trail, we could come back and talk pretty big even in front of you."

"Go on, son," said the leader, still gentle. "You could've

talked loud enough in front of me before. I know that you got nerve."

A smile worked on the lips of Ike. But the torture of his wounds wiped it out. "Anyway," he gasped out, "we went back and got down behind that bunch of black rocks. You remember 'em?"

"I remember," said Joe White. "I figured that was where you and Cloudesley was doing the shooting. It looked made to order for Indian work."

"Sure," said Ike, "but them that was on the trail in the posse didn't seem to notice it none. They was jogging along mighty brisk, gaining every lick on you and the rest of the boys. Right in front of 'em there was riding that young kid with the red bandanna and the old, black felt hat and the frisky gray hoss. He was the nearest, and I figured that I'd take him last, because he looked the easiest.

"So me and Cloudesley got our rifles drilled on the line, and we give each other the wink . . . we was 'bout to turn loose when the young gent that rode in front let out a yell and just nacherally dropped out of the saddle. I dunno how he figured that there was something wrong, but he sure worked it all out. He dropped out of that saddle like he had a slug in him, and he landed flat behind some rocks that wasn't big enough to cover up a tomato can . . . but somehow he made them big enough to cover him, and all that I could see of him was the end of his rifle. He'd got that rifle out and in place while he was falling.

"Meantime, I put a chunk of lead into the hindmost of the gang, and, while he was still falling, I drilled the gent next to him through the shoulder . . . I'm sure it was the shoulder, the way he swung around in the saddle. Cloudesley had dropped two of 'em slick as a whistle on his side. Then both of us pumped our lead into the fifth man. There might be doubts about the other four, but that fifth man was sure dead before he struck the ground.

"Just as he fell, Cloudesley jumps up in the air with a yell. I thought that he had lost his head because of the work he'd been doing with his gun . . . and it was neat enough work, at that . . . but he jumped up with a yell and fell down dead. The kid with the red bandanna had chipped a bullet into him, some ways, though I'd thought that Cloudesley was plumb covered up where he lay.

"It made me so mad to see what had happened that I turned loose a blast of lead at the kid, but I couldn't hit nothing. I just blistered the rocks, that was all. Then, the first thing I know, I get landed in the right arm. The young devil had worked to the left behind his rocks, and he give me mine that way . . . from the side.

"I had enough head to shoot a couple of times with the left hand. Then I got up, left the rifle laying in the notch, and run for my hoss, not thinking of nothing, every lick of the way, but what you'd said, chief, that, if a gent got hurt fighting for the rest, you'd see him through. I got into the saddle and started racing away. Just when I thought that I was safe . . . you seen what happened. But . . . Joe White, make me one promise."

"I'll try to do it."

"Keep clear of that kid with the red bandanna. He's just a nacheral wildcat. Will you do that?"

"I'll see what I can do, son. Now tell me what I can do for you."

"You can wait till you get your chance and then ride down into the hollow back at Piketown and give Pa a good word for me, will you? The old man'll be sort of cheered up if you tell him that when I died. . . ." He stopped and began to gasp for breath. "Chief. . . ." He died before the next word came.

Joe White, without emotion, closed his eyes, then deliberately drew out a pencil and scribbled on the rock nearest the head of the dead man: **Ike Colfax died here, with his boots on. Them that did find him, take a word to his dad in Piketown that he was talking about his old man last of all.**

The next posse to ride that way would find the dead man and the inscription, and so the message would be sure to reach Ike's father.

That accomplished, the leader went up to the ridge above, where his three remaining men were lingering. But they had seen nothing along the slope beneath them. The kid with the red bandanna had chosen to remain strangely quiet on the scene of his victory; he had not followed to make out just what had become of the second man he had shot.

The three were for riding back to destroy the kid and rescuing from him the share of the loot that Cloudesley carried, but the leader ruled them down, and, presently, the party spurred on along the trail.

III

"A Worthy Foe"

There was at least one gain, according to the three remaining followers of Joe White. They had crushed the posse that was immediately behind them, and they had done it without loading themselves down with wounded men. Moreover, even though the share of Cloudesley was lost, they had the share of Ike to split into four portions and redivide. So that, take it all in all, the adventure of the mountainside and the deaths of Ike and Cloudesley were rather fortunate happenings.

But, when Blinky and Jack Lawrence and Sam Hunter came to this agreement, their leader overheard and frowned upon the conclusion.

"A man has just so many killings under his belt," he said, "and every one that he chalks brings him that much closer to his finish. I'd about as soon send a chunk of lead into myself as shoot another man, I'm that near gone."

"What have the killings that Cloudesley and Ike done got to do with us?" he was asked with some heat.

"They're blamed on me," said Joe White, "and it's right that they should be. I got this gang together. I started 'em off on the hunt. All the deaths that come by the way are deaths that I've caused. You boys can shake your heads and swaller your grins, but I know what I'm talking about."

That melancholy viewpoint daunted them only for the moment. In the strange mind of their leader were shadowy and mysterious corners that they felt no ordinary man could understand. He had to have some weaknesses if he were to be human. And these superstitions were his weaker part. So they made no answer, but smiled slyly to one another.

Joe White himself, no matter how convinced he might be that vengeance would eventually overtake him, slackened the pace of the party that night. As he explained, the youngster in the red bandanna would certainly not dare to pursue them single-handed. Besides, if he were human, he would stay to care for his wounded companions of the trail. So the outlaws camped rather earlier than usual, taking less than ordinary care to withdraw themselves to a secluded place.

They posted Jack Lawrence, the oldest head and the cleverest fighter, next to Joe White, as guard during the first watch of the night, and, before darkness had covered the height upon which they were camped, the other three were asleep.

White himself was to be awakened at midnight to take his turn watching. But midnight was long past when Joe White awakened and found the campfire dead and no Jack Lawrence within sight.

Following a first and natural suspicion, he hurried to his feet and looked around him. But all the horses were there. Certainly, if Lawrence had planned a defection from the party, he would not have gone away on foot, carrying his share of the gold coin.

The leader turned back thoughtfully to the fire. It was not completely dead. From a final spark a frail column of smoke was rising, a smoke that they had dared to venture in the darkness so long as the rocks were piled around the blaze to keep it from showing at any distance. He always insisted upon a campfire, even at great risk, on account of the heart that it put into the men on a long trail. At the end of the day, it was a nucleus of home around which they could group themselves.

It gave them a feeling of security, no matter how much of a real danger it might be. It afforded an opportunity for relaxation from a nervous strain.

Now he stirred the ashes, found the living ember, and raised from it a meager, wagging finger of flame. Then he placed over the flame a few dry sticks, crosswise, until the sticks kindled. Presently as big a fire as he dared venture was burning again. It cheered him as much as ever it cheered any of his men. It cast a light, also, by which he could look down into the faces of his men, and, assured by their quiet and their silence that they still slept, he took up the problem of locating the missing sentinel.

For many reasons, the situation was curious. In the first place, it was most unusual that a member of one of his parties should have defied him. In the second place, it was strange that Jack Lawrence should be the man, for he and Jack had ridden upon more than one trail before this, and Jack had ever been the religious soul of obedience.

He went to the outer circle around the camp where Jack had been walking. There was the trail, beaten clearly into the soil. He stepped out a few more paces, and, in the gray of the early dawn light, into which the columns of smoke from the campfire was melting so perfectly, he was able to find where the trail diverged from that circle.

It was not hard to tell where Jack Lawrence had stepped, because the other members of the party wore the usual narrow-toed cowpuncher's boots, but Jack, a born mountaineer, as much at home on foot as on horseback, affected square-toed, heavy boots. These were his tracks striding off down the mountainside. To the astonishment of the leader, there was a parallel series of tracks moving just beside those of Jack, tracks made by a man wearing light boots with high heels, but tracks that told of a long, light stride. The heel imprint was hardly any heavier than the imprint of the toe of the boot.

Down the side of the mountain went the tracks and plunged into the thick obscurity of a hollow. So much the leader discovered. Then he turned on his heel and went back to the fire. A quiet word brought Blinky and Sam Hunter to their feet, each ready for action of any kind.

"Jack's gone off for a walk with somebody that ain't one of us," said Joe White calmly. "I dunno if he's found somebody and gone off to make a bargain with them about betraying us, or if . . . well, boys, I simply dunno what to think. But get saddled and ready to start on the run. There's liable to be blue lightnin' a-popping."

"He can't be making any bargain about surrendering us," said Blinky, who, next to Lawrence, was the oldest and most reliable of the crew. "Ever since Jack killed old Turner in Pine Hollow, folks have had it in for him. If he turned state's evidence, they'd get him and lynch him as soon as he was done talking. Nope, it ain't likely that he's throwed in with the law."

That, in fact, was the opinion of Joe White, but he could make nothing of the double trail. While the others were busy saddling, he decided to make another short detour down the mountain to see what he could see in the growing light.

Dawn seemed to step suddenly upon mountaintops. In a few moments the heights had become fairly bright, and the fire had been reduced to a few smokeless coals under the bacon pan and the coffee pot, so that no white column rising from that summit would give warning to the searchers.

Down the mountainside, then, Joe White stepped off at a brisk pace, skirting a little to one side of the direction of the double set of tracks, and so he reached a little cluster of those invincible climbers of the high places—the lodgepole pines. Beyond was a slight ascent. He climbed that, also, sharply on the look-out, and now beginning to wish that he had taken not his revolver only, but a rifle as well.

But all regret was lost in the wonder of the thing that he viewed from the little ridge beyond the pines. For, looking straight down the long, free slope of the mountain, he saw, on a little plateau, no other person than Jack Lawrence sitting side by side with a slender and younger figure about whose neck was knotted a bandanna of flashing crimson silk. It could be no other, then, than the daring and expert marksman who had dropped from his horse the day before and, shooting almost from the open, had downed both Cloudesley and Ike, although the latter fought behind shelter.

Joe White pondered. He was well beyond revolver range. It would be too late, probably, if he went back for a more effective weapon. And, if he attempted to advance closer, he must step out upon the naked mountainside and be at once descried and at once brought down by a bullet from the rifle upon which the hand of the kid rested.

The kid now rose and stood facing Jack Lawrence—and the hillside above, as well. That movement banished all hope of stalking the pair. And Joe White, raging at his impotence, furious at the sight of one of his men in such close conference with a mortal enemy, drew out his glass and focused it upon the face of the youth.

The daylight had been growing every instant. Now it was sufficiently bright for him to see clearly. The powerful glass brought the face of the stranger fairly leaping into his vision. What he saw was a youngster in his early twenties, perhaps not more than in his later teens. It was a singularly handsome face, dark-haired, dark-eyed, a face full of animation. He was talking eagerly with Jack Lawrence, and Lawrence was repeatedly shaking his head. Was he holding out for a higher price before he would consent to lead the party of Joe White into a trap that day? The outlaw set his teeth at the thought. Darkness would never fall upon the traitor.

At that moment Lawrence rose, and, turning his back upon the youth, walked ten paces away and faced him again. As he turned, Joe White saw that the holster on his right thigh was empty. He focused the glass on the face of Lawrence, and it seemed to him, in spite of the blurring distance, that it held a strained expression of terror.

Each instant, now, the mystery grew. Suddenly, there was an arching flash of metal glinting in the air and falling about a yard from the feet of Lawrence. He lowered the glass a trifle and studied the ground. There he saw a revolver lying in the dust where the youngster of the crimson bandanna had thrown it.

What did it all mean? Now another gun was thrown down by the stranger, about a yard before his own feet. Suddenly the explanation came thrilling home into the mind of Joe White. How Jack Lawrence had been brought to this place from the campfire was still strange as ever. But there was no question at all that he had been disarmed, in some manner, and that he had been helpless in the hands of his captor. There was also no question that he had been bidden to march those ten paces, and that he had then turned and faced his captor with the expectation of receiving at once the death he so richly merited for his life of crime. But, instead, a weapon had been thrown at his feet and another dropped at the feet of the youth.

It was to be no slaughter, but a duel strangely arranged, and yet fair enough. At a given signal, perhaps, or else whenever one of them chose, there should be a reaching for the weapons. Neither of them, as yet, stirred. Then Joe White saw that the stranger stood with his hands dropped lightly upon his hips, the very picture of careless confidence. He himself, in the wildest moment of his fiery youth, had never faced such a crisis in so jaunty a fashion. No doubt he was taunting Jack Lawrence, challenging him to stoop first for his weapon.

Now Lawrence leaned swiftly, and his hand swept toward the ground and scooped up the gun. But the stranger did not stoop. Instead, he flung himself bodily toward the ground as though he were diving into a yielding surface of water. He shot past the weapon, scooping it up at the same time. It spun over in his hand and exploded. Jack Lawrence sagged to the ground with his unfired gun dangling from his loose fingers.

IV

"The Last Blow"

The victim fell in a shapeless heap. There needed only a glance at the manner of his fall to know that he was dead before he struck the ground. The victor leaped up, tossing his weapon aside—a thing that Joe White coolly marked as a rashness of youth—and lifted Jack Lawrence lightly in his arms and laid the dead man upon his back. For an instant he leaned over Lawrence. Then he rose and dragged the shapeless felt hat from his head. Joe White puckered his brows in wonder. It was a strange maneuver. Who could have dreamed that a mortal being would ever remove his hat to Jack Lawrence, dead or living?

But there was only an instant's hesitation. The conqueror turned from the dead man, replaced his hat, and disappeared under the shoulder of the hill. He reappeared almost at once on the back of a horse. Again he turned about and looked steadily up the hill, as though contemplating an ascent and another attack upon the camp. But he changed his mind and, apparently swinging his horse around, rode at a trot down the mountain, dipped over the edge of the little flat-topped plateau, and was gone.

That was the story that Joe White carried back to the two men waiting at his camp. Briefly, without comment, he detailed the strange narrative. When it was ended, he said: "That's the way it happened. How it come about that Jack went down there with him, or how he might of been forced to go, I dunno. I'm still sort of staggering over what I've seen."

106

"Look here," said Blinky, who had not spoken a word of comment, although Sam Hunter had been profuse in exclamations and curses to register his astonishment and dismay. Blinky led the way to a distance of perhaps twenty-five yards from the camp, on the outskirts of some thick-growing shrubbery, perhaps an acre of which extended to the side along the mountain. Here he paused and pointed down to the ground. "After what you've said," he remarked, "I guess that maybe this has some sort of meaning."

What he pointed out was a place where the ground had been slightly scuffed up, once raked as a spur might rake it, and in one place scraped away as the driving heels of a man lying on his back and struggling vainly to get a purchase for turning himself might dig into the soil.

"I dunno," said Blinky, "but just suppose that the kid with the red bandanna sort of smelled us out and sneaked up here, and that he seen Jack walking around, and that he waited till Jack come close by the edge of the bushes and then jumped out and put him down with a tap on the head with his gun. But then Jack came to and started struggling, and got another tap on the head to make him lie still. And then he got marched off. . . ."

"Well," said Joe White, "that was all before midnight, you got to remember; because, if it had been later than that, Jack wouldn't've been standing watch. He'd've been under his blankets, and somebody else would've got what came to Jack. How come that he took Jack 'way down the hill? Why didn't he finish him right here where he first dropped him?"

"Because he's a fool kid," said Blinky. "He's got ideas in his head. He couldn't kill a gent that was helpless. So he couldn't hurt Jack while Jack was lying there with a gun jammed down his throat to keep him quiet. Finally, he made Jack get up and walk down the hill away from the camp, where they couldn't be heard easy by us. Down there where you found 'em, they waited until the sun got bright enough for 'em to see for shooting, and then the kid . . . by heaven, it looks that way . . . made Jack stand up and fight like you seen."

"That's fool talk," said Sam Hunter. "Nobody but a crazy man would do that."

"All kids like him are crazy," Blinky assured him. "Ain't I right, chief?"

Joe White returned no answer. He was thinking back to the days when he had first come into the West, when the Indians had first called him Young-Stallion-On-Fire. In those wild days, this exploit of the kid would have been exactly what he would have chosen for himself. He had sought for useless chances. He had courted danger for the sake of danger. He had made himself drunk, never on liquor, but on the desperate ways of battle. And here, it seemed, was such another come to take his trail. All that he had seen, all that he had heard of the actions of this nameless youngster, agreed with what he himself had been those many, many years ago. He had been bigger, more imposing to look on. In appearance he had been the very antithesis of this slender, dark youth. But Joe White understood men well enough to know that it is the heart and not the bones that make the man.

"You went wrong on another thing," said Blinky gloomily. "You said that the kid would be sure to stick behind on that trail and take care of the gents that had dropped."

"It ain't likely that he'd leave 'em," said the chief soberly. "But maybe some others come up, and he let them take care of the wounded."

"And he come trailing us all by himself?" asked Blinky.

"Don't it look that way?" asked Joe White.

There was silence as they rode out on that day's march. It

was not until noon, when they had paused to drink at a spring and eat cold pone, that another thing was said bearing on the death of Jack Lawrence.

"D'you think, maybe," said Sam Hunter, "that they'd take the trouble to bury Jack where they found him lying there?"

"How come?" grunted Blinky. "What put that into your head, Sam?"

"I was thinking of him lying there on his back and facing this sun all the day. . . ."

"But he's dead, you fool!"

"I know . . . still. . . ." Sam Hunter shrugged his shoulders that the keen mountain sun was burning, despite the thickness of a flannel shirt.

"They'll bury him under some stones that was lying handy nearby," said Joe White uneasily. "They'll sure wait long enough to do that. If they don't, I'll go back and. . . ."

He paused. All three, by mutual assent, looked up through the burned white of the zenith, and there, across the sky, floated black specks, moving in great, loose circles, and drifting steadily west and south. The buzzards were following their strange trail.

They started on, again in silence, which lasted unbroken until the evening and the camp for the end of that day. Not once had they sighted a pursuer. Yet, as the day wore on and the shadows began to gather again like pools of heavy smoke in the hollows, Joe White noted that his two companions looked more and more frequently over their shoulders, searching the trail anxiously behind them.

This troubled him, for the darkness should be looked upon by fugitives as their greatest friend. And, when they begin to dread it, it means that their nerve is going fast. He himself had never ceased to regard it as a blanket of protection dropped between him and his foemen. But Blinky and Sam Hunter rode on with eyes growing greater and greater as they felt the dread of the pursuit gain on them, chilling their very hearts.

They seemed to grow cheerful again, for a moment, when the time came for picking out a camp. What they found was an ideal spot in a little miniature gorge carved across the shoulder of an eminence, so that in the bottom of it they had a place for sheltering the light of the fire from all observation, and the hollow, also, was great enough to cover the horses from view. As for wood, they could get it from the shrubs that grew in dense thickets a scant quarter of a mile away, over the edge of the mountain's side.

To the astonishment of Joe White, both of his men questioned his judgment when he asked them to go out and drag a quantity of fuel with their ropes and their horses. They had no doubt, they told him, that the light of the fire, or perhaps no more than the smell of the woodsmoke, had been the thing that guided the kid toward them on the preceding night. If he came again, all three might be murdered in their sleep by that cunning enemy. They wanted no fire. A sense of security would keep them warmer than any flames. But Joe White, staring at them for a moment in a mute wonder, shrugged his shoulders and bade them go and do as they were told. So they rode off with sullen faces over the edge of the hill and left him to unpleasant ponderings.

It was many and many a year since his judgment had been questioned by a follower of his. He raised a hand and felt the dense, prickling stubble of his beard and the folds and wrinkles of his aging face and the deep furrows that went across his forehead. To be sure, he was not the man he had been five years before. Age might bring him wisdom, but wisdom was a hidden virtue, and, in the eyes of the men of the mountains and the cow ranges, it could never make up for a superior agility on foot, a greater strength of hand, a more hair-trigger acuteness of nervous speed. He was not what he had been. The flashy qualities were growing dull and duller.

Now they feared the very empty night, even when Joe White was in their midst. It was the writing on the wall; it was the clear, loud prophecy of danger. His time was short, indeed, before some keen youth, someone like the kid in the crimson bandanna and the shapeless felt hat, should pull him down and mount upon his dead body, at a stroke acquiring all of the honor, all of the dignity of position that Joe White had built up with the labors of a lifetime.

He roused himself and raised his head from these reveries. The moments had stolen swiftly past him. The color was gone from the sky. He was standing in the grave twilight just before the coming of utter night. And, although Sam and Blinky had had ample time to uproot and bring in to him a whole forest of such shrubs as he had sent them for, they had not yet come in.

Grumbling heavily, with a growing anger at every step he had to take to find out the cause of the delay, he marched to the edge of the mountain—that point from which he could command all the sweep of the slope and its covering of shrubs. But there was no sign of Blinky or Sam Hunter.

He struck the back of his heavy hand across his forehead. Was this another instance of the devilish cunning of the kid? Had he stolen up to them and, by some magical power, succeeded in spiriting away two grown men on this evening, just as he had succeeded in spiriting away Jack Lawrence the evening before? He caught a deep breath and expelled it with a curse.

Then it seemed to him that something moved on the dark side of an opposite peak. He strained his eyes toward it. Yes, passing over the edge of the mountain out of the black eastern side and toward the west where there was still a ghost of light in the sky, he saw two horsemen, one behind the other. And then he knew.

It came home to him cold and sudden like sad news of disaster at home told by a bitter enemy who gives no sympathy while he speaks. He knew the whole bitter truth: Blinky and Sam Hunter had deserted him.

Not that he lacked their aid. Heaven knew that they had been an encumbrance and a burden to him on the trail. Heaven knew that he could make his own way better if he made it alone. But it was the first desertion in the middle of a march. The first rats had left the ship. It was the last blow of a disastrous expedition.

There is a strange impulse in even the worst of men, which, in a time of great trouble, makes them look upward. This instinct made the great outlaw now lift his head and peer up into the midst of the darkening sky. And he saw, sweeping strangely low and huge as a bald eagle at such close range, an immense buzzard, the carrion feeder, sailing above him.

V

"Outguessed"

He made a fireless camp that night. And when, after four hours of fitful sleep, his eyes opened and he knew that he would rest no more, he saddled his horse—an ungainly but wonderfully powerful mustang—and started out on foot, leading the animal.

On the trail which he proposed for himself, the horse would have all it could do to follow, far less carry the great burden of the master on its back. Straight up toward the crest of the ridge above him he went, feeling his way through the darkness with a sort of extra sense that comes only from long trailing. The horse behind him tugged back again and again on the rope, weary from the previous day's work, rebelling against this added labor.

He topped that ridge, sharp as the ragged top of a wind-harried wave, and dipped straight down into the ravine beyond. It was a slippery and dangerous descent, and he walked at the head of the mustang to guide the latter the more surely. Up the farther side he set a course in brief zigzags, until once more they came out against the stars on another summit.

Here he paused. The fearful labor of that climb had started the mustang panting. Now it stood with drooping head, a sure sign of exhaustion in the beast. Joe White himself was dripping with perspiration, and the pulse was pounding in his head, but so far the work of the night had not drained a tithe of his resources. He shifted the pack a little, then changed his mind and took it off completely. While the mustang cooled down, he sorted over his possessions. When he was through, he was carrying only three things—ammunition, gold, and food. All the little luxuries, all the little things that make camping endurable for most men, he had cast aside. The difference of an ounce's weight, in a whole day's march, might mean thirty yards, and thirty yards might be the distance by which a rifle bullet failed to carry to him.

In fact, it was by the calculation of such niceties as these that Joe White had gone free from the law these many years. When he started on again, the night was breaking into a sordid gray, just enough illumination to deceive the eye and the foot. But he had put a valuable section of ground behind him, and before the sun rolled up past the eastern horizon he would have added yet more.

Again he dipped down a precipitous incline, and again he labored up the yet higher and steeper slope beyond. He was headed straight for the crest, and, when he reached it, he found that the next ridge beyond and above him was bald as Cæsar's head, a crisp outline against the morning sky. He knew that he was close to the timberline.

Shortly after sunrise he passed it, and there on the hillside he paused, unsaddled the poor mustang so that the horse could rest more effectually, and cooked his breakfast over a fire made so cunningly, out of such well-selected materials, that the haze of smoke it sent up was invisible two hundred yards away after the first white column had risen.

He lingered after his second cup of scalding hot coffee, bitter strong, had been drunk. He smoked a cigarette and watched the mustang with a cold and watchful eye. The horse was half dead with fatigue. But somewhere in the stanch recesses of its nature he knew that it would find strength to stagger on where a commoner nag with less heart would curl up and die. So he rose in another moment and again struck toward the summit.

Still he struggled on, for, what was a bitter hard mile to his solid strength, might well be an utterly impossible mile to a lesser man, such as the kid, for instance. As for Sam Hunter and fat Blinky, they could not have lasted half an hour in the face of such labor as he was now accomplishing. A fierce thrill of satisfaction went through him as he noted that his powers, although sapped, perhaps, were certainly far from completely wasted. He was a good man, still. He was a better man than any that walked in sole leather among those mountains. Let the kid and all the rest follow him if they dared and could. He even began to feel that providence had had a hand in it. More than once before he had felt a thrill of trust in his luck, and now he had a sublime assurance that the desertion of Blinky and Sam Hunter had come providentially so that his hand might be freed of encumbrance and he could go on to safety.

Although his fame might be somewhat dimmed when it was known that he had lost two of his party by desertion in the midst of a march, still, the fact that he had escaped at all would be taken into account before that day was out. The other two would disagree about their plans, strike a compromise course, and walk squarely into the arms of the men of the law. He shrugged his broad shoulders at that thought, and then smiled grimly. They would deserve their fate by all the laws that kept men true to one another on dangerous trails.

Here the broad tableland was split by a steep-sided gorge that dropped hundreds of feet to a dry bottom. He spent half an hour hunting for the best crossing and then dipped down toward the bottom, working carefully back and forth with the mustang until at length—a triumph of skill and care—he came safely to the level beneath.

In the greatness of his exultation, he could have laughed.

They might have trailed him to a certain place on his way across the mountains, but, after he struck the miles of almost naked rock on the summit, they could only guess at the direction he might take, and, when they struck this gorge, they would be completely at sea. How could they guess whether or not he had gone down or up the edge of the gully, or down to the bottom of it and then up or down, or straight across to the farther side? On the slabs of slippery rock they would not have one chance in ten thousand of finding sign of him.

He determined, however, although the game was now in his hands, to make assurance doubly sure and cut up the gorge, where he could enjoy the shelter of the rock wall from the wind. This he did, sauntering along comfortably until something sang sharply through the air before him, and on a rock ten yards ahead of him there was a thud and then a round spot of white.

He stopped in amazement. Unless he had gone mad, that was a bullet which had narrowly missed him. Yet none of his pursuers could have marched all night, as he had done, guessed at his trail in the darkness, and so come upon him here. He lifted his bewildered head and stared up at the cliff above him. Nothing was there. And now came the sound of the report, a great, throat-swelling echo in the narrow gorge.

Joe White turned his head again and looked to the far side of the gorge, and there he saw a tiny figure of a man perched on a rock that seemed to overhang a dizzy precipice, as though he were about to fall to the bottom as one would playfully drop into a swimming pool. There was the same reckless gaiety about the posture of the man on the edge of the cliff, it seemed. Yet it could be no enemy. It could be no one hunting him. Despite the singing of that bullet, he still shook his head and raised the glass to his eye.

Into the circle of the glass there leaped the picture of the youth with the red bandanna around his neck, sitting, laughing on the edge of the cliff and waving the shapeless felt hat by way of greeting.

He had fired the shot, apparently, as one might shy a stone to call the attention of an acquaintance. With a fury of curses, the outlaw dropped his glass and tore his long Winchester from its holster along the saddle. But, when he pitched the butt into the hollow of his shoulder, there was nothing to shoot at perched on the edge of the cliff. He of the bandanna had disappeared.

Joe White, groaning with despair, drew back with the sweating mustang beside the shelter of a great boulder the size of a small cottage, that had dropped from the cliff top just above and splintered itself on the floor of the gorge.

He was cornered there. All the man on the edge of the opposite cliff needed to do was to raise a column of smoke as a fire signal and gather his friends to his support. Then they could fill Joe White full of lead from the safety of the cliff verge above him. Or, if he strove to break away up or down the valley, the youth, or devil in the shape of a youth, who occupied the opposite wall, could shoot him at pleasure as he ran. It would be a good long shot, but there was no question in the mind of Joe White. A man who could handle a revolver, as he had seen it handled the preceding dawn, could certainly strike down a grown man at such a distance with the most consummate ease.

But, more than all, he was tortured with wonder. How had the youngster climbed or flown to that place of vantage? A superstitious horror jumped into the brain of Joe White. He had to close his eyes and lean back against the rock wall, knowing in that way lay madness.

No, the man of the crimson-silk bandanna had simply out-guessed him, out-marched him—he had run where Joe White had walked. Taking chance by the forelock, he had gone down the gorge and climbed to the opposite side and there marched up and down, knowing that sooner or later Joe White would walk into the trap!

In the meantime, the sun was growing hotter and hotter. As soon as noon came, and the shadow straightened, and the sun beat straighter down into the valley, this place would be an oven. The priceless minutes were running past him like water down a slide, hurrying him toward a wretched, an utterly shameless death.

Quietly, he determined that he would not wait. Since he had come to his death, he would run to it with open arms, not stay here like a rat in a hole to be slaughtered in a corner. He raised his head. Above him, the narrow lips of the cañon fenced a winding way through heaven. He looked into the blue with a strange breathless pang of sorrow for all the beauty which was in the world, and to which he had never given even an idle moment.

Then he leaped out from behind his rock and ran at full speed for the opposite side of the cañon.

VI

" 'On the Brink of Perdition' "

We keep hope into the very shadow of death. With the first stride of his rush Joe White felt such hope born in him. If he could dart across that open space—and how narrow it was!—until it was close to the other wall, the kid could not reach him—would not know, in fact, whether he were going up or down the cañon. And was it not probable that the youngster would have settled himself for a long watch, never dreaming that his foeman would make this sudden resolution, this sudden dash?

But with the very second step his hope left him. Not an instant passed. Something cut the air before him, the brief *whizz* of a bullet was in his face, and there appeared on a rock a yard ahead of him a small white spot where the lead had pulverized the stone and flattened itself to shapelessness with the impact. The next bullet would lodge in his flesh. If it struck at that angle, the wound must be mortal.

He swerved to the right and plunged straight on. But the watcher above was working a smooth repeater at full speed. The bark of the first shot had not arrived when the second slug was down, but this, also, struck the rock just before him, not half a stride away.

Desperate, now, he made no effort to dodge, but raced as he had never run before, heading for the steep shadow that meant safety. Again a bullet whirred past him, and again came that spat of the lead against the stone at his feet.

Now he understood. The young demon on the cliff above

him was shooting purposely just ahead of his victim to make the latter think that he was missing. But each miss was nicely calculated to keep the range and the speed of the runner. Just as the latter was on the edge of safety, a slug would drive him and flatten him there on the bottom of this nameless valley, slain by a nameless man.

He felt like halting and attempting one snap shot at the cliff in the hope of making the one chance in a thousand his and bringing down the hunter. But he knew that so cunning a fighter would never leave himself exposed. Even now, he would be keeping cover. So, with a swelling heart, the outlaw ran on. Again and again those bullets cut down before him, and always, with uncanny nicety in the placing, they thudded on the rocks just half a stride before him.

There was the edge of the shadow. And where the sun did not look, he on the cliff above could not look. With a last effort of despair, Joe threw himself headlong toward that wall of impalpable security—and reached it living. Yes, to his utter amazement, as he leaned panting against the cliff, he was alive and in safety. A great joy rushed into his throat, into his brain. He had not dreamed that life was half so dear to him.

What had happened? Why, at the last instant, many things might have happened. The gun might not have been completely loaded, and, taken away by the pleasure of his sport, the kid might have shot his last bullet. Or, again, what was more likely, the rifle might have jammed.

If that should be true, he would instantly take advantage of it. Vicious and stubborn as his mustang was, the brute had been taught to come to him in answer to a peculiar whistle. Now he gave that signal again and again, and yonder came the mustang, thrusting its ugly head around the corner of the stone. But it came at a walk! So wild was his impatience that he shouted as though the horse might understand words. He had grown childish in his anxiety, for there was packed on that saddle, in coin of the realm, a tidy small fortune—and not so small, at that.

His shout merely made the horse throw up his head and halt, and, as he repeated the whistle that started the beast toward him, he saw that hope must be lost. Again there was the wicked hum of a bullet, so undesirable, so shudderingly unmistakable, once it has been heard. A bullet cracked home on the stones and made the horse wince. Again Joe whistled, but half-heartedly. Again the mustang came on, shaking his brown head as though he were being led against his will into a hornet's nest of danger. Indeed, it must be a slaughter. Once more the rifle barked, and again the bullet hissed down before the nag. Yet the horse lived.

Suddenly the outlaw looked upward with a gasp and a new thought. Could it be that he on the verge of the cliff did not intend to kill—that he was firing these shots to show that he could strike down if he chose, but that he did not care to butcher his enemy in this fashion?

There could be only one explanation to append to this. Delighted by the gambling chances of the chase, that wild youth on the mountaintop was determined to delay the end until he encountered the foeman, face to face, in such a duel as he had fought with Jack Lawrence, for instance.

At that thought, a grim satisfaction welled through the body of the old warrior. He had never yet met his match, and certainly he would not find it in this clever trickster. But here came the sturdy brown horse, still shaking his head, his long ears glued to his neck. He halted beside his master and straightway began to pluck at some grass that hung in a cleft of the rock, working at it eagerly, for he had never lost his old range-bred interest in the problem of food. Yes, now that both man and beast had been allowed to cross the cañon, it was folly or hypocrisy, or both, to deny that the youngster had held his life in the palm of his hand, and then had refused to close his fingers. But it was also impossible to doubt that the confident youth expected to make an easy prey of his famous opponent when they next met—face to face.

What strong Ulysses felt when he held the bow and began to mark down the suitors in his own hall, such was the feeling of Joe White as he set his teeth and raised his stern face toward the upper edge of the cliff. Then he swung into the saddle on the brown gelding and sent him trotting down the gorge.

The respite in coming down from the upper level had been enough to recruit some of the strength of the mustang, and now it was able to strike along the level, first at a trot, then at a swinging lope. A slight downgrade aided him presently to raise this to a gallop. The confidence of the outlaw grew with every passing moment of time.

There was a shallow drift of sand, piled by the wind along this inner edge of the defile, and, while the precipice shielded him from discovery by the eye, the sand would muffle the beat of his hoofs, and the watcher above would be unable to tell whether he were riding up or down the gorge.

In a short time, he on the cliff would become the hunted just as he had been the hunter. Since hunters on a man trail are but little removed from beasts of prey, a tigerish joy and satisfaction in the prospect grew in the soul of Joe White as he galloped.

The mountains were strange to him, but, after a time, as he had expected, the floor of the cañon shelved away, and he climbed easily to the upper level again. Once there, he made for the nearest commanding eminence. It was a stony knob on the hard, swept surface of the summit region, and from this he scanned the landscape. But there was no sign of horse or man. Yonder on the edge of the precipice, then, the youngster was waiting and watching, or, perhaps, journeying down toward the farther end of the gorge.

Joe White shook his great fist above his head and spurred down the slope. He rode at a brisk canter for half a mile. Then he dismounted, and, leaving the mustang to follow him, he began to scout more carefully, taking close observations of all that lay before him. At length he had arrived at what he knew to be the region where the young enemy had lain on top of the cliff, and now he tethered the mustang and advanced along, feeling that the time of the encounter would not be far removed. He found the spot, now, where the spy had been sheltered. It was marked by the impress where the youth had lain prone. It was marked, moreover, by the empty shells that he had thrown there after his target practice.

Joe White lay down in the same place. He commanded a perfect view of the great boulder in the gorge beneath him. Yes, such a shot as the kid was, he could have killed the outlaw easily as he fled across the floor of the valley. The hot pulse came surging into the temples of the outlaw as he thought of the undignified picture he must have made as he ran—not so lightly as he would once have run.

He gritted his teeth and then pushed still farther forward to the rock on which he had seen the kid first sitting. He found that rock on the very edge of the cliff. It had seemed from below a dizzy position, but it was downright murderous when viewed from above. Joe White laid aside his rifle, twisted his holster about so that it would come between him and the surface of the rock, and crawled up.

Yes, there in a crevice, was a little deposit of tobacco where this wild young dare-devil had calmly rolled his own, sitting on the brink of perdition. There beneath were the scratches made by his heels. Resting on the rounded surface of that great boulder, the boulder itself none too securely poised on the verge of the abyss—below him dropped thin nothingness.

Joe White, himself no mean mountaineer, felt the sweat start on his forehead—beneath his armpits. He caught his breath. It was hard enough for him to rally sufficient nerve to lie here prone. But what courage must it have taken to sit erect, yonder, with a cigarette in one hand, waving his sombrero with the other, veritably laughing in the face of death?

He began to back in toward a safer footing, and, as he pushed himself in with his hands, he felt the whole mass of the giant boulder quiver beneath him as though it were poised—all that mass—upon a hair's breadth. Another slight thrust might send the ruin toppling.

Now it was that a voice spoke behind him, a careless, laughing voice: "Joe White, what you been seeing down yonder in the hollow? Your ghost?"

It was the kid, standing behind him, no doubt, with a gun poised, balanced lightly in his hand, and the life of Joe White within the crook of his finger.

VII

"Memory Restirred"

We do not judge men by their acts in the everyday humdrum of life. We judge them by actions and reactions in important crises. That is why we do not truly know so many of our friends, because we have never seen them vitally tested.

If Joe White had been judged by what he did in this emergency, half of his fame would have been lost to him as a fighter at once brave and cunning. He went blind with one consuming terror—not that of toppling with the rock into oblivion, but of receiving the death-wound in his back. And a picture flashed into his brain of a dead body he had found on a mountain trail, twenty years before, a body newly fallen, which, when he leaned over it, revealed a wound in the back. There had passed through him a shudder of scorn on that occasion. A man who died while running away from danger was not worth keeping in life.

Would he himself be found in that fashion by the sheriff and the rest of the posse? Would they judge him and say that he had lost his courage in the end and turned like a coward from a boy—a mere child?

It drove him to madness. He leaped to his feet, swerving as he leaped, wondering vaguely why it was that a bullet did not plow through his brain, through his body, launched by the steady finger of that strange youth behind him. But the bullet did not strike. He faced the youngster, and, through the blurred vision of his fury, he saw that the latter stood idly, with careless hands dropped upon his hips. He saw that, but the meaning of the picture did not come home to him. So blind had been that leap up and that whirl, that he had not even gripped his own gun. Now he did not try to draw it, but struck out with all his weight behind a fist of iron.

The blow caught the other beside the jaw and beat him down to the earth—lifted and flung him headlong upon the rocks—and the great outlaw, standing staring down at the beaten man, felt his rage dissolve. And, as his eyes cleared, he was able to look into the truth of things and saw that he had been right before. The kid was hardly nineteen, and as slenderly made as a girl. He had fallen with his arms thrown wide, his eyes closed. In the fall, his forehead had touched against a ragged edge of stone, and now a thin trickle went down his face. The red made the olive skin seem pale. The old felt hat lay beside his head. The upturned palms showed the hands of an idler, one who had never worked, for work blunts and thickens and mars. No matter how deft he might be with his guns, he was probably a veritable tenderfoot when it came to the wielding of a rope.

Joe White, still staring down, drew a great breath, filling all the nooks in his lungs, and breathed it forth again. Once, twice, this youngster had had his life to take if he pleased, and twice he had refused to touch him. It became a sudden and vital mystery.

He scooped the limp body from the rocks—it was wonderfully light—and carried the kid to the lee of a mighty stone that cast a sheltering shadow. There, as he deposited him, the kid opened his eyes, sighed, and sat up.

Joe White watched for the first word, the first action. But both surprised him. There was no reaching for a gun, no torrent of curses.

Instead, he fumbled for and found the shapeless felt hat

and first replaced it carefully upon his head. Next, he pushed himself into a more erect posture. Then he blinked at Joe White. And thirdly he touched the purple place where the pile-driver fist of the big man had crashed against his jaw. "If you want to go into the prize ring," he said, "I figure that you'd get on tolerable well. That was a considerable wallop, Joe White."

Joe White pushed back his own sombrero and cursed softly as he did so. But he took care to push it back with his left hand and all the while keep his right close to his revolver where it hung at his thigh. In a case like this, one could not tell. The youngster was a freak. His reactions were simply not the reactions of common men.

"Son," said Joe White, "who might you be?"

"Ted McKay," said the boy among the rocks. "I wished you'd known my name before you hit me, though. Might've made you hold up the punch a little."

Joe White bit his lip and studied the stranger. "Ted McKay," he said, "what in the devil is into you?"

"Is it the devil that's into me?" asked Ted McKay, and he grinned a twisted grin at the outlaw.

"Hmm," said Joe White, "how come you to get up here today?"

"How come I to know you hit in this direction?" asked Ted McKay. "Is that what you mean?"

"Put it that way, yes."

"Well, I was moving around last evening, and I come across Blinky and Sam Hunter riding over the hills."

"You met 'em, then?"

"The posse caught up with me after dark."

"They was that close behind me, eh?"

"They'd been riding like blazes," said Ted McKay. "But there was one led hoss in the gang. It was pretty fresh, not

127

having packed a man all day, and so I got that hoss from the sheriff, and I laid a circle through the hills . . . just figuring that maybe you'd do something fancy in the way of laying out a new course before midnight. You see?"

"You didn't need no rest yourself, eh?"

"Oh, I got along. But that was the way I come onto Blinky and Sam. They was riding hard down a trail when I spotted 'em."

"And now they're both buzzard food?" queried the leader coldly.

"Nope, not at all. Blinky had a pretty bad shoulder, and Sam is down with a wound in the leg. But they'll come through, all right, if they don't get lynched before they're brought to trial. They sure ain't popular with the boys!"

Joe White suddenly laughed. "Son," he said, "you're worth knowing!"

"Thanks!" said the youngster soberly, eagerly even, it seemed to the older man. "D'you mean that?"

"I sure do. But go on and tell me how you come onto my trail."

"Why, that was just luck."

"I thought so."

"I figured that, after them two skunks rode off from you, you'd be so glad to get rid of 'em that you'd start out to do something that you couldn't've done while they was along to bother you."

"Hmm," murmured the outlaw.

"What I guessed was that you'd hit across the hills and go for the summit. So I thought that I'd do the same thing. I looked over the hosses, and none of 'em looked very fit for work. And finally I thought that I'd strike off on foot. So I done it."

"Without sleeping none?"

"Without sleeping none."

"You didn't close your eyes last night?"

"Sure I did. I come straight along at a pretty good lick. I figured that, if you did come this way, you'd not be able to go much faster with a hoss than you could go on foot. And, if you was a stranger to these mountains like Blinky said, you'd most likely come bang into this here cañon."

"I see. But you were sort of taking chances, weren't you, son?"

"I was gambling . . . about one chance in four in my favor. But it was worth the chance. I got here, climbed up this side of the gully, got me a comfortable place leaning against a rock, had an hour's snooze, and then woke up feeling pretty much like work."

The outlaw nodded, and his eyes gleamed. When he was in his teens, he had been capable of just such efforts, but the matchless resiliency of youth was long since gone.

"Then you seen me when I come over the edge of the cañon?"

"Yep. I was away down yonder, at that end . . . but I seen you come over the edge, so I sifted up here through the rocks and watched you working down with the hoss."

Joe White shrugged his shoulders. "Would have been a pretty easy shot to pick me off, along about then, wouldn't it?" he said.

"Pick you off?" said Ted McKay. "You sure don't think that I wanted to do that?"

"Well, son, what were you up to?"

Ted McKay sighed. He rubbed the sore chin and eyed the outlaw wistfully.

"I guess you'd think I was a plumb fool if I told you," he said.

"Maybe," said the outlaw. "But gimme a try at hearing."

"Well," said Ted McKay, "I'll tell you how it was. It goes back to about twenty years ago. Once you was riding through the Jeffrey Mountains."

"I know the Jeffreys, well enough."

"You come on a forest fire scooting across the mountains."

"Well?" said Joe White sharply as his memory cleared.

"Well, right there in the forest, just as you was turning around to ride about as fast as you could away from the fire, you met a man and a woman, and they was running on foot. The fire had taken their cabin and their hosses and killed everything. And the man was carrying the baby."

"Good Lord!" And Joe White sighed. "I sort of recollect a little."

The youth stood up, as though the memory of that story had the power to raise him bodily to his feet. "You took the woman, and you give your hoss to her," he said. "And you put the baby in her arms and told her to ride like fury for the sake of herself and the kid. And then, when she started off, you stayed behind with her husband, and you give him a hand through the forest, because he was plumb tuckered out from carrying the kid as far as he had. D'you recollect?"

"Yes, yes," said Joe White. "She sure cried a lot, she was that broke up at leaving him behind."

"But you brought him safe through the forest," said Ted McKay, his voice ringing. "He ran along with you till he fainted, and then you picked him up, and you run with him throwed over your shoulder, and you was just about to be grabbed by the fire that was running after you, when you come out onto the river, and you dived into the river and brought him across it to where the woman was waiting for him."

"I know how she come wading out to us and towed us in. I

was sure spent. I was all done up."

"Well," said Ted McKay, "that gent's name was McKay, although you didn't stop to find out, but sneaked away in the night for fear that they'd start thanking you for what you'd done in the morning."

"Ah," said Joe White, "and you're the kid. How you squalled all the time," he began to laugh, but very softly.

"Yes," said the youth, "I'm the kid." He said it with great tears standing frankly in his eyes. "And when my mother died last month . . . Dad being dead ten year back . . . I started out to find you. She's always wanted me to. The only luck that the McKays ever had, she used to say, was when they met up with Joe White. But I never had got out to find you. I got to admit that I wasn't much help to Mother. I always been sort of lazy, you see. But after she died, I figured out that it might do her some good to know that I'd gone looking for you . . . and so . . . here I am."

VIII

"A Void Is Filled"

"Here you are," echoed Joe White. "But don't it appear to you like you've acted sort of queer . . . the way you've come giving me your introduction?"

"Queer?" said the other. "How come?"

"Why," said Joe White, "you been like a wolf on my trail, kid."

A smile came on the lips of Ted McKay. "Did I sure enough bother you some?" he said.

Joe White rubbed his knuckles across his nose. He summed up dryly, briefly. "I started out with five men," he said. "You've killed three of 'em, and you've drove two of 'em away from me and then knocked 'em both over. And, finally, you've had two chances to drop me dead and you ain't done it. Yep, I'd sure say that you've bothered me some. But what in heaven's name was in your head?"

"I looked at it this way," said Ted. When he spoke in this way, so softly, with such an almost femininely gentle manner, he drew vividly before the eyes of the outlaw the picture of that young mother whom he had seen the long years before in those terrible smoking woods. The memory came back over him like a reincarnation. "If I was just to come riding into your camp, you wouldn't have much use for me. You'd figure that I was too young to be of any account, you know. So I thought that, when I was coming along behind you, I'd try to do something that'd make you see I could be useful to you,

132

because I'd got to be pretty fair with a revolver or a rifle."

"You sure are, son," said Joe White. "You practice pretty steady?"

"My mother always wanted me to be just like you," said Ted McKay, "so she started me in early with guns."

"Wait!" exclaimed Joe White. "You mean to say that your mother wanted you to be just like me?"

"Sure," said the other blandly. "And why not?"

"Why . . . why," stammered Joe White, "there's folks that have some pretty hard things to say about me, Ted McKay. You sure ain't rode very far without meeting up with gents that had hard things to say about me."

"Ah!" cried Ted McKay. "Ain't I heard 'em? And I've let 'em know that they was liars! Why, I've done pretty near all my fighting that way. But my mother and me . . . why, Joe White, didn't we owe our lives to you? And didn't we know what sort of a man you really are?"

"You could explain away everything that you heard about me?" said Joe White, and his own mind went darkly back to terrible chapters in the telling of which he was damned for eternity.

"Sure we could," said Ted with enthusiasm. "Why, we knew all the time that there was something wrong. Mostly, they been blaming on you things that was done by other folks. As for banks that you've robbed, and things like that, don't we know that you take the money away from them that are rich and give it to them that are poor? Don't we know that?"

Joe White moistened his lips to speak, and could not. He looked down and saw the hard rocks shining in the sun. He looked up and saw not the blue of the tender sky and the shadows of his own grim past.

"It puts a lot of heart into a gent," he said, "to hear talk the like of this, Ted. You ain't lying."

The hand with which he gestured was seized in both the hands of Ted McKay. "Joe White," he said, "if you'll let me do it, I want to prove through the rest of my life that I believe in you. I want to prove that, though I've listened to a pack of lies about you . . . lies that even womenfolk I couldn't fight have told . . . I ain't believed a one of 'em. I sure ain't been a very good son to her in lots of ways, but there's one thing that mother taught me so well that I couldn't no ways forget it. And that thing was to believe in Joe White to the end of time. And that's what I'll do!"

Joe White extricated his hand from the grip of the youngster. He wanted to back away. He wanted leagues of distance between them, for the enthusiasm of the other was like a weight falling upon his soul. All the evil that he had done, and that evil was legion, returned, rolling cloud-like over his brain. "I sure take this kind," he found himself saying without heart behind his words.

"But you don't want me!" cried the youngster in anguish. "Is that it, Joe? I ain't proved myself enough of a man to team up with you? But, look here, I ain't trying to be your partner. I'm just asking that you sort of let me fetch and carry for you and work along, until you've given me a fair try-out. Then, if you see that I ain't worth my salt, I'll be going along my own trail and leave you alone. But, I'd sure like to have a try at proving what I can do for you, Joe."

Joe White passed a hand across his forehead. He began to pace up and down, his mind working as it had never worked before this day. It was the thing for which he had yearned all his life—a friend, a follower upon whose truth and good faith he could rely blindly, unquestioningly. What had worn the heart out of him had been the ceaseless vigilance necessary to keep control of the men who rode in his expeditions. Although he had conquered always, the time would come when he would be defeated. This very day had been the scene of such a defeat, and at the hands of this youngster. But, with Ted McKay at his side, or standing back to back with him, what could they not do?

There was another side. As he grew older, he grew more and more taciturn, like an old surly bear, pricked on the sullen angers by the mere weight of years which he carried. Sooner or later all his trust and joy in human society would go, and in its place would grow up a furious hatred of men. There would begin a period of blind, insensate slaughter. He had felt it coming up in him, as it had come to many a warrior of the frontier. There was one remedy possible, and that was the companionship of friends, such a friend as this youngster could become. He turned suddenly and dropped his heavy hands upon the shoulders of Ted McKay.

"Ted," he said, "if you ride with me, it's a trail that don't stop at no home."

"Yes," he answered, "I've thought of that a lot of times, but I can stand it easy."

"There's long times when we wouldn't see no other men or women."

"We don't need to see 'em."

"They'll hunt us down like mad dogs."

"Because they don't believe nothing but lies about you."

There was no downing him. He was like a bent sapling springing back to straightness.

"Then, shake," said the outlaw. As his hand closed over the slender hand of the youth, he said to himself: *Heaven forgive me for it.*

IX

"Ted Recalls a Debt"

They reached a bald mountaintop five days later. By that time the pursuit had fallen away to nothing behind them. There had been a period, during two days, when the searchers were everywhere through the summits. But after that they drew away, thanks to the intimate knowledge that Ted McKay had of the mountains. And the wonder of it, to the mind of the outlaw, was that his companion was unmounted. Yet, going on foot, he made progress that taxed the powers of the brown horse to keep up. It was only when they had crossed the summit region and drawn out below timberline on the farther side of the range that he had a real need of a horse, and then he found a mount with a readiness that amused Joe White.

They sat side by side, cross-legged, each upon his separate rock, and they stared down into the mist-thickened air of the valley, a morning mist that a little later would be turned to nothing by the sun, and only crystal clearness left. While it lasted the mist transformed the valley and the mountains, made the deeps of the lowlands seem bottomless wells of distance. The pale colors of the early sunrise tinted everything. Joe White had sat down, here, by the side of his companion for no particular reason. As he bit at the stem of his pipe and inhaled the powerful smoke, it occurred to him that Ted McKay was singularly silent. So it was that he came to follow the glance of the youngster down into the abyss.

For Ted McKay was like a young swain smiling at a pretty

girl. His cigarette grew cold between his fingers as he stared. The eyes of Joe White, when he looked again among those delicate pastel colors, those breathless prospects, opened to a sudden glimpse of new knowledge, such knowledge as he had guessed when in the gorge five days before he had looked up to the tender blue of the sky before he rushed out in a blind charge to gain safety. He had thought then that, if he were able to live another day, he would certainly spend his time in another pursuit than merely fighting men and stealing money. It came back on him more strongly now. There was something down yonder that gave the youngster the most exquisite delight. But to Joe White there had appeared merely the sweaty task of climbing down from these heights to a better footing below.

"You look sort of happy," he suggested to the youngster.

"Sure." Ted nodded.

"And how come . . . before breakfast like this?"

"Why," said Ted, "sitting up here on the top of the world, and looking down at all them things dressed up in the mist and the color . . . ain't that pretty good to look at?"

"Hmm," said Joe White. "I dunno but I'd rather have a look at a good thick steak right now. It'd suit me considerable better than all the scenery you could pack inside the grip of your eyes."

"Well," said Ted McKay, very worried at this statement, "maybe it would . . . only . . . you could eat a thousand steaks and then forget 'em all. But you can see this only once and never forget it if you live a hundred years."

"How come?" said the outlaw. "Ain't this up here all the time to be looked at whenever you feel like groaning over the distance you got to come to get up here and look at it? Ain't this fixed here all permanent?"

"Look at it one way," argued Ted McKay, losing some of

his awe of the authority of the older man as he progressed with his subject, "and you're right. But look at it another way, and you ain't. No two days are ever the same, any place."

Joe White laughed. "I can show you places in the desert, son," he said, "where you couldn't tell ten o'clock one day from ten o'clock of another day to save your head."

Ted McKay nodded. "I know," he said. "That's the way things get along in the middle of the day. The sun comes along and burns out all the differences. All that a gent can feel or think about is the burn of it on his shoulder and the back of his hands, and the sting of it on the end of his nose if he pushes his hat back, maybe, and so one day looks pretty much like any other day."

"Appears to me"—and Joe White chuckled—"like you was swinging around and talking on my side of this here question."

"You ain't looking right, then," said Ted McKay with more than his usual dignity, "because I wasn't never so far from agreeing with anything you ever said."

"Go ahead, then, and show me what you're driving at."

"I'm driving at this. You can't judge a day by the middle of it. What makes it different comes in the beginning and the ending. You see? Look down yonder. If there was a million mornings to come, and every one of them with mist, there never would come another just like this, and every minute this here morning is changing. Look how the light grows, Joe. Yonder it's getting at the base of the cliffs. And it's sliding down into the gorges where there was solid shadow just a minute back. Everything is turning purplish. You can look everywhere . . . and now up comes the good old sun and turns everything rosy for a minute . . . and then *bang!* . . . there she rolls up the sky, and the color's gone, and you see the mist get tore into bits, and the sky's clear crystal. Well, Joe, d'you think that you'll ever see another morning like that?"

"No," sighed Joe, "unless I have you along, kid, to tell me what it's all about." He was silent another moment. Then, looking across to the kid he saw that the latter was lighting his cold cigarette and frowning down at it gloomily. Plainly Ted was learning new and disagreeable things about his companion, just as Joe White was finding incomprehensible things about the youngster.

"But the next thing," said Joe, eager to change the topic, "is how you're going to get a hoss, and where you're going to get him?"

With one shrug of the shoulders, Ted McKay dismissed his gloomy thoughtfulness. He turned with a grin to Joe White. "Look down yonder," he said. "You see where the big cliffs go down in about three jumps?"

"I see that."

"And you see underneath it where all them little hills spill out like coal from a scuttle?"

"Yes, I see that."

"Well, down in yonder, tucked away where you can't see it, is Theobald's ranch. He's got the sort of hosses that I want."

"He has?"

Joe White winced when he saw how casually, how carelessly, the youngster took up the subject of his first theft—or was it the first? Had not the idle youth gone pilfering long before this? Was not that one reason that he looked so lightly upon the crimes of which people accused Joe White?

"He owes me a hoss," said Ted, by way of unasked explanation. "He owes me a fine hoss, too."

"How come that, Ted?"

"Well, after Dad got burned out . . . that time when I was a kid . . . he took to cow raising, and he done pretty good at it.

Everything was lucky for him until a bad year come along and hit him hard. That was about when I was ten . . . and I remember. He had plenty of land and cows, but there wasn't much sale, and so he had to get hold of cash to float him along, and the gent that he went to for the cash was Theobald. Theobald is rich, you know."

"I don't know," said Joe White. "This is my first trip into this part of the country. Go on."

"Theobald give him the money quick," said Ted, "but he made it a short loan. And Dad thought that was all right, because he could turn around, by that time, and get money from a bank. But a panic came along and scared the banks stiff. They wouldn't lend . . . the time come around . . . and Theobald made Dad put up his little ranch to sell for the note . . . and Theobald got the ranch for the note because there was nobody else around with that much spare cash. You see how easy he scooped us in?"

"But men like him," said Joe White bitterly, "don't get nothing done to them. They don't get a rope around their necks, curse 'em!"

"Him?" said the boy with an even fiercer anger. "Why, he owns a newspaper over in the town, and everyday the newspaper puts in something about what the 'philanthropist,' Samuel Theobald, has done for the town, or is doing for it, or is going to do for it. Every time he turns around he's got a reporter right there to write up the news about him. That's the way the world is treating him. But what he done was worse'n shooting my father dead, because it busted Dad's heart. He didn't have no spirit left. The fire had cleaned him out once. Theobald done it the second time, and after that he was all through. He couldn't no ways get himself together to make a new start. And Mother got to worrying at him, and that filled the house with talk and argument. There was constant fighting inside the front door of our house. Then Dad died, and there we were with nothing. But it was Theobald that put us down. It was him that killed Dad and busted Mother's heart! Now he's down there all dressed up and driving his swell, high-stepping hosses around and riding nothing but clean Thoroughbreds. He's too good by a whole pile to waste his time in riding ordinary cow ponies, he is." Wild malice brought the boy to his feet.

"Set still," said Joe White quietly. "He ain't through with you yet. Not by a good pile."

"If he was young enough for me to fight," raged Ted McKay, "I'd tear his heart out . . . I'd sure have it out."

"Suppose you was to drop down and take his best hoss," said Joe White. "That might do him some sort of a hurt. Then maybe he's got some sons that you might bother a little."

"Sons?" said Ted. "Oh, I thought of that long ago. But he ain't got any sons. All he's got is one daughter. And he keeps her away at school, mostly. She don't talk nothing less than words of about ten syllables, they say. I can't fight a girl, can I?"

"It looks to me," said Joe White, "that you don't think none too much about girls. Is that right?"

The other shrugged his shoulders, his handsome face still clouded with the rage into which thoughts of Samuel Theobald had thrown him.

"What good are girls?" he said. "They can't do nothing like a man can do. I ask you fair and square . . . what good are they? I never seen one yet that could ride a hoss better than fair to middling. I never seen one yet that was worth shucks when it come to shooting. They can't walk a mile without wanting to set down and rest themselves. They can't climb a hill without acting like they'd done a day's work. They can't argue peaceable about nothing, but they got to keep repeating themselves and making no sense and getting mad when folks don't agree with 'em. Why, Joe, I don't see no particular use for women . . . that is excepting them that are mothers. Of course, they're different."

"Of course," said Joe White. "Of course, they're a little different."

"Look here," said Ted McKay suddenly, "are you grinning behind your hands? Are you laughing at me?"

"Me?" said Joe White blankly. "Sure I ain't laughing at you. I know just the way you feel. Wasn't I twenty once?"

But Ted McKay had seen the flickering light of mirth. And he could not forget. Yet he did not refer to it until they were swinging down the steep slope toward the lowlands after breakfast.

"Look here, Joe," he said.

"Well, son?" said Joe.

"I guess you figure I'm tolerable young?"

"Maybe I do," said Joe.

"Well," said Ted McKay, "I guess maybe you're right."

And they laughed together.

X

"Theft on His Own"

On the way down from the ridge Joe White spoke so little and walked with so contracted a brow that Ted McKay was over-awed. He felt that he must surely have offended his famous companion—perhaps by the freedom of his speech—and, there-fore, he resolved that he would not again speak until he was spoken to. And that resulted in a long, dreary silence.

What filled the mind of Joe White was chiefly a profound concern for the welfare of his young ally. They were pro-ceeding now straight for the ranch of Samuel Theobald. That ranch would be the scene of the first crime which Ted McKay had committed so far. One crime, however, would be the opening of a floodgate. Once the career of enmity to the law began, there could be no ending to it. He knew out of the les-sons of his own life how cruelly the first crime—which was justifiable, almost, the result of necessity—led to the tenth crime, which was the result of pure caprice, perhaps. Ted McKay, no doubt, would drift even more easily than he, for there was a fluid temperament in the youngster. He took on easily the tone of those around him.

But how could he stop Ted from the theft of a horse he could find on the ranch of the legal thief and plunderer, Samuel Theobald? The problem filled up his mind all that day. When, in the evening, they camped among the foothills, he sat scanning with his glass the precipitous paths and trails by which he and Ted and the brown gelding had come to this

more pleasant level, and, although he marked no sign of enemies now descending, still that could not increase his cheer.
It was not the physical danger to himself that he was
dreading, but the fear of the future toward which Ted McKay
was rushing.

His reference to it, however, was most carefully guarded.
"I'll tell you what," he said. "If I was you, I sure wouldn't go
over to the ranch of Theobald tonight."

"Why not?" the kid inquired.

"Because not even you, with your eyes, son, could take the
pick of the hosses when it's dark."

Ted McKay agreed. Indeed, his eyes shone as he heard the
suggestion. "We'll go over in broad daylight, then, you
think?" he said. "We'll go over and skin through all of
Theobald's 'punchers and nab the best hoss that we can find?
Well, that sure will give 'em all a thrill!"

And he sat chortling and rocking himself to and fro, with
his arms hugged tightly around his knees. But Joe White,
struck with dismay, could make no immediate answer. Of
course, that was exactly the sort of exploit that Ted McKay
would expect of him. How soon would he be able to open the
eyes of Ted and show him the commonplace truth about himself?

He felt two or three times on the point of opening his heart
and making a clean confession to Ted. But he was held back
by the certainty that Ted would not believe a word against his
idol, even if the very idol itself should speak. When he decided to speak at any cost, he discovered that Ted had gone to
bed and to sleep by the simple expedient of giving one roll in
his blankets and closing his eyes.

So the outlaw leaned his back to a rock and puffed at his
pipe and lived over in grim retrospect some dozen of his adventures, wondering if poor Ted must come to the like. At

length he himself became sleepy and went to bed, to dream of Ted McKay armed with a revolver in either hand, dealing death to scores of onrushing men. Or his unconscious brain skipped all that had followed and went back to the agony in the cañon with a terrible enemy in an invincible position ensconced among the lofty opposite rocks.

He wakened with the light of a new-risen half moon in his face. It was sliding out from behind a wisp of cloud, and it was not an hour old from the horizon. Joe White shivered a bit as he looked upon it. He had heard some talk of a superstition of disasters that come to those who allow the moon to shine upon their sleeping faces. Exactly what the disasters might be, he had never learned. But the rumor had always filled him with dread. It was one of those peculiar aversions that will overwhelm the most normal man. What Joe White dreaded most of all was a moonlight night. All his life he had gone with a feeling that he would die, in the end, by moonshine.

He called, as he sat up: "Hello, Ted! Bad luck if you're sleeping with that moon in your face."

There was no answer. That silence struck a blow at the heart of the outlaw. For even a whisper, in the mortal stillness of this night, should have shaken a man out of soundest sleep, particularly a man of the hair-trigger sensitiveness of Ted McKay. Joe White leaped to his feet as though he had heard the click of a gun hammer in the night. Nearby he saw the misshapen heap in which the blanket of Ted McKay had fallen when Ted had left it. There was not doubt that he had gone by night, wakened by the moonshine, to find a horse on the ranch of Theobald. The light that had wakened the youngster would be the light by which he picked out his mount.

Joe White estimated the height of the moon again. No, it was certainly hardly more than an hour up the sky, and young

Ted McKay could not have more than that head start. Yet, to one of his activity, walking as he walked, an hour was a mortally long period. It might span the distance from their camp to the ranch itself and the theft on the ranch.

Joe White tossed a saddle on the back of the disgruntled gelding after he had kicked the latter into a standing posture. A moment later, he was flying off at a wild gallop, for if he did nothing else in the remainder of his life, if he must use brute force for it, he must keep Ted McKay from that theft.

It was not long before he topped a hill and saw, in a sprawling valley bottom, the moon-silvered roofs and the black sides of the Theobald ranch buildings. Another glance showed him several moving lanterns, and at the sight of them he checked his horse and groaned aloud.

A cowpuncher never walks rapidly, particularly when he is told to do so. He will ride like mad all day, but his idea of a fast walk is a Spanish damsel's conception of a slow stroll. Yet, those lanterns that Joe White saw—and clearly, as they were carried under the cavernous shadow of a great barn— were being carried at a fast clip, sometimes jouncing almost out, and swinging through brief and broken curves as those who carried them hurried on.

It simply meant that a sudden and critical disturbance had caused those men to hurry at full speed out of their bunk-house. They had probably come with guns in one hand, a lantern in the other, not realizing in their quarters the brightness of the moonshine outdoors. If they were gathering in such a fashion and at such a point, was it not probable that Ted McKay was the center of interest? And, if it were Ted McKay, was not there a great probability that poor Ted had been dropped by the rifle of some alert watcher?

He spurred his horse to a gallop and drove forward again.

XI

"A Traitor for Gold"

He halted the mustang at a short distance from the ranch and behind a hummock where he might remain safely screened from view. After that he ran ahead on foot until he reached the side of the great barn where he had seen the lights. Now all the lights were gone from it. He circled around it, running cautiously, with his body bent low. As soon as he cleared the corner of the building, he saw that the ranch house itself was now the center of attention. The windows of one room in particular blazed with light.

Toward this he went, his gun in his hand, for, if it cost him the deaths of ten men, he intended to have Ted out of danger that night. He stepped onto the verandah, moved close to the wall so that there might be less danger of the flooring creaking, and so came opposite the windows.

One glance told the story. Half a dozen cowpunchers stood in the outer circle. Within that circle were the forms of a stout, wide-shouldered, red-faced man whose air of importance stamped him at once as the owner of the ranch, and a slender girl of twenty who was doubtless his daughter. But the outlaw glanced straight past them to the main center of attention. This was the form of Ted McKay—no other—standing with his hands tied behind his back, his battered felt hat still on his head, but pushed far back, and the painfully simple story of his capture was told by the lariat that still dangled from the hand of a cowpuncher nearby, who, from time to time, looked upon the captive with a proprietary grin. The window was partly open. Every voice was clear.

"If you weren't out there to steal a hoss," said the big man with the red face, "what were you doing out there?"

Ted McKay did not answer. He simply smiled quietly upon Theobald and said nothing. The smile seemed to infuriate the big man.

"You're no good, kid," he said. "I've knowed you and your father before you. He was a failure, and you ain't been any good since you was born. Just idling and shiftless. You'll be stretching rope free of charge one of these days, son! If it ain't for hoss stealing, it'll be for slipping a knife into the ribs of some man or other. That's about your size!"

"Father!" cried the girl.

The outlaw looked at her for the first time. She was afire with indignation as she faced Samuel Theobald—slender, as he had first noted, and some two or three years less than the twenty years at which he had placed her age. If she were not a great beauty, at least she was very pretty. She had quantities of copper-red hair and fine big gray eyes under a white brow. Above all, she had what the outlaw always looked first to see in man or woman, a round chin and finely cut mouth. She threw her head up as she faced her father now.

"What are you mixing into this for?" asked the rancher. "What's it mean to you?"

"Haven't you read your own paper?" she asked. "Haven't they told about the way he followed Joe White and killed or captured five of Joe White's men? Haven't they written thousands of words about how brave Ted McKay has been . . . how wildly brave? And now you accuse him of sneaking into a dark corral to steal a horse?"

"You go up to your room and don't let me hear no more talk out of you," said her father brusquely. "The kids these days are all lip and no respect. A gent might think that you'd just been drug up, not raised plumb civilized the way I've done by you!"

"I'll go," she said, "but not before I tell Ted McKay that I know he's innocent."

She stepped suddenly to Ted. She could not shake his corded hands, but she laid a hand on his arm. "I remember you, Ted. I remember playing with you. And I know this will come out all right. There's one friend who'll fight for you!"

She fled from the room with Ted McKay standing stiff and staring after her in a strange dismay and happiness combined.

The outlaw at the window took another look at the glowering face of the rancher and then turned on his heel, sprang from the verandah to the ground, and ran for the hummock behind which he had left the gelding.

When he turned again toward the ranch house, he was carrying a heavy canvas sack, and he rounded the front of the big building in time to see a horseman vault into the saddle and rush down the dusty road for town. He would return and bring the sheriff with him. There was no doubt of his errand.

The outlaw made sure of that. He made sure, too, by the sounds of voices in the house, that the cowpunchers had not yet returned to their usual quarters. So he waited with his back against the wall, huddled into a corner where no one was apt to pass or to see him if they passed, until the jangling and slamming of a side door on the farther side of the building told him that some, at least, were leaving the house.

After that he began to skirt around the verandah again, peering into the windows. He found the rancher exactly as he had hoped to find him—alone in the big living room. He waited for no more, but, going to the front door, he pushed it open and boldly walked in, crossed the hall, and stood in the living room before Samuel Theobald.

The latter was sitting with his hands clasped behind his head, rocked far back in his chair, with an air of perfect beatitude. His bland look changed to the most complete dismay at the sight of the big man from the mountains. Then he swayed drunkenly to his feet, the crimson sweeping out of his face and leaving it the color of ashes.

"Joe White!" he breathed.

"That's me," said the outlaw calmly. "Sit down."

Theobald slumped heavily into a chair, and the other, crossing to the window, pulled down the shade and faced his host.

"Theobald," he said, and the rancher stiffened like a private when the captain speaks, "I hear that you're a gent that drives bargains and makes trades."

"I've made my honest money that way," said the rancher uneasily, "what little I got in these hard times."

The outlaw sneered. "I'm going to make you a business proposition," he said. "I know you're rich, Theobald, but I know you sure would like to make some more money. Now listen to me. Down yonder you got a gent locked up in a room with three or four of your 'punchers guarding him till the sheriff gets here to take him in town to jail. Theobald, is it worth five thousand dollars, arresting young McKay?"

Cupidity banished the fear in the eyes of the rancher. "Five thousand?" he said. Then he laughed. "How come, White?"

"Stand steady," said the outlaw, for the rancher was edging gropingly back toward the door. "Sit down yonder and write out on that piece of paper I see on the desk . . . for five thousand dollars received, I promise to set Ted McKay free."

"And be blackmailed with the note?" queried the rancher shrewdly.

"You know I ain't that kind," said Joe White. "I keep my word. I'm paying you five thousand, if you'll keep yours and go down the hall and tell the boys that you want to talk to Ted McKay. Then, when you get him in here, you can cut his rope and tell him to beat it. All I ask is that he gets a fair run to the window. Does that sound like business to you, Theobald?"

"Does it seem likely that you got five thousand dollars on you in good coin?" asked Theobald sharply.

"Here," said the outlaw, and he suddenly displayed the little canvas bag. "Here's forty-five pounds of gold coin. Look at it." He jerked open the strings and spilled the contents upon the table. Theobald drew in his breath deeply.

"Now move quick," said the outlaw, sweeping the money back into the bag. "I'm taking chances every minute I stay here. They may hear my voice. And my voice ain't unknown. I want that paper, Theobald. Then I'm going to trust you to go down the hall and set Ted free. I'm going to trust your word, and trust to the fact that you know that, if you try to double-cross me, I'll get loose and do for you before I'm through."

The rancher hesitated one instant, then sat down at the desk, scribbled the note, and passed it to Joe White. He took the canvas bag in exchange, and his lips twisted into a grin of uncontrollable, covetous delight at the weight tugging down on his arm.

"I'll bring him right back. Wait here," he said, and turned away through the door.

White hesitated. Then, as the door closed behind Theobald and the bag of money, he stood for an instant with his head lowered, lost in a brown study, while he listened to the retreating footfalls of the rancher. There was something stealthy and hurried in that tread, it seemed to him, and, making a sudden resolution, Joe White stepped to the window, drew the shade up, and leaped lightly to the verandah outside. He drew the window shade down again, stepped to the ground, and behind a broad-trunked oak.

He had hardly taken that shelter, when a dim shape slipped around the farther corner of the house, stole up to the verandah, and crouched down behind it. Next he tilted up the long, dimly glimmering barrel of a rifle and pointed it steadily at the window through which Joe White had just come. The outlaw set his teeth. His rage grew when a second form hurriedly followed the first and dropped down beside him. There remained no doubt about it. The rancher had attempted to trap the man whose money he had just taken. He was about to spring that trap from the inside, drive his prey through the window, and there the outlaw was to fall, riddled with the unexpected fire of rifles that waited for him at that point. Joe White ground his teeth, and his hand trembled in the strength of his grip on the revolver butt. They were hardly a yard away. Two strokes of the heavy gun, and they would fall silently, with crushed skulls, yet he held his hand, praying that he might have the power to withstand bitter temptation.

Then the sudden shriek of a woman, a young girl in mortal terror, came thrilling through the night air and brought the two watchers shuddering to their feet.

XII

"With Gloria's Aid"

What Ted McKay knew was simply that the big rancher, his face blotched and his features singularly contorted, appeared at the door of his room, panting as though he had just run violently for a great distance. Yet there had not been a sound as he approached down the hall of the house to open the door. He motioned, and the two cowpunchers, who had been regaling themselves with a game of cribbage and cursing while they watched over the prisoner, rose and stepped to the master.

"Come with me," whispered the rancher.

"What about McKay?" they asked.

"Ain't his hands tied?" murmured Theobald. "Besides, he don't matter. There's bigger game on foot, sons. Come with me and. . . ." The rest was lost in the breathless whisper as the rancher drew the two through the door and closed it behind him.

The prisoner, left entirely to himself for the first time, looked about him. There was nothing in sight that he could use for the severance of the bonds that held his arms behind him. He tried the ropes with a desperate pull. The only result was the loosening of the skin at his wrists. He desisted, with a faint groan, and walked to the window. He might shatter the pane and climb through and run for it, but the first noise of the falling glass would be sure to bring men on his heels, and, if they saw him running, they would shoot, and shoot to kill.

He turned in renewed despair as there came a click of the

turning doorknob. The door opened and into the entrance came the daughter of the rancher, Gloria. She was transformed wonderfully from the girl he had seen only a few moments before. Her cheeks were on fire. Her eyes were blazing green. The very golden red of her hair seemed more shimmering bright as she hurried stealthily toward him.

He stared at her, benumbed. Then a sharp tug, the hiss of a knife blade on the rope, and his hands came free with the crimson trickling slowly down from the injured wrists.

"Now, go," she breathed. "Run, run! I only had this minute. But first the way to a horse . . . right behind the big barn . . . beside the corral fence . . . there's a saddled horse with the reins thrown . . . he's the very horse you tried to get . . . it's my horse . . . I give him to you . . . I've just saddled him for you . . . there's a gun in the holster . . . and ride for it."

The whispered words poured out in a swift torrent that he could hardly understand. All that was intelligible was her excitement, her beautiful excitement. He hung before her, breathless. He wanted to say he knew not what.

"Go, go! Go while they're after the other man," she stammered. "Oh, if they find out what I've done. . . ."

"What other man?" he gasped.

"Why, the big man. In the living room. . . ."

"Ah, Joe White! Have they trapped him?" He started for the door.

"Are you going in there with your naked hands?" she murmured, and clung to him to stop him. "Go, go as fast as you can. Or else stay here behind this locked door as you in honor bound should stay unless you go where I tell you to."

Dimly, he understood the logic of this strange demand. He hesitated. "Why are you doing this?" he managed to ask.

"I don't know," she breathed. "Because I'm mad, perhaps. I only know that I think there's something better in you

. . . something that no jail should hold. But will you go? Will you go?"

She had dragged him to the door. She glided before him into the hall, and there she whirled and faced the commanding bulk of her father towering above her with a sawed-off shotgun—that most deadly of all short-range weapons, the only weapon in whose use no skill was required—balanced in his hands.

Her shriek tore at the ear of Ted McKay. The next instant he had struck past her head and into the fleshy face of the rancher—left and right flashing out like two flying pistons, and the hard knuckles biting through the pad of flesh and against the bone of the skull. The sawed-off shotgun was flung up crazily. The contents of both barrels went off like roaring thunder down the hall. Then Ted McKay was past the barrier and racing like a greyhound for freedom.

He turned the corner of the hall. He met a cowpuncher running low, with a gun in either hand. Ted McKay vaulted over him, landed on both feet, and dashed on, with lead coughing vainly from the guns behind him. He leaped the last ten feet, struck the door before him, tore it from its hinges, and so passed out into the blessed open air of the night.

That open air was torn with shots and shouts. He heeded them not. Yonder was the only possibility of refuge. He turned the corner of the barn. There, glimmering in the moonlight, was that same slender-limbed bay whose beauty of head had caught his eye earlier in the night. Into the saddle he went at a leap. The bay started off like a watch spring uncurling. And, gathering up the reins, they flashed across the first field, cleared a high fence of the terrible barbed wire with a sailing leap, and so on into the open, on into freedom.

And Joe White?

He had crossed the ridge beyond when he saw a horseman

spurring hard across the hollow, a horseman who turned to the sound of coming hoofbeats and threw up a gun to fire.

"Joe!" said the youngster.

Throwing away all caution, bringing the pursuit inevitably on their heels with his voice of thunder, Joe White roared: "Thank the Lord . . . Ted McKay!"

"But what will he do to her?" asked Ted, when the sun was coming up, bright and lonely in the east.

"Nothing," said Joe White. "I been a-wondering, Ted, if you wouldn't be going back there anyway . . . and not for the old man?"

"Me? Go back there?" said Ted McKay. "Why, they know me for a thief. Nope, captain, got only one way to ride now, and that's beside you."

Joe White, lifting his grizzled head sadly to the sun, knew that it was, indeed, true.

The Overland Kid

A Reata Story

Originally published as "Reata and the Overland Kid" in the January 20, 1934 issue of Street & Smith's *Western Story Magazine*, this story was the sixth entry in the popular Reata series written under Faust's George Owen Baxter byline beginning in late 1933. The first story in the saga was "Reata," which was reprinted in THE FUGITIVE'S MISSION (Five Star Westerns, 1997). The second, "The Whisperer," is to be found in THE LOST VALLEY (Five Star Westerns, 1998). The third, "King of the Rats," is to be found in THE GAUNTLET (Five Star Westerns, 1998). The fourth, "Stolen Gold," is to be found in STOLEN GOLD (Five Star Westerns, 1999). THE GOLD TRAIL (Five Star Westerns, 1999)contains the fifth, "The Gold Trail." The conclusion, "The Peril Trek," will appear in THE PERIL TREK: A WESTERN TRIO. In "The Overland Kid" Reata has been successful in retrieving the money stolen from the Decker & Dillon Bank, but he is being pursued.

I

"Lost Loot"

Dave Bates found the sign of four horses crossing a bit of almost green grass. He followed that sign because he was following anything. He knew that Gene Salvio and Harry Quinn were slaving away in a similar manner perhaps miles away. Yes, necessarily they were miles away, since both sides of the Chester Draw had to be searched. A hundred and eighty thousand dollars in gold dust had been snatched away from them by a stampede of wild mustangs, and that might be considered merely chance, an unfortunate stroke of natural luck, but this luck no longer appeared merely natural when the three horses that had been laden with treasures were not found among the weary, worn-out remnants of the horse herd.

So the three had scattered to search for the gold savagely. Since they had owned it by theft, the idea of losing it maddened them. Nothing seems so doubly ours as that which we have taken without right. And now and again, as one little clue after another petered out, Dave Bates turned his thin half face toward the western horizon, hoping against hope that he would spy somewhere in it the wavering dimness of the two columns of smoke that he and his partners had agreed upon when they had separated as the signal that one of them had discovered sign of at least one of the missing horses.

After the sign of the four horses crossed the grass, Dave Bates turned again to stare around the horizon, but the sunburned hills rolled in straw-colored waves far out of his view into the horizon, and toward the other there was the sudden lift of the mountains. There was no thin stain of smoke in between.

He resumed his trail, not hopefully, but attentively, and now the hoofmarks of all four horses crowded in between two boulders where many another animal had traveled, also, cattle and deer and sheep and beasts of prey having turned in this direction to take the natural gate through the fence of great stones, so that the grass was quite worn away, and the ground here was thinly padded with dust that had not blown away today. On that surface, faint as a gray chalk mark on an old gray slate, thinly traced among the tramplings of the horses, he saw a sign that made him jerk up his mustang and fling himself down on the ground.

The sun was barely up. The eastern light flooded aslant across the earth, and, therefore, helped to outline and imprint every ruffling of the dust. It helped to bring out the pattern of a fine tracery that caused Dave Bates to leap suddenly up into the air and shake his fist in the direction toward which the prints of the four horses and this other almost indiscernible trail vanished.

Then he hastily gathered two piles of brush, lighted them, threw on green boughs, and watched the columns rise high into the air until the wind struck them, slowly bowed them over, and caused the white heads to vanish continually in the sky. Then he pulled up his belt a notch, sat down, and lighted a cigarette.

Sitting down was no good. It never is to a man who has been long in the saddle. So Dave Bates stretched his lean little body on the grass and braced head and shoulders on a mound. He was weary, but his horse was so much wearier that the poor beast hung its head without desire to eat. There was a telltale quiver in the front knees of the mustang, and

Dave Bates considered that tremor with perfect understanding, but with a cruel indifference. The pain of the horse did not trouble him, because he was on a trail of gold. The weakness of that mustang was a handicap, but other nags could be had not far away. He knew a ranch where there was always a plentiful supply of horseflesh, not pretty to look at, but good enough material to pass under the spur.

Now, as he smoked, he studied the thin drifting of clouds across the sky; now he stared again at the hills and at the mountains. The bigness of this scene seemed to him appropriate, because of the largeness of the adventure on which he was embarked. There was not a great deal of good in the nature of Dave Bates, but there was a trace of poetic appreciation of destinies.

It was Harry Quinn who arrived first, spurring a staggering mustang into a gallop. He flung himself out of the saddle when he saw his companion.

"Hey, Dave!" he shouted. "I thought you found something! What the devil!"

"Yeah, and I found plenty," said Bates. He continued to smoke.

"Where?" cried Harry Quinn, his broad, red face wreathing into an expectant smile.

"What's the good of showing it twice?" asked Bates. "Wait till Salvio comes in, and I'll show you both at the same time."

Quinn glowered, then he flung himself down against the same mound that supported the head and shoulders of Bates. Both of them eyed the vast emptiness of the sky, and spoke about one another.

"You was always a sour kind of a hound," said Harry Quinn.

"I wouldn't wanna be sugar in your soup," answered Bates.

"No?" snarled Quinn.

"Aw, shut yer face," answered Bates. "I'm tired of your yapping. You make me kind of sick. Shut up, will you?"

Quinn raised himself on one elbow. "Sometimes I got half a mind to . . . ," he began. His hands worked, but he would not let himself finish the sentence.

"I feel the same way. Sometimes I wish I was a snake so's I could poison you," said Bates.

"You *are* a snake," said Quinn, "but you'll bust your fangs, if you try to stick 'em into me."

"What's the good of yapping?" asked Bates. "You know we can't take a pass at each other so long as Dickerman's our boss."

"Yeah, and I know that," agreed Quinn. "That's what mostly makes me sick. Someday I'm goin' to be free from him."

"Sure. That's what the duck said when the fox had him by the throat," said Bates. "Hear anything?"

"No, nothing.

"Pull the cotton batting out of your ears and let the two sides of your brain work at the same time, if your brain *has* two sides to it," said Bates cheerfully. "There's sure a hoss coming this way, and it oughta be Gene Salvio."

It was. He topped the rise and came down toward them, his horse in better condition than either of the other two, partly because he was a finer horseman, and partly because he rode slightly better horseflesh. When he came up and threw himself to the ground, he looked at the two of them in silence as they rose to their feet. In the feline beauty of his face, no one could say that there was a happy expectation. It was rather the look of a man who expects danger to come suddenly near him and who enjoys the thought.

"It's him," said Quinn. "He spotted something here."

Bates went to the spot between the two boulders and there dropped to one knee. He pointed down at the ground.

"You two *hombres* come and see for yourself," he said.

They came. Salvio kneeled in turn. Quinn put his hands on his knees and leaned far over to examine the sign.

"Look at it," said Bates calmly.

Quinn, staring at the fine imprints, said suddenly: "It's a fox track. What about that?"

"No growed-up fox ever stepped as fine as that," said Bates.

"A young fox," said Quinn.

Gene Salvio ruled this out. "A young fox cub don't travel alone, and it has more fur on its feet. It wouldn't make a frog track like that."

"Like a toad hopped along," agreed Quinn.

"Except the marks ain't side by side," pointed out Bates.

"Well, what is it?" asked Salvio.

"Yeah, what you got all heated up over this for?" asked Quinn angrily.

"Look again and use your brains," said Bates. "There ain't more'n one thing in the world that would make a sign like that."

"I dunno what. It's more the size of a bird track than anything else," said Salvio.

"Ever seen a bird leave toe marks like that?" demanded Bates.

"Well, you tell us, and maybe *we'll* have the laugh," growled Quinn.

"It's the trail of a dog, a dog so small that you could take him up and put him in your pocket. And that dog belongs to the gent that grabbed the three hosses out of the stampede."

Salvio and Quinn, straightening, stared at one another.

"By the leaping thunder," groaned Quinn, "he means

Rags! He means Reata's little sharp-nosed dog, Rags. Bates, you mean that Reata has got his hands on our pack hosses?"

Bates pointed to the ground again. "There's the sign of four hosses in the dust," he said. "That would be the three hosses loaded with our stuff, and the fourth would be Sue, the roan mare. Look for yourselves and you'll see . . . here . . . and here . . . and here . . . where one of those hosses steps out longer than the others. And shuffles the feet kind of into the dust. Well, you all have seen the way that the roan mare steps, long, and kind of loose and sprawling."

Quinn was groaning deeply in his throat. Salvio said not a word and uttered not a sound, but his face was pale and tense as he bent over the sign that Bates pointed out. Finally he straightened. "It's true," he said. "Reata told us that he'd get that stuff away from us . . . and he's got it. Then *he* is what sent that hoss stampede smashing down the Chester Draw?"

"Ain't it like him?" demanded Bates. "He never draws no blood, but he gets things done the way he wants 'em. Ain't it like him, is all that I'm asking you?"

"It's like him and it *is* him!" exclaimed Harry Quinn. "He's got the stuff, and he'll keep it."

"He won't," said Salvio. "It wouldn't bite me so deep if I thought that somebody with a claim to it was going to have it. No, the fool is going to take the gold back there to Jumping Creek to the Decker and Dillon Bank, where we got it in the first place."

"It's true," groaned Harry Quinn. "He's going to try to go straight."

"Aye, and that's the only place that he's a fool," declared Dave Bates.

"How come?" asked Salvio.

"Well, you've known Dickerman for a long time," said Bates.

164

"Sure, I have," agreed Salvio.

"Then you tell me if any of Dickerman's men ever managed to break away from him? Come on, boys, this is the trail we ride down. Get onto the Hyman ranch and we'll have fresh horseflesh under us, and then. . . ."

"Aye," put in Salvio gloomily, "but I'd rather be trailing a regiment than Reata all by himself. He ain't so much noise, but he's a lot more danger."

II

"The Hymans"

It was in the break of the dawn of this day that Reata had come in sight of the Hyman ranch. The house stood in the lee of a round-headed hill that would cut off the worst strength of the north wind. It wasn't a house; it was rather a mere shanty. Small as it was, the weight of the flimsy roof seemed too great for the sagging walls, and even the stovepipe leaned awry on its loose guy wires. But what mattered to Reata was not the look of the house, but the look of the horses in the fenced field near the house.

When he saw those horses, he stopped the roan mare, loosened her cinches, and then went to the nearest of the three led horses. They had dropped their heads as low as their knees the instant they were halted. Visibly they were badly done in and could not go on much farther. From a saddlebag of this first horse, Reata took out a small chamois bag. The leather was badly streaked and discolored, with distinct green stains here and there on the surface of it. The mouth of the bag he untied, then unstrapped his belt. Inside of it was a soft pouch, and into the pouch he poured from the sack a stream of glistening yellow dust and tiny nuggets. Three or four pounds of gold went into the pouch before it was filled. After that he sealed both the pouch and the bag, replaced the latter in its former receptacle, and then walked on.

Out of the grass, the tiny little dog, its body as sleek as a rat's, its face furred over like the head of a wire-haired fox terrier, jumped up and trotted ahead of its master, seeming to know exactly which way the man would go.

Reata was very tired. If the three pack horses were totally spent, even the roan mare, ugly, wire-strung, tireless creature that she was, was now half spent, but her eyes remained bright, and so were the eyes of Reata. And his step was light and easy, the step of a man who has boundless resources of nerve energy when the strength of the body fails. Under his eyes were the blue shadows of fatigue, but they would not have mattered except to a very close observer. They would have been overlooked. For the man seemed what he was, a perfect, though not very large, machine. A trainer of athletes would have chosen him by his step on the ground without ever looking up at the taper of the wiry body into the capacious shoulders that sometimes seemed a little too big for the rest of him.

It was a half mile, nearly, to the door of the ranch house. Reata walked that distance, because the instant he saw a prospect of getting fresh horseflesh, he would not put the burden of a single extra ounce on the saddle of the roan mare, although she stepped up freely behind him, never letting him get more than a pace ahead.

A great, tousle-headed, thumping fellow in his early twenties came out of the door of the shack as Reata approached. The youth was big from his feet to his hands. He was square-built, and every inch of him rigged with muscle and that natural strength that some men have without training to develop it. When he saw Reata, he merely stared.

"'Morning, partner," said Reata.

"Hey, *you* been movin' pretty fast and far. What's been chasin' you?"

"I've been in a hurry," said Reata politely. "Is the boss around?"

"Why mightn't I be the boss?" asked the other.

Said a harsh, nasal voice inside the door of the shack: "Comin' right out, stranger!" Then a tall man appeared in the doorway, a man with prematurely white hair and a sun-blackened face. "Don't give any strangers none of your jaw, Rudy," said the older man. "How are you, partner?"

"Pretty fair," said Reata. "I'm all right, but my horses are done in. You've got plenty in the corral. How about three swaps and one buy?"

"Yeah," said Hyman, and he eyed the long, low lines of the roan mare and her ewe neck and her starved sides with perfect disfavor. "Yeah, I wouldn't swap nothing but a dead sheep for that one. But the others look like they're worth something. I'll give you hosses for the three of 'em . . . with a little boot throwed in."

"How much boot, and what horses do I get in exchange?" asked Reata.

"In a hurry, ain't you?" asked the other.

"You can see that."

"You'll have to pay for the hurry," said Hyman. "What four do you want out of the corral?"

"There's two bay geldings, and a brown mare, and a thin-sided gray with a Roman nose. I'll take those," said Reata.

"Hey!" exclaimed the son. "Who told you about 'em?"

"Shut up, Rudy, and go and get them hosses for him," said the father. "As sure as my name's Joe Hyman, this gent's got an eye for hosses in his head. I wouldn't try to put nothin' over him in a trade, I wouldn't. Go catch up them hosses, and you come inside here, and we'll feed and talk about the boot."

"I'm not eating," said Reata. "We can talk just as well out here in the open."

"Sure, we can. That thin-sided gray you was talkin' about is a thumpin' good hoss, partner. Worth two hundred dollars of any man's money."

"Let it go at that," said Reata calmly.

Joe Hyman blinked as he saw how easily the asking price was accepted. "About the others," he added gloomily, "I dunno. You got some bad-spent hosses here. That roan ain't worth nothin', for instance."

"She goes along with me," said Reata. "No, she doesn't stay. I'm talking about the others."

"She stays with you?" asked the rancher, staring. "What's she got to her?"

"Oh, she's just an old habit," said Reata.

"Yeah," pondered Joe Hyman. "An old habit with her four fine legs to travel on, eh? Yeah, I can see something to her now. Well, partner, you sure know your business. What's your name?"

"Tom Graham."

"Graham, my name is Joe Hyman."

They shook hands.

"I sure like to deal with a man that knows his hosses," said Hyman. "But, now, you take them other three, they're spent pretty bad. Maybe they won't ever be the same again."

"Look 'em over for a moment," said Reata. He added truthfully: "Those are hand-picked horses, brother. There's not a fault in any of 'em. Turn them out in the pasture and you'll have to sit out five minutes of bucking before you can ride them tomorrow."

"Yeah, they got eyes, and maybe they got nerve, but maybe they're busted down inside. You can't tell about a hoss as hot and tired as them three until it's been cooled out. I wouldn't want to trade with you under . . . well, fifty dollars a head." He clicked his teeth on these words, for he knew that he was asking outrageous boot.

To his amazement, Reata said: "That's pretty close to robbery. Every one of those three is better than anything in your corral, partner, and you ought to be able to see it. But I have to pay for being in a hurry, as you said before. Have you got a scales in the house?"

"I sure have. Why?"

"I'm going to pay you in gold," answered Reata. "Bring out the scales, will you?"

The tall man stared at him for a moment, then, without a word, strode into the house and came back carrying a small balance scales and several small iron weights.

"That's three hundred and fifty dollars," said Reata. "Call a pound of gold two hundred and fifty dollars, and I'll owe you, say, a pound and a half."

"Hold on," said the rancher. "Gold, you know, it ain't the same as money."

"No, but it's much better," said Reata.

"It ain't so handy," said the rancher. "I'd have to have more'n a pound and a half."

"Two pounds," said Reata, and he looked Joe Hyman so straight in the eye that the rancher flushed a little.

"Well, all right," he answered, and placed a two-pound lump of molded iron in one side of the scales. Into the other side, from his money pouch, Reata turned a thin stream of shining gold dust. The little heap mounted. The breathing of Joe Hyman became very audible. The scales shuddered in his hands.

Only when the iron-weighted side of the scales began to rise did Reata pinch the mouth of the wallet shut, tie it carefully, and restore it to his belt.

Joe Hyman kept on staring. With one hand he stroked his throat as though the effort of swallowing had pained him.

Then, looking down at the gleaming heap of gold, he murmured: "You struck it, eh?"

"You can see that I'm in a hurry," said Reata.

"Think of getting it out of the ground," murmured Joe Hyman. "Here I go and sweat my heart out all the years of my life, and what do I get? Hellfire and hell cold, and nothin' much more, and sowbelly, and potatoes boiled with their jackets on, and that's about all. Well, you went and struck it rich, eh?" He turned and walked slowly into the house.

Rudy Hyman came up with the four horses on the lead at this point, and, giving the lead ropes into the hands of Reata, watched him tether the horses to the roan mare. He did not help in the shifting of the saddles, for Rudy was a person who detested work that was not demanded of him. Instead, he went inside the house, and there he found his father seated at the scarred, dirty little kitchen table with the double scales before him, and the yellow heap of wealth in one side of the scales. Rudy felt a prickling go through his flesh and come out like electric rays at the roots of his hair.

"Hey," he whispered.

His father looked up at him with burning eyes. "You . . . you lump!" he snarled at Rudy. "Here's what other gents go and dig out of the ground. What do you dig?"

"Shut your face," said Rudy politely. "What . . . you mean that he paid in that?"

"He overpaid about half. In this. He's struck it rich somewheres."

"Gold!" said Rudy, and even out of his shapeless mouth the word issued with a sort of deep music.

"He's got more of it," said the father with another sudden glance at his son. "I dunno . . . maybe he's got a lot more of it on him . . . for the taking."

The face of Rudy pulled all to one side. He grabbed at a

rifle that leaned against the wall.

"Not that way, you fool," said the father. "Blood's the only thing that weighs heavier than gold. Use them big hands of yours."

III

"Rope Artist"

Rudy came out of that house bent on trouble and bent on money, and there is no more deadly a combination to behold in the heart of any man. But when he looked at the slender body of Reata, a sort of sneering pity wakened in his heart. He looked down on Reata at such an angle that he could forget that the spirit may be stronger than the flesh. His wrath he summoned up again as he saw Reata buckling on the fourth saddle, the one he had taken off the roan mare. This time he was cinching it on the back of the tall, thin-sided gray.

"Look here!" exploded big Rudy Hyman.

"Yes?" said Reata.

"Talkin' about the money, the old man tells me that he's gone and been a fool."

"He was overpaid. Is that being a fool?" asked Reata.

"That there gray . . . it's worth a pile of money. And you give us three wore-out old rags of horses besides, and think I'll take 'em?"

"I did the business with your father, Rudy," said Reata patiently.

"You're going to do it all over ag'in with me!" shouted Rudy, and strode closer.

The father, deep within the shadow behind the door, looked on and smiled. He was not very much ashamed of his son, and he was very proud of him. When it came to action, he had seen Rudy take two ordinary men and bump their heads together.

"I don't do the same business twice over," Reata said calmly.

"You don't? You're goin' to stand there, a snipe like you, and tell me what you don't do?" shouted Rudy Hyman. And now, having worked himself up to the proper pitch, he reached out to collar the smaller man. His hand gripped the empty air.

"Steady, old son," said Reata without alarm. "Don't get trouble started, because you're barking up the wrong tree this time."

"Barkin' up the wrong tree, am I?" asked Rudy. "Then I'll take some of the bark off the right face!"

Suddenly he smashed a fist for the head of Reata. That head swerved aside at the last instant, and Rudy, in the full driving lurch of his punch, stumbled on nothingness, as it were, and then tipped sidewise and landed flat on his face.

Just what Reata had done to Rudy, old Joe Hyman could not make out, but he opened his mouth and his eyes, and then he grinned. After all, he thought, no matter how the fight went, he would be a winner. If Rudy won, they would make a handsomer profit. If Rudy lost, he would have received a lesson that would make him a more endurable companion in the house.

As for Rudy, he came up from all fours with a howl. Something mysterious had happened, but he trusted more in his two huge fists than he feared any mystery. So he came lunging in headlong this time, and found himself suddenly hoisted into the air. Yes, all the two hundred and odd pounds of him were suddenly floundering in the emptiness of space, and whirling. Then he dropped with an impact that knocked the breath whistling from his body. Rudy knew, as he gulped back the lost wind, that he was beaten. He was aware that there was a knowledge in the slender hands of the stranger that was more powerful than all his beef and bone and brawn. But Rudy felt that he would rather die now than live to be shamed, so he snatched out a revolver to finish the battle while he lay on the ground.

What happened then was most mysterious of all. The hand of the stranger had disappeared into his coat pocket as Rudy reached for the gun, but it was not a revolver that Reata produced. It was merely a length of coiling line that appeared to Joe Hyman, studiously looking on, no bigger than very large twine. But it flew from the hand of Reata as though it were heavy wire. It caught not the body, but only the gun hand of Rudy, and the tightening strands of the noose squeezed his fingers flat together and made the gun drop on the ground.

Reata picked that gun up and tossed it to a distance. "That was a bad play, brother," he said. "When you get out among rough men, one of these days, you'll be killed first and talked to afterward, if you try one of those little tricks of yours. So long, Rudy. You're big enough now, and you'll know better later on."

With that he mounted the thin-sided gray. The lead ropes tightened, and one after the other, with a lurch, the horses broke into a trot and then into a canter. But the roan mare followed her master uncompelled, shuffling over the ground at a gliding trot that made the canter of the other horses look perfectly futile.

Joe Hyman stepped out of the door and stared at the departing stranger, not at his son, who was rising from the ground slowly, nursing his crushed and skinned hand. As Hyman stared, he made sure that the gallop of those three led horses was not free, as it should be under the weight of saddles only. It was labored and stiff, and short-paced. They were weighted down, but where? Why, the weight must be in the strong saddlebags. It could not be elsewhere. And what could it be, of small compass and so much bulk, heavy as lead itself?

The answer stunned Joe Hyman as his brain stumbled on it. Gold! It was gold that the three led horses labored under! No wonder that this stranger was willing to pay a price and a half, or two prices, for the horses he wanted. A frantic impulse came to the rancher to saddle a horse and fly in pursuit, but he checked that impulse. He had seen too well how the stranger had been able to handle big Rudy, his son.

Rudy was growling: "There you sat inside the house and let him get away . . . you with a rifle right ready at your hand, cleaned and loaded!"

"It was your job, Rudy," said Joe Hyman. "How come you let a little runt of a gent like that throw you up into the air and flatten you out on the ground afterward? What kind of a gent are you, to call yourself a fightin' man?"

Rudy rubbed his sore hand and stared at his father. "Dog-gone me," he said, "if I don't think that you liked seein' him do it! Dog-gone me if I don't think that it was fine with you!"

"Me? Sure, it wasn't fine with me," said the father. "But just the same," he added with a grin, "it'll give you a coupla ideas. And you know what it is, old son! Ideas is worth a lot more'n big hands and iron jaws."

It seemed for a moment as though Rudy would rush like a bull on his father. But his recent lesson had forced a new control on him. "Look," he said huskily, shaking his head, "I was plain licked!"

"You were licked brown and plenty," said his father. "Go fetch in some wood, and I'll start breakfast goin'. This ain't such a bad day, after all. I got three hosses worth twice of them that I sent away, an' I've got nigh five hundred dollars in gold dust, besides. No, it ain't a bad day."

"And what did I get out of it?" demanded Rudy.

"Why, you got a bit of sense knocked into your head. Hurry up with that wood!"

It was a good bit later in that morning that Joe Hyman had a chance to see three more very tired horses. They were ridden by three grim-looking men who swept down the slope and up to the door of the shack, into which Hyman himself stepped to view them more closely. He knew one of them. That chunky fellow with the thick chest and shoulders and the bulldog jaw—that was Harry Quinn.

Quinn, waving at him, shouted: "You seen a gent go by here with three hosses on the lead and a little mite of a dog along with him?"

"Sure, I seen him," said the rancher.

"You didn't give him no hosses, did you?" demanded Quinn.

"I didn't give him none. But I sold him three," said Hyman. "What's the matter? Ain't he a friend of yours?"

"You sold him three hosses?" groaned Dave Bates, writhing his thin face bitterly.

"Four, now I come to think of it. But he took the roan mare along with him, though there wasn't no saddle on top of her. That makes five hosses, all added up in his party now."

"There," said Salvio, pointing. "That sorrel gelding is one of our three."

"One of *your* three!" shouted Joe Hyman, his hair fairly lifting. "You mean to say that them was stolen hosses that he traded in to me?"

"They was stole, and stole from us," answered Quinn. "What you mean, doin' business with every bum that comes down the road? There's seven, eight hundred dollars' worth of hossflesh that you owe us, Hyman!"

The rancher stared, agape.

"Don't be a fool, Harry," said Gene Salvio. "We want new horses, and we don't want a lot of argument. Hyman, show us the best three horses you have in that corral, and we'll leave the three we've got under us with you. They're better than your stuff, but we won't charge you any boot. Hop to it, and get 'em out here fast. Come on, boys, and get something to eat. There's no use howling about what we missed. We gotta get some strength under the belt and ride ag'in."

They stormed into the house, and quickly the fire was roaring in the flimsy little stove, and the coffee pot was on, and sliced bacon was hissing in the broad frying pan.

The three best horses in the corral were promptly brought to them by a very subdued Joe Hyman and a frightened son, to whom he had merely whispered: "One of them gents is Harry Quinn. And Harry Quinn is hitched up to the queerest and the strongest gang in this neck of the woods. Yeah, or any other neck. Talk small and look smart when you're around these *hombres*. You might hear something."

They did hear something before Salvio and the other two went cantering away.

"You going to remember that hoss thief the next time you see him?" demanded Harry Quinn.

"I'm goin' to salt him down with lead and keep him for you to look at," vowed the rancher.

"I'll tell you a name so's you can label him," said Quinn. "He's Reata!"

"Hi!" shouted Rudy. "Him that killed Bill Champion?"

When the three galloped their horses down the hill, Rudy was grinning.

"Look! I was all busted up," he said. "And now I ain't nothin' but proud that I was throwed around by the gent that killed Bill Champion."

"Sure," said the father. "At the same rate, you'll die proud and swift one of these here days."

"Nope," answered Rudy. "Before I ever fight a gent ag'in, I'm goin' to have his name all wrote out and learned by heart."

IV

"Sun Talk"

Salvio and the rest kept no direct or headlong course. As Bates said to Salvio, they were engaged in a stern chase, and one that was always sure to be hard. It was apparent that Reata was driving southeast toward Jumping Creek. The town of Rusty Gulch lay almost due south. The thing for them to do was to get word to Dickerman, and Dickerman could send out men to intercept the flight of Reata.

"Send word? You'd think we had telegraph wires strung up between us and Rusty Gulch!" exclaimed Salvio. "Even if we did, wouldn't a message like that be pretty fine? Think it over, partner . . . 'Reata running for Jumping Creek to pay back the stolen gold. Send out armed men to stop him.' That would look pretty good, coming in over the wire, wouldn't it?"

"Sometimes you kind of beat me, Salvio," said Dave Bates. "You've clean forgot that we have the heliograph. Right there on the shoulder of Mount Passion there's one of Dickerman's men. And I know how to write out the code."

"Do you?" said Salvio. "Damned if I can ever get the thing memorized. That place on Mount Passion ain't more'n five miles out of the way. And you're the lightest in the saddle. You ride down there and send in the message. If you don't find our trail, I'll call you in before night with a couple of columns of smoke."

Dave Bates, at that, waved to his two companions. There were never any kind or lingering farewells among them, because the only thing that held them together was the will of Dickerman.

Diverging on a long slant from the trail which Salvio and Harry Quinn held to, Bates aimed his course at a mountain with a cleft head that stood at a considerable distance to the south, just far enough away for its rolling sides to be a thin mauve between the brown of nearness and the blue of far away. When he reached the upslope of the mountain, he pressed his mustang hard. It did not matter, perhaps, how quickly he used up horseflesh on this part of the trail, because, if his message went through, perhaps the major part of the work in the stopping of Reata would be done by other agents of Dickerman. So the horse climbed into a thick pine wood, slipping and stumbling over the uncertain floor of the thickly laid needles, and so came out on the flat western shoulder of the mountain.

A shack leaned here against a tall boulder, and in front of the shack sat a very old man, stretching a coyote skin on a light frame. The veteran was so very old that all his face was checked and counter-checked by wrinkles that seemed to have been incised with the edge of a sharp knife. Age was not loosening, but drying his body; it had been plucking gray hairs out of his beard for so long that the outline of the chin was plainly visible through the hair.

He looked up silently at the stranger and waited. Dave Bates sprang down from the saddle, threw the reins, and waved his hand to the trapper.

"I've been looking for you," he announced.

"You have, have you?" said the old man. "Maybe you've been wantin' to get me news that my grandfather's gone and died and left me his million. Ain't that right?"

"What I wanted to talk to you about was junk," said Dave Bates.

"Well, a gent can talk about pretty nigh anything," said the trapper. "I recollect prospectin' all one year with Sandy McGurragh, and we used to talk about what would happen if there was a war with Mexico, and we used to plan that war, and by the time the year was over, we was both generals setting up there in Mexico City, all covered up with gold braid and laughin' at the world. That was what we done with a year of talkin'. And I suppose that junk would be good enough to talk about, too."

"It depends on where a gent aims to put the junk," said Bates.

"Where would *you* start the business?" asked the trapper.

"What about Rusty Gulch?" asked Bates.

The trapper loaded a short-stemmed pipe and lighted it carefully and tamped down the flaming coals with a thick-skinned forefinger before he squinted at Bates through the cloud of smoke and answered: "Rusty Gulch, eh? Ain't there a junk dealer in Rusty Gulch already?"

"A junk dealer that knows his business, " said Bates, "is always dead ready to take in partners, you know."

"Maybe, maybe," said the trapper, narrowing his eyes more and more. "But how would you go about asking him?"

"I'd come up the side of Mount Passion and find a helio-graph," said Bates.

"Would you find one there?"

"I'd find an old man setting in front of his house, stretching a coyote skin and smoking a pipe," said Bates, "and he'd know how to start my message shooting south to Rusty Gulch."

"I could guess a few things about you," said the trapper. "But I dunno you very good."

"D'you want Pop to introduce me before we're friends?" asked Bates.

At this the trapper shrugged one shoulder and made a slight gesture with his hand.

"All right," he said. "You fire away and tell me what you want."

"I'll write it," said Dave Bates.

Being a man of method and some business, he carried a small notebook with him. He sat down with the book on his knee, scribbled a message first in English, and then on another sheet slowly transcribed it into code. When he had finished, he tore out the first page, put a match to it, and watched it turn into a fluff of yellow flame and then a little gray-black cinder that dropped to the ground. He tore out the code message and gave the paper slip to the trapper.

"Start shooting that," he ordered.

The trapper looked down at the message with a grin.

"What kind of hell pops after I send this?" he asked. He went into the shack and came out with his apparatus, which surprised Bates by its size and weight.

"We gotta have luck," said the trapper. "Sometimes the other gents that had oughta pick me up seem to be asleep most of the day. Yonder on Turner Peak is where I oughta get a flash back, if I'm having luck."

Dave Bates, looking across the vast charm of the Turner Valley, studied the head and side of the opposite mountain through patient minutes. Then a muttered exclamation came from the trapper.

"He's got me!" said the trapper.

It was a moment later before Bates saw a rapid winking of light from near the head of Turner Mountain. But the trapper was satisfied.

"We're goin' to step the message right across the mountains and down to Rusty Gulch," he said. "Sun talk is talk that don't make no noise, but it says a terrible pile. How big a pile is this goin' to say, stranger?"

"This here sun talk," said Bates, pleased by the phrase, "is all about gold and hosses and men."

"Sure," said the trapper. "Gold is always what lies behind the sun talk. So long, then. Give Pop my regards, will you? Tell him that I ain't goin' to keep up this job very long. The game is getting sort of scarce on Mount Passion. Tell him I want a change."

V

"The Overland Kid"

It was almost at the time when the sun talk was passing with a silent glittering from mountain to mountain that the Overland Kid came into Rusty Gulch. The Overland Kid sauntered through the town with an ample step and a wide smile, but, when men caught his eye, they generally became a little uneasy. That was because of a habit that the Overland Kid had fallen into. He looked at a man and printed the picture far back in his brain. It was necessary to recognize trouble as soon as trouble recognized him. And when he looked at a man, he sized the other fellow up and generally found him wanting. That was why strangers were uneasy when they met the Kid's eye. They felt themselves added up and knew that the total was not very big.

The fact that the Kid was so young, so smiling, and so handsome made him seem all the more dangerous. Only the veriest tenderfoot would have been fooled by the Kid's good looks and genial manners, and in these days he found, more and more, that he had to hunt for trouble hard before he could find it. He always managed to succeed in his search. Before long, he could warm up any community, and then the ground grew so hot underfoot that he had to move on.

The Kid did not look upon himself as a badman; he simply considered himself a bit careless and casual. Perhaps, after all, that was the truest way of looking at him, as well as the kindest. He was one of those precocious youths who make older and more normal men shake their heads, because the ordinary way is the best way, and youngsters who shoot up into a sudden maturity remind us of weeds that may kill out useful plants.

Nature had been too kind to the Kid. She had given him his height and breadth, and plenty of substance, too, when he was barely fifteen. Then she had filled him out with strength, and drawn his nerves tight and true, and rigged him with all the power and aptitude that a human could want. By sixteen he was a very finished product for the range. Perhaps he should have been closed up in the rigorous schedules of a good school, but the range was his school, and by sixteen he had received his diploma in riding, roping, and shooting. He got better and better in all three, but the Kid realized, it seemed, that this was an age of specialization, and he chose to specialize in guns.

He did not limit himself. Shotgun, rifle, revolver, he was at home with anything. He had three passions, and these were the three. For each he had a peculiar love. The revolver was a fine tool for close work. The rifle had about it a dignity. It conquered distances; it required exquisite precision, and nerves of chilled steel. But always he yearned for a time when a crowd of enemies might assail him and he could turn loose with a sawed-off shotgun and plenty of ammunition.

It will be seen that the Kid was a fellow of parts, and although he was a scant twenty-one, and although his perpetual smiling often made him seem even younger, the hard, bright glint of his inner nature would often peep out at his eyes, and, as has been said, chill the very spinal marrow of other men.

He walked right through the town of Rusty Gulch, and even went by all the saloons without being tempted, and on the outer and farther edge of the town he came in sight of the building that had been described to him—a huge old barn that had been turned into a house, a big, gloomy place with a tall wooden fence surrounding the yard behind it.

The gate was open, and the Overland Kid walked inside. It was all as he had been told it would be. There were the many and big piles of junk rising here and there from the ground, some of them partially covered with big tarpaulins. A ranch and a farm could be largely furnished with implements from those that the Kid saw rusting in that junk yard. Off to the side an old man was sorting a heap of weather-reddened chains—fifth chains, and singletree chains, and logging chains that required all the strength of the old man to haul them into place.

The Overland Kid stopped in mid-stride when he saw this man. For his senses were very acute, and in that fellow, who must be Pop Dickerman, he guessed at evil so dark and so profound that a disgust that was almost as old as fear came over him. For although the Kid had done many bad things in his life and although he had done little or nothing that was good, it must not be forgotten that he did not consider himself a lost cause. Perhaps that was the most dangerous thing about him. Badmen who justify themselves are the very worst members of society.

In that moment, while he stared at Pop Dickerman, the Overland Kid summed up all the features of that long and downward face, the grizzled, rat-like fur that masked it, the eyes that were too close together, too small and too bright, and the very red and smiling lips. For even as Pop Dickerman worked along, without an audience, he was wearing a smile that turned up the corners of his mouth.

When he saw the Overland Kid, he straightened, looked at him, and nodded. Then he went on with his work, for Pop Dickerman was accustomed to having people come out to his junk yard and look through the piles of rubbish, as the Kid now started to do.

The Overland Kid first found a hand rake; next he discovered an axe handle; and from a big heap he extracted a single tile. He went to the junk dealer and laid the three on the ground. Two or three scrawny cats came out from behind Dickerman and sniffed at the three things, and looked up into the face of the stranger as though they were beginning to understand something about him.

Dickerman said: "Rake . . . axe handle . . . tile. Hey?"

"That's it," said the Overland Kid.

"What might that spell?" asked Dickerman.

"You tell me about it, partner."

"R-a-t, it looks like to me," said Dickerman.

"Well, that's a word," said the Kid.

"Sure it is," agreed Dickerman, nodding, and then rubbing his hands together as he looked over the big dimensions of the Overland Kid. "That's a word that might mean a whole lot, depending on where a gent learned how to spell it this way."

"Turk Loomis, he's the *hombre* that taught me how to write like that."

"The Turk, you know him, eh?" said Dickerman.

"Yeah, I know him."

"You a friend of Turk's?"

"Him?" said the Overland Kid. "I wouldn't be a friend of his. The dirty sneak! Why d'you ask any white man if he's a friend of Turk Loomis?"

Dickerman made a slight clucking sound and kept right on smiling. "That's all right. But Turk must think a lot of you, or he wouldn't 'a' sent you to me."

"Aw, you know how it is," said the Overland Kid. "The bum got into a jam, and I happened along. I was on the road, d'you see, and I just happened along when Turk needed a happening. That was all. There were three greasers climbing his frame. I took 'em off, was all."

"Took 'em off or picked 'em off?" asked Dickerman with a greedy flicker of light in his eyes.

"I picked off the top man," said the Overland Kid, "because it looked like he was ready to prune the head off the tree with his knife. The other two was shaken off in the fall, and started running."

"One of 'em didn't run, eh?" said Dickerman.

"I dunno about the other one," said the Kid carelessly.

"One of 'em won't never run again, maybe," said Dickerman.

"How would I know if a greaser would run or not? I ain't a watchmaker. I don't care whether they run or stop and stay stopped."

"You didn't know Turk when you seen him in trouble?"

"Nope. I never seen his oily mug before."

"Why did you step in for him, then?"

"Aw, I dunno," said the Overland Kid. "You know how it is. Greasers are all right. They're all right in their place. But I kind of hate to see 'em climb somebody's frame. You know how it is."

Dickerman nodded, not in agreement, but in a further understanding of this youth.

"Well, what about it? What happens?" asked the Kid.

"What do you think ought to happen?" asked the junk dealer.

"How would I know? Turk tells me to come up here to you, and I come."

"As fast as the rods would carry you, eh?"

"I don't ride the rods," said the Kid. "I sat on cushions most of the way, and then it looked to me like more air would be better for me, so I came blind baggage the rest of the way."

Dickerman grinned as he answered: "Sure. You wouldn't

ride the rods. Now I take another look at you, I see you wouldn't spoil your clothes that way."

"Well, say something."

"I'm trying to," answered Dickerman. "I see you been in some hot weather."

"I always wear a pretty good coat of tan," said the Kid.

"I was telling by your eye, and not by your skin," said Dickerman. "Come inside and have a snack. You're hungry."

"I'm not so hungry. I'll go with you when I know why."

"Your belt's up two notches," answered Pop Dickerman, "and you haven't eaten since you left Turk Loomis's place. You better come in and have a snack."

"All right," replied the Kid. "I don't mind taking a chance, now and then."

This insolence Dickerman did not appear to notice, but, as he turned his back to lead the way, his upper lip twitched once and made the fur bristle on his ratty face.

Perhaps it was because he was angry that he glanced up at this moment toward the head of the northern hill that looked down over Rusty Gulch. He saw there a little rapidly winking point of light.

"Here . . . quick!" snapped Dickerman. "Come along. I got something to do."

His long stride became almost a run as he led the way through a back door into the kitchen.

"Start up a fire in the stove," he directed. "Bacon and eggs and things in that pantry yonder. Help yourself. I got a job to do right away." And he shambled swiftly away on his noiseless carpet slippers, closing all of the doors soundlessly behind him.

It was fifteen or twenty minutes later before Dickerman had finished his work on the roof of the house, and then, sitting in an upper room, decoded the jumbled letters which had been spelled out to him by the heliograph. The sun talk, deciphered, read:

> **Reata found us on way and swore he would get the stuff and take it back to Jumping Creek. He stampeded our horses and got away with everything clean. He is traveling hard for Jumping Creek. He has fresh horses. We are trailing him close. Work from that end. His line is from Chester Draw.**

When Dickerman had finished this translation, he sat for a moment with his head straining farther and farther back toward his shoulders, and an expression of frightful anguish on his face. His mouth opened, and his bright fangs worked a little in excess of his pain. Afterward he mopped the sweat from his forehead. He picked up the sheet of paper on which he had been working, burned it, and stamped the ashes into the floor. Then he went down the stairs toward the kitchen.

The arrival of the Overland Kid at this time was so much to the point that Pop Dickerman was already taking the coffee pot off the stove. On the table stood a frying pan that held no fewer than eight eggs, and an equal number of strips of bacon, flanked by a loaf of bread.

The Kid said, glancing toward the junk dealer: "Kind of gripe you to see me spreading all this chuck?"

"No," said Dickerman instantly, "bums are cheap . . . but a gent has to pay for the top sawyers. I always pay big!"

VI

"A Shootin' Job"

There was a burning impatience in Pop Dickerman, but he controlled all the fire of it carefully until his guest had finished the solid food and come down to his third cup of coffee. Then, relaxing in his chair and making for himself a cigarette with a careless flick of the fingers, the Overland Kid began to smoke and sip coffee.

"You keep some cats in this house," he said. "But you don't look like food done you much good. You look kind of lean and yellow to me. How come that first-rate chuck don't put some red in your skin, Dickerman?"

"Me? I got no stomach," said Dickerman hastily. "A little milk and stale bread. The doctor, he says it's better for me."

"Hey, but why d'you keep all the eats around, then?"

"For my friends," said Pop Dickerman. "I got a lot of friends that have appetites, partner."

"A lot of friends like me, eh?" said the Kid.

"Some of 'em like you," agreed Dickerman. "What might your name be?"

"Any old name would fit me pretty good," said the Kid. "I ain't so old as some. A few gents call me the Kid. Some call me the Overland Kid, because I travel quite a lot, and sort of fast."

"The Overland Kid," said Dickerman. "Aye, and I've heard of you. Turk Loomis, he ain't a fool. He never sent me anything but the first class. Now, how do you feel about a job?"

"How does the job feel about me?"

"The job feels good about you."

"Why?"

"Because you shoot straight," said the junk dealer. "And this is a shootin' job."

"How high does it shoot?"

"You ever hear of a fella by name of Reata?"

"That's a greaser name for a rope."

"Aye, and there's a man that wears the same name because he's got a reata, and he knows how to use it. You never heard of Reata?"

"No. Never. What's he like?"

"Like a bullet between the eyes," said Dickerman softly and thoughtfully, "or the poison in a rattlesnake's tooth, or the point of a flash of lightning."

"Kind of fast and mean, eh?"

"No, he ain't mean," said Dickerman. "He don't look mean. He looks kind of mild. He ain't big. He don't weigh more'n a hundred and fifty pounds, kind of light in the legs and big in the shoulders, but nothing to talk about. But all of him is made up of steel springs and rawhide."

"He may be a good man, but he's too small for a pinch," said the Overland Kid, who had battled his way through this world until he had a very definite opinion of himself.

Dickerman, at this, considered for a moment. Then he said gently: "You ain't a sleepy sort of a gent. You're wide awake. You can take care of yourself. But lemme tell you something. While you was setting and saying good morning to him, Reata would pick that gold filling out of that tooth."

The Overland Kid straightened and was about to make an angry denial. He contented himself with saying: "Well, maybe. I've got to see that."

"Wait a minute," said Dickerman. "Maybe I can tell you

something more. This Reata, he never carried a gun. But . . . well, you've heard of Bill Champion?"

"I dunno that I have."

"You keep thinkin' and try to remember."

"Hold on. Yeah. I've heard something about him. He's the gent that can't miss with a rifle or a Colt, and he ties up iron bars like they was twine."

"He used to," said Dickerman. "He used to do things like that. I got a little museum over yonder that maybe you'd like to see some time. There's something of Bill Champion in it."

He went to the corner of the room, where he opened a door and exposed a deep cabinet whose shelves were lined with a motley array of objects. A time-yellowed and polished skull grinned at the Overland Kid from the shadows.

"Hey, who's the dead man?" he asked, startled.

Dickerman picked up the skull with his long, claw-like, dirty fingers, and he smiled and brooded over it, and turned it this way and that with a sort of affectionate slowness.

"That's the skull of Jim the Spider," he said. "Maybe you never heard of Jim, neither. But Jim the Spider was a great man in the old days. He lived mighty quiet, but he made lots of money. Poison was the Spider's way. You stop at his house tonight. You get mighty good food and a fine bed, and the price is dirt cheap. And then you start along and you come to the hills beyond the house, and a pain grips you. And the world turns black, and you fall on your face and look up at the sun and don't see nothing, because you're dead! And Jim the Spider comes along a little later and takes your wallet and leaves you dropped down into a crack in the rocks. Jim was a mighty bright gent, and he used to set out in the sun and smile at folks, and he was fat and easy-going. You'd be surprised how big the face was that was hung around this here set of bones."

Dickerman put the skull back, and from the rest of the

litter selected a pair of bent iron bars. He held them up, solid, massive weights. "They got Bill Champion into a jail once. But he bent a pair of the bars and pulled out another one and went away."

"I kind of remember more about him," said the Kid, frowning. "Seems like gents have told me about him. Like they'd tell about a ghost. Where does he mostly hang out?"

"In hell," said Dickerman cheerfully, "where Reata put him. Him and his size, and his guns, and his big gray stallion, and Reata with his rope . . . but Reata was the one that did the killing, and Bill Champion was the gent that died."

"It ain't possible!"

"No? Well, none of the things that Reata does is possible," declared Dickerman. "There ain't hardly a one of them that folks would believe in, but they keep right on happening. There ain't a man that I know about that I'd send up ag'in' him . . . but I'd send three in a set, and I'd pick you for one of the three."

The Kid stared, and then finished his coffee. He felt rather cold of spirit, and hoped that the coffee would give him a greater warmth of heart.

"It sounds damned queer," he said.

"It's queerer than it sounds," said Dickerman. "Will you ride that trail for me, Overland?"

The Kid was frowning as he answered very slowly: "All the days of my life I never turned my back on any kind of job like this. But gimme another sort of a slant. The Reata gent . . . suppose that he was bumped off, it's murder, ain't it?"

"He's carryin' stolen goods," said Dickerman.

"*Your* stolen goods, maybe?"

"Stolen goods," repeated Dickerman, "and, if the law comes up with you after you put a bullet through him, the law'd thank you mighty big and fine, Overland."

"Dickerman," said the Overland Kid, "you look poison mean to me. But I reckon that I need a job. How high do you pay?"

"I ain't a rich man," said Dickerman, "but I'll pay ten thousand dollars for Reata dead."

"And I am to split that three ways?"

"Your partners on the job, they each get a split. You get a half, and they each get a quarter. That's five thousand for you."

The Overland Kid nodded. "I'd be a fool if I didn't take this here job," he said. "Damn if it ain't a big country, Dickerman, for a gent like Reata to be wanderin' around and me never heard of him."

"Nobody much will ever hear about him," answered Dickerman, "because he's smart enough never to brag. He never hunts for no trouble. He waits for it to sneak up behind him. Then he stretches it out cold. I guess he never drew a drop of blood in his life, hardly. But he turns gunmen into wooden soldiers."

"I've heard enough about him," growled the Overland Kid. "When do I start?"

"Finish your coffee, give yourself another cup, and then come outside. I'll have a hoss waitin' for you."

The Overland Kid, having poured himself another cup of coffee, went to the closed door of the closet that contained Dickerman's museum pieces, and, having pulled the door open, he stared at the crowded shelves until it seemed to him that the hollow eyes of the skull were regarding him in turn with an animate interest. Then he closed the door suddenly.

Since he was alone and could give way to a shuddering feeling of horror, he actually backed up across the room. He forgot his coffee finally, and, suddenly snatching the door open, he stepped out into the bright heat of the sun and stood fast, his eyes closed, letting that warmth soak into him. For it seemed to the Overland Kid that a cold shadow of decay had sunk into his very heart, and that it would need hours and hours of the most burning sunshine to thaw out the sense of death that lay in him.

He wondered a little that Dickerman had showed him that collection. But then he realized the point. Whatever happened, he was not to be sent out on the trail of Reata until he was thoroughly convinced of the importance of the mission and the danger that lay before him. He had been shown a terribly difficult objective; now it would lie in his own discretion to handle the long chance in the best possible manner.

When he looked up again, he saw old Dickerman coming toward him, leading a bay gelding of sixteen hands or a bit more, a powerful and high-blooded brute that kept shouldering against the old fellow, jolting him to a stagger as he bore back as well as he could against the reins.

The sight of the horse instantly lifted the heart of the large young man. There was a mount that would be able to carry even *his* weight with consummate ease. The saddle was new and good. The bridle was plain and strong. There was no show about this outfit, but it was the best of everything, and he saw the butt of a rifle thrusting out at the end of a long saddle holster that extended down the right side of the horse.

"That's a horse after my own heart," said the Overland Kid. "I'll sure take good care of it for you!"

"Take care of it?" Dickerman chuckled. "No, sir, but use it up like scratch paper. Use it up and throw it away. There's plenty more where that one came from. There's tons and tons more horseflesh like this here, but there ain't many more men like you, Overland. You use this hoss like it was nothin', and I'll think all the better of you."

The Overland Kid stared. He began to see more clearly

that there was, indeed, a great goal at the end of this trail.

Dickerman went on: "Now write down in your head some things I'm goin' to tell you."

"Blaze away," said the Kid, filled with increasing respect for this strange and evil old man.

"You know the country from the Chester Draw to Jumping Creek?"

"I know it like a book."

"You've ridden it?"

"Every inch of the way."

"That's the line that Reata is riding. You're goin' to stop him. There's three good men of mine behind him. They're spotting the trail, and they're ready to fight hard. You ride straight east from Rusty Gulch till you come to Tyndal Creek. You know that place?"

"I know that place."

"Go down to Tyndal Creek till you come to the bridge, and a quarter of a mile below the bridge there's a grove of a lot of tall poplars. You come up to that grove, and you come slow. And as you come, you whistle, d'you hear? The tune you whistle is 'Auld Lang Syne.' If you whistle it loud enough and long enough, there's two men will come out of that wood, and one of 'em is dark, and he's Blackie, and the other one's short and blond, and his name is Chad. Two good men, and two good hosses, and two good rifles. If you whistle that song, they know you come from me, and you can boss 'em. Tell 'em what I've told you. And that's all." He added suddenly: "Waitin' for anything?"

"No."

"Then get out of here and on the way!" shouted the old man. "Ain't every minute drainin' the blood out of my heart? Reata has seven or eight hundred pounds of gold that belongs to me. Go and get it!"

VII

"The Ambush"

Tyndal Creek raced its white horses between banks of green, shouting on its way with never a thought that it would leave the mountains and join a sullen, muddy river, and so go down to its destiny. And up the side of Tyndal Creek the Overland Kid rode the bright bay until he came to a bridge and, beyond the bridge, to a gleaming, tall grove of poplars. That moment of the day was windless, but the leaves were never still, and shook out a constant noise like the falling of a still, small rain.

When he was near the woods, the Overland Kid, as he had been instructed, began to whistle with all his force, "Auld Lang Syne." He whistled it, and he sang it, and he rode his horse up and down within fifty feet of the woods.

Presently he was aware of a tall, dark man with a straight line of black mustache ruled across his face who had appeared on the verge of the woods and was leaning one hand against a tree. He leaned on his left hand. His right hand hung just off a conveniently angled leg holster that carried a revolver. These were small things to notice, but the Kid had an eye for them.

"Seems like a pretty good day for a song, all right," said the stranger. "Kind of clears up your throat, don't it?"

"Blackie," said the Kid, "we've got to ride. Where's Chad?"

"How would I know?" asked Blackie, showing no surprise that his name was known.

"You know Dickerman, and you know he sent me," said

the Kid. "We've got no time to waste. There's blood running out of Pop Dickerman's heart every minute you hang back."

"Let him bleed for a while," said Blackie. "He'll never bleed his heart white."

The Overland Kid laughed. "All right," he said, "I dunno that I care so much for company. I'll ride alone if I have to."

"Come and take a look at this *hombre,* will you?" said Blackie, looking calmly over his shoulder.

A shorter and very blond man appeared beside Blackie.

"He looks kind of young to me," said Chad, for it surely was he. "He looks too young to know much, I'd say."

"I'm old enough to know a tramp from a white man," said the Overland Kid readily enough.

"What d'you know here, then?" asked Chad, sticking out his jaw and stepping a pace beyond the verge of the trees.

Then the Overland Kid could see all of him. He was not more than eight inches over five feet high, but there must have been nearly two hundred pounds of him. He was smoothed over, not with fat, but with a deep gloss of muscle. The Overland Kid dropped off the bay horse, threw the reins, and walked up to Chad.

"You look like a big pile of cheese to me," said Chad, and smote the Kid on the nose.

The Kid staggered back. He was, in fact, thrown a little off balance, and his arms flung out wide as he strove to recover himself. But he was by no means as far at sea as he seemed. The lore of a thousand barroom and lumber-camp fights was stored in the back of the Kid's brain, and he shrewdly noted how Chad rushed in with red lust of victory in his eye and his guard down, ready to throw punches with either hand.

The Overland Kid clipped him high across the temple with a damaging left. With the same hand he shifted on Chad's wind as the shorter man came to a halt, and, as Chad tried to jump back, the Kid shifted again and brought over his right to the button. The blow sounded like a butcher's cleaver chopping through a bone. Chad dropped flat on his face.

The Kid held out his red hands toward Blackie. "Come on and get your letter of introduction stamped, partner!" he called.

Blackie had not moved. "You got brains, and you got a pair of hands," he said. "But if it comes to *real* trouble, that damned crow knows more about you than I do."

For a crow, as though alarmed by this fighting, had sailed out of the top of a tree and was flapping heavily just overhead.

The Kid snatched out a gun and put a bullet through the bird. It was a lucky shot even for him, but everything came right, and the first shot did the trick. The crow tumbled heavily, head over heels, and thumped the ground with a good solid *thwack*.

"There's the crow handy for you," said the Overland Kid. "Now you go and ask him what you want to know."

"Anything that bird told me now would sure be dead right," said Blackie. His own remark amused him so much that he smiled all on one side of his sour face.

"See if you broke the kid's jaw," said Blackie. "Maybe we're goin' to ride with you, after all."

At this, Chad sat up unassisted. He rose and rubbed the side of his face with one hand and his stomach with the other, but his voice was perfectly genial and cheerful. "A good little man ain't got any business with a good big man," said Chad. "Never did have, and never will have. About this here ride you was talkin' about, partner. When do we start?"

"Now," said the Overland Kid. "But wait a minute, first."

He held out his hand, and Chad, after a bit of a grimace, suddenly took it.

"It ain't the first time I been licked," said Chad, "so you

don't need to feel so proud. I thought you had the dust in the brain, or I wouldn't 'a' come in so wide open."

"I got a lot of lickings myself," said the Kid, "before I learned how to fake a beating before I felt it. Come along, Chad. I'll tell you the news on the way."

The pair of them were out with him in five minutes. The first thing that the Kid noted was that they were mounted almost as well as he. By that he knew instantly that, if Dickerman had many men, these were among the most chosen.

"Dickerman hosses, eh?" he said.

"Same as you," answered Chad, whose jaw was swelling fast, but whose spirits seemed much higher than those of Blackie. "Now tell us both a pretty story, partner."

The Overland Kid told them his pretty story, as Dickerman had said that he should do. When he finished, Blackie surprised him by saying: "This *hombre,* Reata . . . this one you say don't wear no gun . . . I never heard of him before. But if Dickerman says that he's poison, poison is what he is. There ain't nobody like Dickerman to know about things like that. If he's riding from the Chester Draw to Jumpin' Creek, he'd likely come through Jericho Pass, wouldn't he?"

"That's the way I've been figgerin' it," answered the Kid.

"Sure, he'll go through Jericho Pass, unless he wants to throw away a whole lot of time," said Blackie. "We'll lay this *hombre* there and cook his goose."

So they went up into Jericho Pass, where the hills split away and a way was found among them, narrow and straight. There they lay through the hot, still middle of the afternoon, their horses tethered back among the rocks, and their own positions chosen with skill for cover and the distance they could command. They had their rifles ready, every man.

They even had chosen the targets.

The Overland Kid had said: "You shoot for the head, Blackie. Chad, you try for the head of the hoss. I'll try a heart shot on this here Reata. We'll get him, hoss and man."

Afterward, the conscience of the Overland Kid bothered him a little. But he pacified himself by declaring to his soul that a man handling stolen goods did not need a great deal of consideration. And yet—well, he felt that it would be much, much better if he could have a chance to get at Reata man to man and take his equal chances.

Remember that the Overland Kid had never yet been beaten by armed men in fair fight, and the sense of invincibility was strong upon him. His nature, too, was about equally divided between day and night. What the Overland Kid had never learned was that it is really possible for men to be good. He thought of goodness as of a hypocritical pretense. Since the days when his stepmother had beaten him; since the days when he first had to fight his way through a grim world; since the days when scars first began to appear on his body, he had known nothing but battle, and treacherous battle, at that.

Then Blackie gasped: "There! He's comin'!"

The Kid saw him a moment later, a man on a tall, thin gray horse with an unsaddled roan scarecrow following without a lead, and three other saddled horses moving as though weary, apparently carrying loads, although nothing in the way of a load could be seen except their empty saddles. In front of all, at first barely visible, was a true midget of a dog, trotting in the lead. Now the rider and his horses came close and dipped out of view into the hollow immediately beyond.

The prize was almost in the hand of the Overland Kid. He smiled a little grimly to think that this fellow Reata was so surely riding to perdition. Well, we never know where we are riding.

The Overland Kid looked back, and a mile down the road he saw the flimsy little wooden bridge that spanned a deep ravine. When he trotted his horse across that bridge, he had been aware of a small qualm in the bottom of his heart, for the bridge had wavered a little, horribly, under the weight of the horse. A quick thought of death had come to the Kid at that moment. And now Reata. . . .

The little dog came over the rise briskly. He was the queerest and the ugliest thing that a man could wish to see in many a long day, with his rat-like body and long, sleek tail, and his little fuzzy head so unlike the rest of him. He stopped, looked about him, sniffed the air, and suddenly turned back with his tail between his legs.

Well, Reata would not be able to read the air, and Reata would not be able to run for his life. Bullets would attend to that business. Still no Reata appeared. Long minutes dragged on.

"I'll tell your what," said Blackie softly from the side. "This here *hombre* has stepped down there at the run of water in the hollow to let his mustangs drink."

That had to be the explanation, and it smoothed the wrinkles of worry out of the brow of the Overland Kid for a time. But as the minutes lengthened again, he grew very restless.

Even he, however, was shocked by the exclamation of Chad: "Boys, the little dog warned him, and he's gone the long way through the pass!"

At that, the Overland Kid leaped to his feet, and saw swinging into the smooth of the trail behind him, already well started for the flimsy little bridge, the rider with the five horses, and the horses galloping furiously for safety.

VIII

"At the Bridge"

To an ordinary rider of the wilderness, that retreat of the small dog from the narrows of the pass would have meant little. A snake might have crossed its path, for instance. But to Reata every move of Rags had become eloquent with almost the detail of words. And that roached-up back, that tail between the legs, that stealthy haste meant to him, plainly, danger. So Reata had halted his horses for one instant only, and, when no men appeared, he understood that men must be waiting up there among the rocks. For that reason he took no chance. Men who wait in a boiling cauldron do not do so for a good purpose. Reata turned aside and carried his horses and his treasure through the winding way of the second pass.

When he got onto the plain beyond, he put his mustangs into a gallop and sped for the bridge. Even so, he was rather desperate, and he was not surprised when a shout rang thin and far through the air behind him. Looking up and back, he saw three riders racing their horses down the slope from the pass, and they came with a speed that made him groan.

He could cross the bridge safely enough, but horses carrying a dead weight cannot keep pace with horses that bear a smaller burden of living, acting flesh. He ground his teeth as he surveyed mentally the picture that lay on the other side of the ravine, beyond the slight rise of rocky ground. There was simply a broad and open sweep of rolling ground, with a few patches of trees here and there. He could not find shelter for five horses in such a region, and he could not keep those riders from catching him swiftly and surely.

He might as well stop now and surrender. Only that instinct which keeps a lost man swimming till the last ounce of strength has left him induced Reata to ride on, urging the tall, thin-sided gray, and dragging the mustangs after him with their priceless load. Behind him he could hear the hurrying rhythm of the hoofbeats. Glancing back, he saw the three riders bending far forward, like jockeys. More like wild Indians they seemed to him, and something about the recklessness of their going told him the sort of treatment he would have at their hands.

He had heard—he never would forget it—that Pop Dickerman could not be beaten. How word could have traveled to Rusty Gulch as quickly as this he could not guess. But the thing must have been done. These must be men of Dickerman, posted to intercept the line of his retreat.

The bridge was nearer. It was so rickety that, in spite of his haste, he dared not take it at a gallop, so he slowed the horses to a walk that cost him agonies. Always the rush of horses behind him grew louder and louder, and he heard one devil yelling like mad with excess of exultation. Reata looked up grimly, and it seemed to him that the tall, jagged pillar of rock that stood by the bridge was like an old funeral monument. Battered and worn, the whole top of it sagged outward, as though ready to fall on the bridge.

That mental image gave him his idea. As he reached the end of the bridge, he leaped to the ground and shouted and struck at the gray to send it ahead over the mound of rocks on the other side. There the horses would be safe from rifle fire. Then he leaped for the stone pillar and went up it like a cat. He was glad, not frightened, when he felt the great shaft of stone quiver slightly beneath him. The whole pillar was in an advanced state of decomposition, the frost cracks sunk deep into the core of the rock. So he came to that point near the top where a huge bit leaned out above the bridge. He poised, sprang with his whole weight against the slanting fragment, and felt it go away from before him as though it had been wood instead of solid stone.

He barely managed to reach back and grapple a ledge of the pillar, and, dangling over nothingness, he saw the two-ton fragment topple and strike the bank beneath. There it burst in two with a loud report, and into the sound came the dismayed yelling of the three horsemen. The second half of the stone rebounded and struck fairly on the end of the bridge. There was a sickening, crunching sound, as though bones were being devoured by gigantic jaws.

The bridge was broken, but not yet down. It was sinking merely, and the timbers gave out a half-screeching and half-groaning sound as they gradually collapsed. Then the entire ruin pitched down into the creekbed, a hundred feet below.

Reata had drawn himself up to safety on the rock by this time. And now he rapidly commenced his descent. Rifles were crackling before he got to the ground. Yet none of the bullets whirred anywhere near him. Instead, when he looked up, he saw that the gray horse had not led the others clear over the mound. It had paused on the top, as though the better to outline the horses for a target against the sky, and the rifles of the three pursuers were taking advantage of that fact. They had halted their horses not far away when they saw that they could not get across the ravine by this pass, and now Reata saw one of the burden-bearing mustangs rear, plunge, stagger. Another squealed as Reata heard a rifle bullet audibly thump into its body. The gray suddenly bent its knees and dropped its head. Then the whole group of horses surged across the mound of rocks, out of sight.

Could Reata reach them? He tried, running, dodging like a snipe that flies downwind. One bullet kissed the air beside his cheek. Another tipped his hat forward. And then, with a fast leap, he was over the rock ridge in the safety of the farther side. Safety? Safety for him, no doubt, since he had the roan mare ready to carry him away, refreshed as she had been by traveling this part of the day without carrying even the weight of a saddle.

But the treasure of the Decker & Dillon Bank was gone, it seemed. The tall, thin-sided gray that had gone so gallantly all day long, carrying Reata and leading the other mustangs, now lay on its side, dying. Two more were failing fast. The brown sat down in a ludicrous and thoughtful attitude. Another had blood gushing from a hole in its side. There were three almost dead horses here, and that left two animals sound to carry Reata and seven or eight hundred pounds of gold.

The thing could not be done. There was no way in which he could manage to make headway sufficiently fast, for there was another bridge not so far up the deep trench of that ravine, and he could hear the rattling hoofbeats as the three riders stormed along with their horses in that direction.

Before Reata lay this despair, and a smiling, peaceful landscape, singularly smooth and unbroken except by an occasional grove of young trees. To make all seem more peaceful, there was a rancher roping down a load of hay that he had just pitched onto his two-horse rack at the side of a wide field of standing shocks.

Calmly the rancher went on with his work, an old man, straight enough in the shoulders, but with a shining bit of silver beard on his chin. The wind blew strongly toward the ravine, and he could not have heard the guns.

Reata looked up toward the sky with a quick groan of impatience. Three horses down—three horses dead. He stood over them with a blind, gathering rage in his heart. Murderers of men, they are black enough, but murderers of poor dumb beasts. . . . Not for the first time he regretted that he had given up guns forever, never to touch them with his hands if he could avoid it, never to fondle their shining deadliness.

He could save himself, but what did he matter to these scoundrels? They wanted the stolen gold of the Decker & Dillon Bank. They wanted that—and they would have it. Automatically, nevertheless, he loaded the gold onto Sue, the roan mare, and onto the remaining mustang. It made a severe load, and he did not add his own weight, but strode forward, with Sue following him and the other mustang after her.

He went blindly forward. There was nothing to see except the load of hay, and, therefore, he went toward that, and saw the farmer standing up, hands on hips, staring toward him. The picture brought another idea to him that made him hurry forward on the run.

There was still a little time, but very little, before the galloping riders would have crossed the second bridge and ridden over the ridge of rock into distant view of him and his proceedings. He waved as he came up.

"Yeah, I been seein' you," said the old man. "Looks like you left some hoss meat behind you over yonder. But maybe you take kindly to the coyotes and wanna leave some food for 'em. You even left some saddles yonder."

The old man was apparently as keen as a hawk when it came to long-sightedness.

Reata panted: "Did you ever hear of the Decker and Dillon gold robbery over yonder in Jumping Creek?"

"Maybe I have," said the rancher. "You got any news about it?"

"I've got seven or eight hundred pounds of that gold

loaded on these two horses, said Reata. "I'm trying to get it to Jumping Creek, and there are three devils riding me down. They've shot three of my horses, and I can't make any speed with these. I broke down the bridge across the ravine there, but they'll come over the second bridge in a minute. What I want to know is this . . . will you let me throw the gold into your hay load and take it away? They'll never suspect you."

The old man took out a plug of tobacco, worried off a corner of it, and deliberately stowed the chew in the center of one cheek. "Well," he said, "how come you was able to bust down the old bridge short of dynamite?"

At this delay, Reata groaned. But he explained: "I climbed that pillar of rock by the head of the bridge. The top of it was almost broken off. I finished the job, and the fall of that part of the column smashed the bridge to flinders."

"That was to keep them gents from swarmin' right over you?"

"It was," said Reata. "They'll be in sight in a minute, and then it will be too late to do anything. Will you take this gold, or. . . ."

"Dog-gone me if that wasn't smart of you," said the rancher. "I was tellin' the boys not long ago that one of these here days the rock was goin' to fall and smash the bridge for us all. But what was a gent to do? It's county business, keeping up the bridges, ain't it?"

"Man!" cried Reata. "Will you take this stuff or won't you?"

"It ain't no part of my property," said the rancher. And he shook his head.

Sweat poured down the face of Reata. "You're giving a fortune into the hands of three hounds and a rat-faced devil who set them after me. What's your name?"

"Dan Foster is what my ma called me," said the rancher.

"Foster," said Reata, "I can see why it is. You'd take the stuff, but you know that your measly little pair of mules wouldn't be able to pull the hay and that much added weight."

"Hey! Hold on," said Dan Foster. "I never said no such thing as that! Them mules. . . ."

"It's all right," said Reata. "I know your heart's in the right place, but you know mighty well that the mules couldn't pull that load even with you on top of it, let alone seven or eight hundred extra pounds."

"They can't, hey?" asked Dan Foster. "Well, dog-gone my hide, but they can, though. That near mule, that Beck, she could pack the whole dog-gone outfit all by herself, once it got to rolling. And that off mule . . . that Bird . . . she's as good as Beck, except she ain't fast enough to. . . ."

"It's all right," said Reata. "I know you'd do what you can, but I don't blame a man for not wanting to shame his team."

"Hey, throw up that stuff and I'll show you!" shouted Dan Foster. "Dog-gone me if I don't show you that this here load of hay ain't no more'n a feather to them mules. Why, the sun has dried all the heart out of the grass. But they'd pull the load of it, if it was this big and all new alfalfa. Throw up that stuff. Gold or not, it ain't too good for Beck and Bird to haul!"

Reata eagerly took the heavy little forty-pound sacks and swung them up to Dan Foster, who took them and plunged them into the loose fluff of the hay.

As he handled them, he complained: "Gold! The stuff that some folks bust their hearts for. But you can't eat gold, and you can't drink the stuff, and nothing comes out of it, nothing but dead hosses, like them yonder, and dead men, like you and me are apt to be, stranger."

"Where does that load go?" asked Reata as he swung up

the last chamois sack and watched it disappear.

"This here hay goes into Tyndal, to the livery stable," said Dan Foster. "Timmons, he always thought a hoss took more kind to the hay that I cut out here than they take to most fodder. I dunno but maybe he's right, too. Seems to stick to the ribs of a hoss."

"I'll meet you at Tyndal at the livery stable of Timmons this evening," said Reata. "Good luck to you, Foster!"

"The same to you," said Foster. "Wait a minute and see Beck and Bird start this here load like it was a feather."

"I'd like to stay," said Reata, "but I'm overdue on the other side of the skyline. So long!"

He started the roan mare away with a good, sweeping gallop, and the mustang that remained of the four followed willingly enough now that the heavy weight had been taken from its back. But always, anxiously, Reata looked to the north and west toward that rock ridge beyond which lay the ravine. Now he saw them coming, the three horsemen bending low to gain greater speed. The roan mare would hold them easily enough, but not the mustang, even with an empty saddle. He untied the horse and let it run, and then gave Sue her head.

IX

"The Search"

Once in sight of the prey, the Overland Kid and his two new friends stormed like mad across the rolling ground. They saw the second horse turned loose. But the long, low roan mare skimmed away from them with an amazing and an effortless ease. Two minutes of that running convinced them that they would never overtake Sue, and Reata in the saddle on her, with the little dog Rags before him. So they turned savagely, and quickly Chad had a rope on the mustang that Reata had cut adrift.

Like three wolves they searched her. But in the saddlebags they found nothing whatever.

"She was loaded, this here," said Chad. "The way all them hosses ran except the roan, they was loaded pretty fair."

"With gold," said the Kid.

The two men stared at him.

"Gold?" whispered Blackie, opening his eyes and his mouth.

"Gold," answered the Kid. "He's cut loose from it. It must be somewhere back there near the dead hosses."

"Aye, or in that hay wagon," said Blackie. "That's a thing I might think of if I was Reata. He knew there was a second bridge up the way. He knew that he didn't have much time, all right."

They seized on the idea eagerly, and rushed for the wagon of Dan Foster. When Blackie reined his horse across the trail—it could not be called a road—Dan Foster threw forward the long brake lever and let the weight of his foot ride on it until the wagon drew screeching to a halt.

"Hello, boys," said Foster. "How comes everything with you young gents? And what is all the hurry with everybody today?"

"The feller yonder started it," said Chad, pointing.

"Yeah? Him that is slidin' over the rim of the hills yonder?" murmured Foster. "Well, I never yet seen a gent in a hurry that there wasn't trouble somewheres around. What's he done?"

"Robbery . . . murder . . . god-damn anything you want to name is what he's done," said Blackie.

"What's he robbed?" asked Foster. "Stage or something?"

"What did he pass up to you here on your wagon?" asked the Kid.

He was guessing. Foster looked at him straight in the eye and knew it. "What could he be passing up to me?" asked Foster with an air of great surprise.

"Stuff that weighs seven or eight hundred pounds," answered the Kid. "You know what it was. Boys, we got to search that load of hay."

"Come on up and hunt, " said Dan Foster. "I got an idea that I speared a field mouse with one of them forkfuls of hay, but I dunno for certain. If you find the mouse, I'll give it to you. You can cook it for supper, the three of you."

"He's kind of talkin' down to us, ain't he?" asked Blackie, looking at the old man with a dangerous eye.

The Overland Kid rested a hand on his hip and stared at Foster.

"I dunno," he said. "This *hombre* sounds honest. What does he sound like to you gents?"

"Seven or eight hundred pounds . . . why would Reata give

it to this old bum, anyway?" asked Chad.

"How would the god-damned mules pull that much extra? This here is a whopping load of hay for the two of 'em, anyway," said the Kid.

"Aye, but the sun has lightened it up a good bit. It's pretty dry," said Blackie.

"Foster," said Chad, "if you got anything from that other gent, and we find it when we go through this here load of hay, we're goin' to cut you up in the back and pull your skin off over your head! Now's the time to talk up. If he give you something, say the word and you go free . . . except for the stuff."

"Thanks," said Dan Foster. "I was tellin' you before that maybe there was a dead mouse in his here load of hay. I ain't sure, but I think I heard a kind of squeal when I was hoistin' up a forkful of the hay."

"Mean old gent, he is," said Blackie. "I got a mind to dump his load off onto the ground for him anyway."

"Leave the old hound alone," said Chad. "We ain't got the time to waste on him, anyway."

"Sure, we ain't," agreed the Overland Kid, who had been studying the thin, dry face of the old man all of this time. "Leave him go. Back there where the horses are lying . . . back there we might find something worthwhile."

They left old Dan Foster accordingly, to go on his way, which he did without in the slightest degree rushing the mules. But back by the verge of the ravine, the three riders dismounted and there searched thoroughly.

The saddlebags of the dead horses were empty. Perhaps, therefore, Reata had dropped the sacks down among the crevices of the rocks? They searched and they probed for a long hour, and still they found not a sign of the treasure.

Then the Kid sat down on a rock and made a cigarette that

he lighted without haste, and smoked in a leisurely manner.

"Restin', eh?" said Blackie, sneering.

"Thinkin'," answered the Overland Kid. "A gent's brain can travel a lot faster than a hoss's hoofs, if you only stop to know it."

The other two said nothing to him. They drew back a little, as though to establish the fact that they would not commit themselves to anything, as though they hereby established a protest against anything that he might attempt.

The Kid began to talk aloud, softly, slowly.

"This *hombre* is everything that Pop Dickerman claimed for him," he decided. "He comes up right under our noses, and then he slides out and away again. When we got a bridge to cross to get at him and eat his heart out, he busts the bridge down. And we kill some of his hosses, and he makes the load disappear. Now, what does it sound like to you?"

"I dunno," said Blackie. "It sounds like a beat to me."

"It sounds like he made fools of us," said Chad. "Maybe he dropped the gold into the ravine. There's water down there would cover it."

"He wouldn't do that," argued the Kid. "A gent like him, he'd find a way of makin' that gold walk sort of in the direction that he wanted it to go. He finds himself with only two hosses out of three. Two hosses can't pack eight hundred pounds deadweight very fast. A gallop would break their backs in no time. What does he do, then? Why, Blackie, you had it the first crack out of the box!"

"The gent with the load of hay?" asked Blackie.

"Him? Sure it's him that's got the stuff, and the old goat, he took and bluffed us out!" shouted the Kid. "Come on, boys. We're behind time, but we can trail the sign those wagon wheels leave on the ground. Come on, and come fast! The more I think about it, the surer I am!"

They remounted silently, and rode grimly on through the end of the day. It was not hard to follow the tracks of the wagon. They wound with leisure across the hollows and up the slight rises of the land until they pointed, straight as a string, toward the glimmering lights of a town.

X

"Gold Hunger"

Not half a mile from the edge of the town, in the midst of a small hollow, where the twilight seemed to be more darkly pooled, the Overland Kid and his two friends came on the hayrack of Dan Foster again. They let the mules trot down the pitch and tug up the farther slope, and then the Kid brought Foster to a stop.

The old farmer was perfectly calm. "Hello, boys," he said. "Lookin' for more news? Or are you thirsty? There's a dog-gone cool can of water hangin' on the side of the rack wrapped up in sacks. There on the near side you'll find it, hangin' where the hay drips down over it."

"Go aboard, partners," commanded the Overland Kid, and was instantly on top of the load to set the good example.

Gold goes the bottom of lighter stuff, but so did the Kid through that load of light, fluffy hay, and it was he who first closed his hand on a chamois sack whose sleek feel and softness and the warmth that had been given to it by the hay made it seem like a living thing, some burrowing, fat-sided rodent. The Overland Kid lifted it out and held it up in the darkening light of the day.

"What's this?" he demanded of Foster.

"I never seen the inside of it," answered Foster honestly. "What you think it might be?"

Both Blackie and Chad had, by this time, found other chamois sacks. There was no need to ask what was in them. The weight alone was enough to tell. Chad yelled like an

Indian and danced up and down until the hayrack began to rock a bit under him.

"Shut up," said Blackie. "Gold shows a red light that folks can see pretty far, anyway. You have to bring 'em down with a lot of yellin'?"

"What're we goin' to do with this old hound?" asked Chad, pointing to Dan Foster.

The rancher sat half turned on his driver's seat, biting off a fresh chew of tobacco. He remained singularly unconcerned.

"He's gotta stay with us a while," answered the Kid. "Old-timer, you took this stuff off of the hands of Reata, did you?"

"I didn't know the name of the gent," answered Foster, "but I seen that he was in a terrible hurry. Why, he reminded me of a time when I was. . . ."

"Be quiet!" said Blackie. "Listen. Hey, you've brought up somebody with your yellin', Chad!"

On the breath of silence that followed, the Overland Kid could hear clearly the drumming hoofs of horses at a slow gallop, and now he could see them coming down the track of the wagon wheels toward the town.

"Three gents bound for Tyndal," said the Overland Kid. "Leave them go by. If they ask why we're here, say that we're restin' the mules a minute before pullin' on toward the town. Foster, your business is to keep your mouth shut."

"Sure," said Dan Foster. "I understand that, all right. They're just some more cowpunchers that've heard about the Gypsy show that comes tomorrow."

"What Gypsy show?" asked Blackie. "You don't mean Queen Maggie and her gang, do you?"

"Aye, that's the lot of thieves that I mean," answered Foster.

Here the three fresh riders dipped into the hollow and swept up beside the wagon.

"Who's there?" called one of them.

"By thunder, it's Salvio!" said Blackie. "Hey, Gene! Is that you, Harry Quinn? We're Blackie and Chad, and here's the Overland Kid. Glad to see you, boys."

"It's Blackie talkin'," remarked Salvio. "What're you *hombres* doin' up here?"

"The front part of the trail you been backin'," said Blackie. "And there's another thing . . . we've got the goods!"

"What goods?" asked Dave Bates. "What goods you talkin' about?"

"In chamois sacks," said Chad.

"Then you've got a dead man in that load of hay," exclaimed Harry Quinn. "Reata's dead, and damned if I ain't sorry to know it!"

"Reata ain't dead," said the Overland Kid. "We gave him a brush and killed some of his horses. He passed the stuff on to this old gent. And I'll be damned if he didn't almost get to town with the loot. But we had a second idea, and we nailed the old fellow this time and found the stuff in the hay. Look here, Blackie. Are these fellows really in on the deal?"

"Pop's right-handers is what they are," said Blackie. "Overland, this is Gene Salvio. Here's Harry Quinn. And this here is . . . sure, it's Dave Bates. Hello, Dave!"

After these greetings they held a brief consultation. They could transfer the gold from the wagon to their horses, but what could they do with Dan Foster, who would go on to Tyndal and give the alarm to the townspeople?

The Overland Kid said: "We could get the old boy to promise to keep his mouth shut. That would be all right."

"Reata's right there in the town, waiting for him. When he shows up without the stuff, Reata's going on the back trail," said Gene Salvio. "The question is, do we want that devil clawing at us, or don't we?"

"Hey, look here" said the Kid. "There's six of us, ain't there? Are you talking scary about one man?"

Salvio turned sharply on him in the twilight, but said nothing.

"He don't know about Reata," said Dave Bates soothingly. "He don't know, or he wouldn't talk so easy."

Harry Quinn put in: "We can cache the wagon in a clump of trees and go on to that old shack up Tyndal Creek. You know the one, Gene. The hosses sure need a night's rest, and tomorrow we can pull out and head along for Pop. Ain't that sense?"

"That's good sense, and that's what we'll do," said Salvio.

"I don't know," interrupted the Kid. "I'm not sure that's the best dodge."

There was a brief and heavy silence.

"Oh," said Salvio, "you don't know, eh?"

"No," answered the Kid. "I don't know. Want me to say it three times, or will twice do?"

He could feel rather than see the rigidity of Salvio. But Blackie broke in: "Wait a minute, Gene. The Kid's a newcomer, but he's sure first rate. Take that straight from me. Overland, you'll know Salvio better after a while. I say that he's Pop's right-hand man, almost. Ain't that good enough to hold your hosses?"

"Pop gave me this job, and I'm going to do it," insisted the Kid, the bulldog in him yearning for a fight.

"Suppose that you and me step aside and have a little talk," suggested Salvio with gentleness.

"Nothing would please me better," said the Kid.

Dave Bates stepped between them and held up both hands.

"You two *hombres* quit it," he commanded. "We going to spoil this job by brawling with each other? Get some brains in your heads and quit the yapping, will you? Harry's got the right idea. We go on to that shack up on the creek, and we take the old man along with us till the morning. Ain't that good sense? Now, you two shut up. You can go and claw yourselves to death whenever you please afterward."

This speech was so extremely to the point that the Overland Kid had to admit the force of it. The whole plan of Quinn was clearly the best. For the horses of Salvio and his two mates were plainly done in. Their heads hung low, and the Overland Kid could hear the dripping of the sweat that ran down their sides and dropped from their bellies onto the ground.

Quinn got into the driver's seat and ordered Dan Foster to drive his wagon into a clump of trees not far away.

"I'm goin' to spend the night with you boys, eh?" said Foster, as cool as ever. "It'll make the old woman worry a pile, but that won't hurt her none. Maybe it's goin' to do her a lot of good. Giddap, Beck. Hi, Bird! Go on, gals!"

The mules hit the collar; the wagon reeled and then lurched ahead. The outfit was soon brought to a halt in the midst of a black growth of trees. There they hunted through the hay load for the rest of the treasure. Twenty-one sacks had to be found; they were forced to pitch most of the load to the ground before they got the last of the gold loaded onto the backs of the horses. The mules were unhitched, and with Dan Foster riding astride on one of them, the whole party traveled on until they heard the rushing noise of the waters of the creek. They passed through more trees, and on the bank of the stream they found a little abandoned squatter's shack— one room and an attic.

Salvio took command and gave orders to Blackie and Chad to unload the horses, to Quinn and Bates to start cooking a supper, and then Salvio himself and the Overland

Kid hobbled the horses to graze in the long grass of the clearing.

When they had finished this work, the Kid said: "All right, Salvio, any time you say."

To his surprise, Salvio laughed with a genuine amusement. "You *like* trouble, don't you, Kid? Well, I'll do what I can for you later on. We've got our hands full now. And maybe we'll have Reata on top of us before morning."

"Any way that suits you suits me," said the Overland Kid regretfully. "But about this here Reata. There's only one of him, ain't there? Is he likely to come with a crowd behind him?"

"He works alone, but one of him is sure plenty," answered Salvio. "Maybe he looks small to you, but, when his hands start movin', he's plenty big. Who's the fool that's making that noise?"

For a wild shouting and singing had broken out from the shack, and, when the Overland Kid went inside with Salvio, he had sight of Chad leaning over the contents of a whole sack of gold, which he had poured out on the little home-made table in the center of the room. Chad was dipping his hands in the yellow heavy dust and lifting it up, and letting it stream down, bright as rays of lamplight in the dance and flicker of flames that came from the fire that had been kindled on the open hearth at the side of the room.

"He's drunk," said Salvio calmly. "And a gold drunk is the worst kind of a drunk in the world. We gotta keep our eyes on that gent tonight, or he'll do something crazy. Pass the word around. Chad's going to give us trouble before the morning comes."

It was not Chad alone. Every man in the place was watching, with a wide, thirsty grin, the colorful sheen of the gold dust under the manipulations of Chad. Yes, there was apt to be trouble before the morning came. The only man in the shack who seemed indifferent to what was going on was old Dan Foster, who regarded the gold no more than if it had been so much bright dirt.

"Well, a gent can't eat it," he said.

"Eat it?" cried Chad. "*I* could eat it! Look! Here's a price of a man. Here . . . what I got in my hand. It ain't much. But it's a man. You can buy a gent's life with that much. And here's a house and lot. Here's a wife, with this much. You could get a fine one with that. And here's a. . . ."

He went on raving. The Overland Kid, very thoughtfully, turned his hand to account in the cooking of the meager supper. He felt that there were only two real men in the place. He was one, and Gene Salvio was the other. And they would need their manhood by the morning.

The Kid stepped to the door, and through a cleft in the trees he saw the lights of Tyndal glittering not very far away. Suddenly he was thirsty in body and in soul for the sight of other faces—the faces of honest men who were not maddened by the gold hunger. He would slip away after supper and get his foot on a bar rail for a half hour or so and have a drink or two, and become a different man. That would mean more than sleep to him.

XI

"The Gypsy Camp"

Reata, as he came in toward the town of Tyndal through the dusk of the day, saw a camp of covered wagons and tents just at the side of the town, revealed by the light of a fire in the center. When the flames lifted high, the entire camp could be seen, but at other times the night poured in over most of the circle, and only a bit of it would be illumined. Around the edge of the wagons, hobbled horses were being guarded by small boys, half-naked, little barefooted youngsters. One of them he saw dancing in swift circles to the shrilling music that ceaselessly continued from the camp.

They were Gypsies, he knew. He turned a little aside. If there were Gypsies in this part of the country, they were almost sure to be Queen Maggie's band, and it was in their hands, of course, that he had left poor Pie Phelps with Steve Balen's bullet through his shoulder.

But did he dare enter the camp to make inquiries? With Queen Maggie he might have some influence, and, as long as Miriam was with the crew, they did not dare to go counter to the wishes of the star of their troupe, who took in more money with her bareback riding than all the rest of them combined. There was Georg, too, whom he had saved from a knife in the back, and who seemed the sort to remain lastingly grateful. But there were many others to whom he had been anathema, and he could not tell what their attitude might be now.

The answer was a yell of delight. The boy caught hold of

his stirrup leather and began to jump up and down, waving his hand and yelling: "Reata! Reata! Reata!"

Others of the horse herds came racing. Their shrilling voices picked up that name and made a chorus of it.

Reata, suddenly assured and confident, came into the wagon circle with a swarming throng of small fry about him.

He saw the big fire in the center of the camp, with huge, black pots hanging into the flames, and the unwieldy bulk of Queen Maggie in her man's coat and hat striding about it, the cigar at its usual angle in her mouth, and the famous iron spoon like a scepter in her hand. She was turning from the fire now, shouting out in the Gypsy jargon, and waving the spoon so that it flashed in the firelight.

The grown members of the band, men and women, were swarming toward him. Danger? Aye, there was more danger in every one of these people than in nest of rattlers. Not a one of them but carried a knife or gun or both; not a one but knew very well how to use the weapons. As those excited, swarthy faces came toward him, and as he heard the harsh gabbling of their unknown tongue, he could not tell whether they came in amity or in hatred.

Well, he was inside the wagon circle now, and it was too late to retreat. Then he saw that the cat-faced monster, the strong man, with his whiskers bristling and with the end of his yellow headcloth fluttering behind him from the speed of his running, dash through the crowd, bowling people away to this side and to that.

Reata was on the verge of snatching out his lariat and making a deadly cast with it. To be sure, there was joy in the strong man, yet it might well be the savage joy of one about to lay hands on an enemy. But Reata resisted the suspicious impulse. He let himself be seized, unresisting, in those terrible hands, and he found himself snatched out of the saddle and lifted high. Under his heels was the flat of one hand, and another grasped him by one calf. Looking down from this height, he saw little Rags, with a yelp of fear, jump from the saddle onto the shoulder of the strong man, thence onto his head, where he remained with his face pointed up toward his master.

In this fashion Reata was borne on toward the central fire, while the music that had been dying down began to shrill out louder than ever, and a rapid roll commenced to beat on a pair of kettle drums.

"Georg! Georg! Georg!" the Gypsies were shouting.

He saw Georg coming, then, leaping and sliding through the crowd, his handsome young face illumined, his hands thrown up to greet Reata.

There was no question that, because of the saving of Georg, the entire tribe had forgiven the past offenses of Reata. They were giving him such a welcome now as they might have extended to a prince of their tribe. The strong man lowered Reata suddenly to one shoulder. Up on the other he snatched Georg, holding the pair lightly, easily. It was like being carried by the substantial power of a horse.

In this way Reata was brought to the fire and marched around it, with all the tribe laughing and shouting. Then he was put down before Queen Maggie. She was puffing hard on her cigar, clothing her head in a strong white mist, while she nodded at Reata.

"What trouble are you bringin' me now?" she asked.

"A question or two," said Reata. "And I want to see Pie Phelps. Is he here? Is Miriam here?"

"Over yonder in that tent, likely fixin' herself up a little brighter," said Queen Maggie. "Set yourself down. The rest of you . . . whoosh!" She waved her iron spoon. The whole gang of the Gypsies, big and little, scattered, laughing. Only

Georg remained to grip the hands of Reata and exclaim: "Ah, brother!" Then he, too, was gone with the rest.

"Phelps is all right," said Queen Maggie. "He's gotta keep his arm still for a while. Are you hungry, Reata? Set down in that chair of mine. I'll make you a sandwich."

She took up a loaf of bread, slashed it in two lengthwise with a stroke of a great butcher knife that she pulled out of a carving block, and then, out of one of the black pots, she ladled a dipperful of chicken and tomato stew, that she heaped along the length of the bread.

"Sink a tooth in that," she commanded. "Here's some coffee." She ladled him out a great iron cup of the black coffee, and Reata sat down to eat like a wolf.

The smoke and the heat blew about him. A vast relaxation spread through his body and his blood. He was instantly rested, as though he had slept for hours. That was what it meant to feel the Gypsy circle spread around him like a guard after his recent long adventures in the land of danger.

"Trailin' trouble up and down the country?" said Queen Maggie. "There ain't nobody else like you, Reata. I've tried to get your throat cut before, but now I'm glad to see you ag'in. I'd put a red silk sash around your head, Reata, and make a gray-eyed Gypsy of you, son. My man didn't give me no children, Reata." She sighed, and then swore. "But I reckon you wouldn't be happy here with us. Romany, even, ain't wild enough for you. The tribe can't travel as free and as fast as Reata rides on the roan mare. Well, here's where I'm ending my talk, because Miriam's comin'. Look at her . . . how she's slicked herself up for you."

The girl came into the firelight, smiling a little. She was as bright as the fire flames in a yellow dress, with an orange silken shawl over her shoulders, and the stones that hung from her ears were as blue as her eyes. He felt the old shock that never failed to go through him when he saw the blue of the eyes under that black, glistening hair.

She took his hand as he stood up, and smiled gently at him.

"Why wouldn't you kiss him, Miriam, you fool?" asked Queen Maggie. "A man likes to be made over."

"Nobody minds you, Maggie," said the girl. "Why do you keep talking? But now that the tribe is all one friend of yours, are you going to be long with us, Reata?"

"Only till I finish the heel of this loaf and that cup of coffee," he answered. "I have to go on into town. But can I see Pie Phelps?"

"He's asleep," said the girl. "I'll call him."

"Let him sleep. Just tell him I was here. Maggie says that he's coming on well. What's in Tyndal that I ought to know about?"

"Steve Balen's there. I suppose that's why you've come?" she asked.

"Steve Balen?" he repeated. He thought of the long, lean body and the grim face of Balen. Of all the enemies who enriched the world with danger for him, there was none more formidable than Steve Balen. "No, I didn't know that he was in Tyndal."

"He," said the girl, "and Lester. Colonel Lester is there. They've given up the Reata trail, folks say. Wayland is with 'em. It's only ten miles from here to Jumping Creek, and the colonel's pretty daughter has ridden over to see her father and go back with them all tomorrow." She looked narrowly at his face.

He had winced a little. Into Tyndal he certainly must go to meet old Dan Foster and get from him the gold that was sunk in the load of hay. Once in the town, he could turn over the gold to the custody of Colonel Lester and Steve Balen, and the rest of those men who had been hunting on his trail. But the thought irked him. It was his plan to carry the stolen treasure clear back to Jumping Creek and deliver it there at the doors of the bank.

These things were in his mind, far back, when he heard Miriam talk, but that image which he saw, coming in a bright flash between him and the Gypsy, was the face of Agnes Lester. He could not say that it was more lovely, but it brightened in his mind and made him thoughtful.

"Aye," said Miriam quietly. "She's the one, then?"

He stood up. "Lester, Wayland, Balen . . . why, the town is full of the devil for me, Miriam. But I have to go in. And I'm coming back one of these days, if you'll want to see me."

Her eyebrows lifted a little. She shrugged her shoulders. "Why," she said, "there's never a time when I'm not glad to see a friend."

He was gone a moment after that, with the small dog in the crook of his arm, and the roan carrying him, and the Gypsies clamoring after him, pleading with him to stay.

Queen Maggie said, around her cigar, the force of her speaking driving out the smoke in ragged puffs: "Ah, and what a fool *you* are, Miriam! Go on after him. Be nacheral and knock that fool smile off your face. You'll be in your tent in a minute more, cryin' like a baby, and I'll go and drag him to see you. I'll shame you. I'll let him see that you're eatin' your heart out."

"Aye, but what could I do?" said the girl. "Suppose that I kept him here . . . suppose I were able to . . . wouldn't it be like tying a pigeon to the ground so that the hawks could start stopping at it? He has more enemies in the world than you've got fingers and toes. I'd have a happy man for a month with me, and a dead man in my heart the rest of my days. Georg! Georg!"

The Overland Kid

That slender youth came with a leap and a bound.

"Go after him, Georg," said the girl. "Shadow him. There's going to be danger enough looking him in the face, but you can guard his back, maybe."

XII

"Enemies Meet"

There was in Reata a feeling of suspense, as though he would himself have but a small control over the events that were immediately before him, as though a curtain of shadow fenced him in with hands behind it prepared to strike him. He thought of Miriam as of a happiness to which he could never return, and, when he considered Agnes Lester, he had to realize that in the eyes of her father he was himself no better than a thief.

When he found out where Timmon's livery stable was, he went straight to it.

In spite of Reata's delay at the Gypsy camp, Dan Foster, with his wagonload of hay, had not yet come to the stable. Perhaps it would be a risky thing to put up the mare inside a building when he might need her speed at any moment, but it was too great a temptation to bed her down in softness and warmth and give her a proper feed of cured hay and oats. So he put her up in a corner stall with only this peculiarity in his treatment of her—the lead rope was hanging down, but anyone who examined it carefully could have seen that it was not tied into the manger rail. She would stand there, untied, until he came for her or called for her later on.

After that he went to the front of the stable, where big, rawboned Timmons himself was impatiently waiting for the arrival of Dan Foster and the hay.

"Here I'm late for supper," said Timmons. "The wife's goin' to have cornbread, too, and it ain't the same after it's been out of the oven for a spell and started to get cold. It ain't never the same afterward. It gets kind of soggier, and no rise into it. But, dog-gone me, I gotta wait here for an old gent and his load of hay to fork it off into the mow for him."

"I've got to wait here for a friend," said Reata. "I'll tell him when he comes that you'll be back in just a minute."

"Sure! Do that, and thanks," said Timmons. "You'll know him by the white jag of beard on his chin and the twinkle in his eyes. You take a man that gets so old that he's always late with his work, and he ought to stop workin'. But these here old codgers all think they're as good as the next man. So long."

Timmons went out, and he had hardly dissolved into the darkness when a splendid young man on a big horse flashed at a gallop out of the night and knocked a hollow thunder out of the floor boards of the stable. He pulled up his horse with a suddenness that made the gelding skid a dozen feet over a wet place where a buggy had been washed not long before. But even while the horse was sliding, the rider was reaching for a gun.

He had recognized Reata, and Reata had recognized in him the big leader of the trio who had blocked him in the pass and shot down his horses later on in the day. They had seen each other only at a considerable distance, but the eyes are sharp when they look at enemies.

Even before the Colt came into the hand of the Overland Kid, the lariat of Reata shot out like a loaded whiplash. The Kid ducked flat across the pommel of his saddle; the noose rapped the back of his neck with its thin, heavy coil, and he pulled his gun to make the kill, then and there. In that fraction of a second he had a chance to think—to remember what Pop Dickerman and Salvio had said to him of Reata, to consider how their eyes would be opened when they learned how

Reata had gone down. He thought of that, and also that he would send the bullet smashing home into the middle of that brown, cheerful, intelligent face. With that the flash of the drawn gun was whipping across the saddle horn, ready for the shot.

Certainly there had not been time for Reata to gather in his lariat and make a second cast. There had not been a tenth part of the time necessary for that, but as the rope slid down to the ground, it dropped near the prancing, dancing, nervous front feet of the gelding, and Reata made the most of that good chance. He put a flying noose over one of those hoofs, and then over the other, and jerked back with a suddenness that did not give the lariat a chance to loosen and pull away. The gelding, at the very moment when the Overland Kid was ready to shoot, lurched forward on its knees, and then pitched on its side.

That would have thrown the ordinary rider. The Kid managed to fling himself loose in the very nick of time, and landed staggering, with not one, but two guns now in his hands. Reata used the hand end of his lariat, where, for a better grip, the rawhide was swelled with an insert of heavy lead. It was not a great weight, in fact, but great things could be done with it by Reata. He snapped that butt end like the accurate lash of a black snake in the hands of a muleskinner, one who can, when he will, cut the horsefly away without touching the skin of the mule, or who can make the whip bite out a solid chunk of the hide. That was how the last eight feet of the line curled outward from the hand of Reata, and the loaded butt end snapped solidly on the skull of the Kid.

A flick of a finger armed with a thimble can hurt a very hard head. And the snapping of Reata's line nearly broke the skull of the Kid. He had not even seen the thing coming. He had barely hit the floor, ready to shoot, when something invisible *whished* in the air and a heavy blow struck him on the side of the head and knocked him to his knees and fathom-deep in shadowy darkness.

The guns were snatched from his hands while his wits were still whirling. He made a vague effort to struggle, but had his wrists roughly jerked back and lashed together behind his back. Then a hard hand twisted him forward into the darkness of the aisle between the horse stalls.

One step more and Reata would have had his man securely away into the dimness of that aisle, but at the last instant, while he was on the edge of the dim lantern light, that man who of all the world detested him most had to step across the entrance to the stable and look in on him.

It was Tom Wayland who paused in mid-step, struck by a vision, a nightmare—for he had seen the unforgettable face of Reata himself in the dimness of the stable interior. Big, handsome Tom Wayland pulled a gun, but he did not rush at once into the place. He had no intention of rushing. Before this, on occasion, he had charged against Reata, and the memories were not encouraging, The pulling of the gun had been an instinctive gesture of defense.

Then, turning, he raced with all his might down the street. He wanted to stop and call to every man he passed, but he realized that only experts in battle could ever handle Reata. So he made for the hotel, where he ought to find Steve Balen and some of Steve's chosen posse men lounging in the lobby of the hotel, all very gloomy because Colonel Lester was taking them away from the trail of the will-o'-the-wisp, Reata.

Into the lobby of the old frame hotel Tom Wayland burst, therefore, and saw before him not only Steve Balen and his posse about him like savage cubs about an old wolf, but also there was the pompous figure of Colonel Lester himself, in the middle of a declamation of some sort, making his heavy jowls quiver with the indignation of his speech. And, drawn by the gleam of golden hair, Tom Wayland's eye found the colonel's daughter sitting back in a shadowy corner, quietly listening, apart from the group.

She was always apart from every group, it seemed to Tom. He was sorry that she had to be here now. She never talked very much about it, but she had queer, distinct ideas about the honor of a man, and perhaps she might not think a great deal of a fellow who brought information to a small army about where they could find a hunted criminal. However, this news was too important to be withheld for an instant.

He rushed to Steve Balen and exclaimed to him: "I've found Reata . . . I've found him . . . !" His lack of breath stopped him.

Balen did not even rise or lift his head, he merely canted it a bit to one side with an air of great attention.

But Colonel Lester sprang up and exclaimed: "Good! Tom, you're worth a thousand! Ten thousand! Agnes, pay attention! Tom Wayland has found the vicious rat of a Reata when we were about to give up hope!"

Tom Wayland saw that she was standing, too, and she did not seem to be expecting good news.

She gripped the back of her chair hard with one hand, and the other was at her throat. She stared. She was like one who waits for a dreadful, an inescapable blow.

"Down the street . . . right down the street!" gasped Tom Wayland. "I saw him walking back toward the stalls. Pushing another man before him. A big man . . . hands tied behind his back. It was Reata who shoved him along! I know it was Reata! I know he was the man!"

XIII

"In the Dark"

Reata had marched his captive straight back through the aisle between the stalls, and out through the rear door of the barn, and so into the gloom of a group of trees that grew in a dense cluster in the middle of the big corral behind the livery stable.

In the narrow clearing in the center of the trees, he tied the Overland Kid to a tree and then faced him close, for there were only a few gleams of starlight that entered the blackness. It was hard to make anything out of the big, blunt chin that should have given him immunity to punishment even in a prize ring.

Reata said: "I was expecting somebody at that stable . . . you came in his place. What's your name?"

"I dunno," said the Kid. "Maybe I might as well tell you a name. But what's the good to me?"

"You're going to hold out, are you?" said Reata.

"Yeah, and why not?"

"Stranger," said Reata, "out there in the open, this side of the creek, there was an old man with a load of hay."

"Was there?" asked the Overland Kid.

"There was an old man with a load of hay," said Reata. "What did you do with him?"

"I dunno."

"You cut his throat," said Reata. "You've had your teeth in his throat. . . . but I'll have mine in your heart! If you touched the poor old fellow, if you even lifted a hand to him,

I'll knock. . . ." Passion strangled him.

The Overland Kid heard that irregularly drawn breath, and knew that he was inches only from death. There was one great mystery. The gold seemed to come second to Reata. The welfare of the old fellow was what he spoke of first and last. This could not be a sham. A queer suspicion came to the Overland Kid that he was confronting a new kind of a man, different in his thinking as he had been from others in the cat-like speed and surety of his hand.

For, in the dazed mind of the Kid, his real self was back there in the entrance of the stable, standing over a body that lay dead on the floor from a bullet that had smashed through the center of its face. It seemed to the Overland Kid that was what must have happened and this other thing was no more than a dream. He could not have been struck down, horse and man, after that first cast had missed him. But the thing had happened. All in a second after he reached for his gun, his horse was down, and he had been struck half senseless by an invisible blow. He would not have believed the reality, but he could remember how Salvio and the rest had talked. They were fighting men, all of them, but they had talked of Reata as of the devil himself. This devil now was standing close to him, breathing deeply with a savage rage. And fear leaped suddenly into the strong soul of the Kid.

"But there are others of you?" said Reata. "There are enough of the rest of Dickerman's rats to pay . . . what I want out of you is talk. You hear me?"

The Overland Kid said nothing.

"You're going to talk. You're going to say everything you know," insisted Reata. "Don't think you're not. I'll . . . I'll burn the face off you, stranger, if I have to . . . but you'll talk!"

The Kid said nothing, and in response he heard a savage little whine of rage. Then a match was scratched and held close to him. He could see by the light of it the gray eyes of Reata, now swimming with yellow fury, and Reata could see the strained, set face of the Kid, with a certain dullness and immobility about the eyes, as though already he were striving with all the might of his will to forget his body and thrust its concerns off into nothingness.

Reata said: "I start at the chin, stranger. That'll toast for a while, and then I shift up to the ears. After that, a bit of flame up the nose doesn't do any harm. Mind you . . . I'll burn the face off your skull."

Terror and horror came up in the Kid's eyes for an instant.

"Then talk!" said Reata.

The Overland Kid said absolutely nothing.

The match went out and dropped down into darkness.

"I've given you your last chance," said Reata. "Now I'm going to do what I said I'd do. If you yell, if you make a noise, I'll drive a slug out of your own gun into your heart!"

He scratched another match. His glaring face, strained, terrible, drew close to his captive, and then the Overland Kid made that face disappear from before his mind. He forgot it. He rendered his flesh insensible. A faint smile came on his lips as if he had been an Indian brave nurtured by a long life of resolution to the enduring of the pain. But all that obsessed his brain was that he must not be untrue to his partners. They were a pretty bad lot, those fellows who worked, like him, for that king of the rats, Pop Dickerman. But no matter what they were, they were his companions, and he could not betray them.

Stories rushed up into his mind out of his past about men who had betrayed other men—aye, under torture. It didn't matter. The betrayal was there, and every traitor was a Judas, a Judas. He had heard frightful tales and seen frightful things, but nothing more dreadful than a traitor.

Well, if he breathed the flame when it was put under his nose—if a fellow could take one deep breath of flame, it was the end, he had heard. There would be endless agony before that, but he would keep the hope of putting out his life like a light.

Then he was aware that something had happened to Reata. The head of the man jerked back as though he had been stabbed. He gasped: "I can't do it! I can't do it!" And the second match dropped out of his hand.

The Overland Kid heard a faint, groaning sound of curses, and those words again. And he said, in a voice that shook a great deal: "Listen, they call me the Overland Kid. The old man . . . nothing happened to him. There wasn't a hair of him touched."

What was he saying? Well, admitting, by inference, that they *had* put their hands on the old man, or on his wagonload of hay—and of gold. Yet, he could not feel that he had been treacherous in speaking like this. He had merely made a fair exchange for something that Reata had spared him, and for something else—a new idea at which he was still vaguely grasping.

"Old Dan is all right?" said Reata. "Thank God for that. I half thought. . . ." He hushed himself again, and then, after a moment, he added: "I know you're one of Dickerman's rats, and I ought to tear you to bits. But there's something right about you, Overland. I don't know what, but it's in you. I ought to leave you tied here and gagged all night. A gent that stands all night, or hangs his weight against his ropes, he knows he's been through something before he's found. But how long would it be before you were found?"

The Overland Kid waited, silent. It seemed to him that through the darkness he could feel the throb and the pulse of Reata's struggle. Then Reata was saying: "I'm a fool. I'm the biggest fool that ever lived. But suppose you got loose from this, would you forget that you'd seen me here in town?"

The Kid answered: "I've got to be square with my partners, but I could forget that I'd seen you here. Sure. I could forget that. I *want* to forget it!"

"Will you get out of town and go back to wherever you're headed, and not use the knowledge that you've seen me?"

"I'll do that."

"Then . . . well, there you are."

Suddenly the Overland Kid was free. He heard a slight, rapid clicking sound.

"Here's your guns back, so no questions will have to be asked. You can load 'em later on out of your belt. So long, Overland."

"Wait a minute," gasped the Kid. "I'd like to . . . well, I'd like to shake your hand on all of this."

"Shake hands?" said Reata, his voice rising a shade and hardening to scorn. "You would have shot me. You came half an inch from doing it. You're one of Dickerman's rats. Shake hands with you? I'd rather shake hands with a slimy water moccasin!"

And Reata was gone, and behind him he left on the soul of the Overland Kid such a burden as never had oppressed it before.

Slowly the Overland Kid went back toward the barn, his head hanging. As he reached the rear door of the barn, hands suddenly grasped him, and guns glimmered dimly about him in the starlight.

"We've got him!" breathed a voice. "Hey, Balen, we've got him!"

"You fool!" exclaimed another. "He's twice the size of Reata! Leave him go. Sorry, partner. Took you for another gent."

The Overland Kid said nothing in answer. He walked on down the aisle of the barn. There were scores of men on the watch for Reata. Why? Because the world hates a white man, no matter how white, if he simply chooses to go his own way? He took his saddle horse and went out of the town of Tyndal, deep in thought.

XIV

"Gold and Guns"

Reata went into the first saloon. He knew there was danger, but he wanted a drink. He needed a drink, a deep drink of rank, stupefying whiskey. So he went into a saloon and stood in the corner at the bar, and ordered the stuff like medicine.

There were a dozen other fellows in the place, all men off the range, noisy, their faces covered with the red-brown varnish of long exposure to the sun. Their hands were dirty with the sort of black that harness oil works into the very tissues of the skin. Reata liked standing there among them. They were honest. They were straight. They were simple. Aye, hard as nails, but straight as a string, every man. It was like standing in sunshine in the open air after long confinement in a sick room to be back among such fellows as these.

He thought then of the days when he had been building the cabin where he and Miriam were to start life together up there in the mountains alone, with the trees about them, and the lake gathering inside its white margin all the blue of the sky, drinking up all the color until it was as dark and rich as sapphire. It had been glorious. It was a salvation of the soul even to think about it. He could let his memory wander from day to day, and almost from hour to hour, up to the moment when Miriam had told him that she could not go through with the thing, that she was already bored with him. Aye, a Gypsy girl, and he had wanted to close her up in one spot for the rest of her life. He was a fool! Yet it had been a beautiful folly.

Someone said behind him: "Hey, there's one of the Gypsies. Goin' to do some stunts for us to get the drinks?"

"Nope, he'll pass the hat afterward. Go ahead, Jimmy. Show us your stuff!"

It was Georg, the new wild rider of horses for the Gypsies, who had taken the place of the dead Anton. He had come into the saloon, and was bowing to all the men assembled. Then he was throwing three knives into the air, one after the other, making the steel blades spin into flashes of fire, like bodiless flames that hung in the air. Those were big knives, too, and, when a fourth one joined the rest and walked up higher than the other three, almost to the ceiling, turning in a slower cadence, the cowpunchers gave the juggler a good, hearty hand.

The four knives seemed to be enough to keep the Gypsy worried, however. And one of them dropped. He collected the rest from the air with a sudden, embarrassed gesture, and scooped up the fallen blade where it was lying on the floor at Reata's feet.

As he leaned over, he was saying, in a sibilant whisper: "On guard, Reata." And as he rose: "They're after you. Front door and back door." Then again he was at work, spinning the knives in the air.

His performance ceased to exist for Reata.

"They" were after him, and that must mean Colonel Lester and the rest. "They" had spotted him, then? Well, if they had the front door and the back door blocked, if they were about ready to burst in on him, there was another exit. He hopped over the bar, while the barman yelled out in surprise. And right through the open window behind the end of the bar Reata dove from a handspring, feet-first, shooting out into the darkness as though into water.

It was not water that received him, however. But heavy bodies flung down on him, crushing the breath out of his lungs, and powerful hands grasped him as though they were striving to tear the flesh from his bones.

"Hold him! Hold him!" gasped the voice of Colonel Lester. "You were right, Balen! The window was his trick. A light, here!"

A lantern was unshuttered, and it flashed with dazzling brightness into the eyes of Reata. He lay still, without a struggle. The fools were after him again. The halfwits were blocking his way and keeping him from working at *their* real problem. He had to lie still and submit.

They made a great parade of their achievement. That was the colonel's fault, not Steve Balen's. The colonel wanted to be revealed driving the criminal before him down the main street of the town. He had Reata's hands tied behind him, and an armed man at each shoulder of the prisoner, and a lantern before, and a lantern behind. Just in front of the second lantern strode the colonel, sticking out his chest and pulling in his chin, and looking straight before him, with a long rifle carried at the ready in his hands. It was a good parade all the way to the colonel's hotel, and the people of Tyndal turned out to gape at the spectacle.

When they came to the hotel, there was a dash of trouble that made the colonel purple, and Tom Wayland white, for as the parade crossed the lobby of the hotel, Agnes Lester came out of nowhere and ran up to Reata, crying out: "It's an outrage and a crime . . . and I know that you didn't steal the Jumping Creek money, Reata!"

The colonel got his breath to shout her down and send her to her room. Then he marched Reata upstairs. In the colonel's mind there was a vivid picture of that other occasion when he had had Reata securely confined in a room from which, in all seeming, it was impossible for anything but a bird to escape. And yet Reata *had* gone free, and left Steve

Balen tied up in his place.

This time the colonel would not make any mistakes. If he could not return to Jumping Creek, bringing the stolen gold, at least he would take back with him a man that the law had never been able to hold in its hand before. He would take the matter into his own consideration and be himself responsible for what happened. So he had a seven-foot two-by-four scantling brought to his room, and to this Reata was lashed, not by the hands and feet alone, but with sixty feet of strong rope wound around and around him. His hands were held straight down at his sides by the strong twist of the rope.

When Reata was well secured in this fashion, the colonel said to Steve Balen: "Now, you tell me, Balen. I want you to tell me. Is there any way that a man can conceive . . . is there any way at all for this scoundrel to get out of my grasp this time?"

"Not that I know of," said Steve. "Not unless help flies in at the window or walks in through the door."

The colonel sat down in a comfortable chair and took a shotgun across his knees. "I lock the door on the inside," he said. "You and the rest keep guard under the window. I lock that door on the inside. Now tell me how help can come to Reata?"

Balen shook his head. "I dunno that I can tell you," he said. "Nobody can tell you, because there ain't any way that Reata can get loose, unless he can break that rope with his breathin'."

The colonel laughed very cheerfully. "Go out, then," he commanded. "I'll take charge of this man and be responsible for him."

When Balen was gone, Colonel Lester locked the door behind him and resumed his place in the chair, shotgun in hand. Beaming grimly down at Reata, he said: "Now what's in your mind, my fine young fellow?"

"I'm wondering about a thing that almost beats me," said Reata.

"Aye?" said the colonel, sensing an involuntary compliment. "And what is that?"

"I'm wondering," said Reata, "how a girl like Agnes can have a stuffed shirt like you for a father."

The colonel leaped from his chair. He was on the verge, for an instant, of dropping the butt of his rifle into the sneering face of Reata, but he recollected himself in time, and, with a black face, sat down in his chair again. He began to see a delightful picture—of Reata hanging by the neck with a black cloth over his face, his body slowly turning on the tension of the taut rope.

It was at about this time that Blackie, out there in the shack on Tyndal Creek, waked rather suddenly in the middle of the night. They were standing watch, two hours a turn, through the night, and, having finished his session, Blackie had fallen sound asleep while Chad took his turn. Something pulled at the unconscious mind of Blackie, and, waking with a start, he saw with his first glance—by the last glimmering from the fire on the hearth—that the heap of chamois sacks of gold, in the corner of the room, had seriously diminished.

Blackie sat up agape, and reached for his Colt. He heard from a corner the snoring of Harry Quinn. The Overland Kid was asleep near the fire, having come in late from town in a silent mood. And overhead in the attic, old Dan Foster was snoring, also, keeping a soft accompaniment to the noise that Harry Quinn made. But where was Chad, the man on guard?

At that moment he came in, hastily squinted once around the room, and then picked up two bags of the gold and turned stealthily toward the door.

Blackie could understand what that meant. He jerked up his revolver and shouted: "Murder!" Then he followed his own word by driving a bullet right through the back of Chad. The thunder of the gun instantly filled the room with echoes and with upleaping forms.

"Chad! He's stealin' the gold!" yelled Blackie, springing to his feet.

Chad, knocked flat by the impact of the bullet, had struck the side of the door in his fall, twisted, and gone down with a crash in a sitting posture facing Blackie.

There was a great, stretching smile on the face of Chad, or something that looked like a smile. Even as the heavy slug smote him, he had dropped the two bags of the gold that he was purloining and snatched out a gun. That big Colt now lay on the floor beside him, and he picked it up with a slow hand and raised it.

"Get him!" yelled Blackie, and made a stride forward, shooting. He smashed his first bullet into the jamb above Chad's head. He saw the second crush into Chad's breast. But death would not come to the man. The revolver that he was lifting came to a level with Blackie's breast, and then spat fire. Blackie fell on his face, and Chad lowered his gun and leaned slowly to the side, still grinning.

They were both dead. A bit of dry wood thrown on the fire by the Overland Kid soon showed what had happened, and, before the two bodies could be laid out side by side and covered with a blanket, old Dan Foster looked down through the attic trap door and drawled: "Now we got a little blood on the gold, eh? Maybe there'll be a mite more before the wind-up!"

Back in the hotel room of the colonel, Reata, giving up hope, had closed his eyes and gone to sleep. He was wakened once by a sharp sound of voices beneath the window; he heard the stern words of Steve Balen, commanding someone to get away and keep away, and then the soft, musical voice of Georg making answer.

The Gypsy was trying to make a rescue, but he had failed. Every other agency would fail, also. Help had to come from himself. And what could that help be?

He went to sleep again, and, when he wakened, he had a sense that he was between the brightness of two suns. Then he saw that the sun had risen, in fact, and was high enough to shine brightly through the eastern window. But to the right of Reata there was another glittering fire, and this, he saw, came from the colonel's concave shaving mirror that he had carelessly placed on a low stool. It was standing up, and the broad face of it fully collected the rays of the sun and focused on the carpet a dazzling patch of yellow-white light so strong in heat that a very thin smoke was rising.

That sight gave a thought to Reata. Knives are not the only thing to sever ropes—flame will do it, also. He glanced toward the colonel and saw him fast asleep, his body sagging far to one side in his chair, and the shotgun appearing in the very act of sliding off his lap. If the gun fell, the noise of it would rouse the colonel and wreck Reata's plan. Or perhaps other noises from the wakening town would rouse him, for, although this was summer, and, therefore, the dawn came very early, the town of Tyndal was already beginning to stir.

Slowly, with infinite effort, Reata rolled himself over until he could adjust his body so that the fine, full focus of the light gathered by the shaving glass dropped exactly on a turn of the rope across his chest, where he could watch it. The heat began to bite the fabric of the rope at once. The focus with which it had fallen on the rug of the room had been quite inexact; this perfect pinhead focus was hotter than fire, and instantly the surface of the rope commenced to glow.

He could blow down on that glowing point and increase the burning. If only it would flame, the rope would soon part. But there were two difficulties. The sun was rising, and, therefore, the focus of the light from the glass was altering slowly, so that Reata had to keep shifting his body closer to the mirror, an infinitesimal bit at a time. Besides, as the heat grew greater, it burned not only the rope, but also Reata's shirt, then his flesh. The pain seemed to him to be drilling straight through his body.

He could not help remembering how he had threatened the Overland Kid the night before. Now the same agony he had promised was being given to him. Would the smell of the burning rope rouse the colonel? For the drifting smoke filled the room with thin wreaths, and some of these passed right before the face of the colonel.

He groaned. He stirred. He half lifted a hand, and the shotgun slid a little farther forward to the edge of his knees.

Then, with a very light, dull, popping sound, the rope parted across the breast of Reata. The pain continued, for the cloth of his shirt was now in a glow that was spreading fast. But two or three wriggles caused the rope to loosen in all its length, and a moment later he was free to sit up, to clutch at his shirt, and put out the spot of fire, and then to rise to his feet.

XV

"Free"

He picked up the coils of rope that had bound him. Then he lifted the shotgun from Lester's lap, and the removal of the weight caused the colonel to rouse with a slight start. His great, vague eyes blinked for an instant before he could appreciate that picture of his own shotgun being pointed at him by the hands of Reata.

"Steady, partner," said Reata, "we've both had a good sleep, but now it's time for me to go. I think you'd better have another nap, though. So I'm going to fix you so that you won't slide out of your chair. If you budge," he added sternly, "or if you try to yell, I'll lift off your head with what's inside this shotgun!"

The colonel opened his mouth, but no sound issued from it, while Reata tied him with a cruel firmness into that big, comfortable chair.

"Now," said Reata, "I'll have to borrow this first-aid kit of yours. This bandage, you see, and a bit of this salve, because I seem to have been sleeping too close to the fire."

He had his shirt off and the bandage around his chest in a moment. When he was dressed again, he wadded the colonel's own handkerchief into a knot and thrust it between his teeth as a gag.

"What a fool you are, Lester!" said Reata. "What a fat-faced fool! What keeps me from rapping you over your hollow head, except that you happen to have Agnes for a daughter? *Adiós,* Colonel!"

He unlocked the door and stepped into the hall. It was empty. So were the stairs, and the lobby below. By the back door, Reata stepped out into the young morning and went around to the livery stable. Through the rear door of that he entered, and little Rags was instantly jumping about his feet in a silent frenzy of joy. Then the roan mare was pricking her ears and wriggling her nostrils in a silent whinny of greeting, like a whisper.

On the edge of the manger, Reata laid a little heap of gold dust taken from his money pouch. It was not much, but it was enough to pay the livery bill five times over. After that, he saddled the mare at his leisure, and rode out behind the town and around it toward the open country.

He could see the Gypsy camp in the distance, with the smoke of the morning fire beginning to mount up in a straight line through the windless air. He would have been glad to pause an instant there to assure them of his safety, but he could not spare even the time for this. For the possibility was—a thin possibility at that—that the Overland Kid and his crew were still near the town, and, if so, each moment from now on counted with a doubled value.

He struck out in a shallow semicircle until he came to the trail of the wagon. On that he dropped Rags, and the little dog led him straight on toward the town, across a hollow, and finally off to the right, toward a group of trees. Inside that grove, Reata found the wagon, with most of the hay thrown off it. Beyond the trees there was a very dim trail over hard ground, on which he dropped Rags again, and so it was that he came within calling distance of the waters of the creek, and still Rags went scurrying on toward the trees that screened the banks. Just before them a horse whinnied, short and soft.

So Reata called in Rags, with a wave of his arm. With the little dog sniffing the way before him, on foot Reata penetrated the wood, with Sue gliding noiselessly behind him, and, presently, he came on a semicircular clearing about a shack that stood on the very bank of the stream, with a pair of mules in harness before the house, and six saddle horses.

He had come in the very nick of time, if anything were to be done, for he saw Gene Salvio and Harry Quinn and Dave Bates, in turn, carrying out those familiar little chamois bags and loading them onto three of the horses. When that was ended, Bates remained with the horses, calling over his shoulder: "You gents figger out what's going to be done with the two stiffs. Dump 'em in the creek, is my idea!"

"Your idea's all wrong," said the voice of the Overland Kid, sounding dimly from inside the shack. "We ought to burn down the shack. That'll rub away any identification marks. And unless those are wiped out, the law's goin' to be down on us for a double killing one of these days."

A warm argument started inside the shanty at this. But Dave Bates shrugged his shoulders at the noise and began to roll a cigarette. He was in the act of sealing the wheat-straw paper when a thin whisper sounded over his head. A wisp of shadow struck down across his eyes. Then the thin line of Reata's rope jerked his arms to a helpless rigidity against his sides and, as he fell, jerked heavily back, and before he could cry out, a flying loop of the rope fastened with strangling force around his throat.

He was not allowed to strangle, however. The flying hands of Reata loosed that lariat from its grip, and, snatching a rope from the nearest saddle, he instantly secured and made Bates helpless. Dave Bates whispered: "What a fool you are, Reata . . . wastin' time, when one jab of your knife would make me still enough."

It was like Dave Bates, Reata thought, to have such a stinging bit of advice on his lips at such a time. Of the lot of them, Bates was the best. There was something decent about the little man. Then, still on one knee, Reata looked up to see the Overland Kid in the doorway of the shack, looking straight at him, and in the act of drawing a gun.

He was finished, he knew. For a fellow like the Kid would not miss at such a point-blank distance. Yet it was strange that the movement of whipping out the gun was not completed. For a terrible half second the two men stared at one another, and then the Kid turned his back on the outdoors, and, blocking the doorway with his heavy shoulders, and big body, began to say: "Burning is the only way. You can see that, Salvio."

"Aye," Salvio was answering. "Maybe burning is the only way. But maybe we oughta put the buddies up there in the attic, and besides, here's old Dan Foster that can talk about us all."

"Dan's given his word not to talk, and I'll take his promise," said the Overland Kid.

Reata, stunned, bewildered, was catching up the lead ropes of the horses. Then, drawing them away after him, on the verge of the clearing, one gesture brought the roan mare to him. Mounting her, he fastened to her saddle the end of the last lead rope. Six horses were now strung out to the side and behind him.

Every step was taking them out of sight among the trees when he heard a screaming voice behind him: "The horses! The horses! Hi, it's Reata! Rifles! Salvio, look!"

It seemed to Reata that he could never get the led horses into a gallop. They walked, they trotted, at last they were in an easy canter. They left the woods. They stretched their legs in a longer and a longer stride, widened the distance between them and the edge of the woods—and then the rifles began.

Salvio, Harry Quinn, and the Overland Kid had run out

from the trees, and, lying flat, they opened fire with their guns.

But the distance was great, and now the ground dropped away into a dry-bottomed draw that sheltered Reata and his horses completely. The firing had ended. Only, out of the distance, he heard the savage, despairing yells of Salvio and Harry Quinn.

XVI

"At Jumping Creek"

Decker, round-faced and empty-eyed, and Dillon, white-headed and tiny and stern, faced one another across the mahogany sheen of the long table in the president's office of the Decker & Dillon Bank. Six other men sat with them, men with a grim and determined look which they shared in common. For the Decker & Dillon Bank was passing into the hands of the receivers.

Decker was silent. His life was wiped out. He was too close to sixty to begin again. He felt that he had the form and the look of a man, but that there was nothing whatever inside him.

As for Dillon, he was closer to seventy than to sixty. It was not the end of life for him. It was actual death and burial when he walked out of the bank and stepped onto the street. But he made a little speech. "It goes to show," he said, "that men are fools when they work a big thing on a small margin. We needed a hundred thousand to meet everything outstanding. We had twice that much in the vaults in pure gold, and you know it.

"We had a business running, too, that would bring us in sufficient profits, inside of two years, to meet every debt we owe. But you fellows don't want us to have that chance. You want the business for yourselves, and you're going to get it. But what I tell you is that you take over the bank and the curse I put on it. If a life of honest labor. . . ."

A man at the foot of the table said: "Dillon, you know that we've made up our minds. There's no use gabbing and being sentimental. Matter of fact, we would have acted before this, if Colonel Lester hadn't been gadding about the country, chasing a will-o'-the-wisp. Now we've determined on action. Lester himself will be back here before long, but we have the power and the authority to act without him. If you'll finish your speech, we'll get down to details."

"You see, George?" said Dillon, looking with a strange smile at Decker.

"I knew what it would be," answered Decker. "We might as well wind things up. Go ahead with them. I'll sign where I'm told to . . . and there's the end."

It was at this time that a stir came in the outer rooms of the bank, and then a murmur, and suddenly a shouting of people all along the street. One word came clearly through the thick walls to the ears of the listeners.

"Reata!"

"What's that?" asked one of the bank's creditors, jumping up from his chair. "Reata? That's the name of the rascal that Lester has been wild-goose chasing all over the range. Don't tell me that he's managed to bring the fellow in."

Here a hand knocked heavily on the door, and, when it was unlocked and opened, the cashier stood on the threshold, babbling vague sounds, brandishing his two hands.

"The gold? Returned?" shouted Decker.

He managed to get out of his chair, but his knees were bending so that he could not budge. It was little old Dillon who got out of the room into the corridor beyond and found shouting men who were carrying into the bank small chamois sacks, the leather curiously discolored and streaked and stained with green.

Twenty-one of those sacks were piled on the floor of the

bank. Old Dillon stood over them, with his arms folded tightly across his breast, for he felt that otherwise his heart would break with swelling joy. He kept a terrible scowl on his forehead, and then ran his glittering eyes over the faces of his mute, gaping creditors. At last he was able to point to the door. "The gold has come back," he said, "you'll all have your bills paid. But now . . . get out of my sight and get out of my bank."

Afterward, as the crowds thickened in the street, they were able to find out who had brought the stuff back—Reata.

But where had he gone? No man could tell. While the search for him went on, Colonel Lester and tall Steve Balen rode with their men into the main street of Jumping Creek. Agnes Lester was with them, high-headed, and very strangely smiling, so that her father could not endure to look into her pretty face.

Before they had gone two blocks, they had heard the story. The lost gold had been returned. And the very man they had been pursuing as the thief had brought it back.

The colonel, when he heard this, looked about him wildly, as though all sense, all truth, all logic had vanished from the world. "But this is not possible!" he shouted at last. "An infernal thief . . . a criminal . . . a scoundrel who has actually dared to defy . . . who has escaped twice from. . . . But his profession is stealing, and he *can't* return the gold he has taken away! It isn't sense. It means nothing. It. . . ."

Steve Balen ventured to interrupt him.

"He's made fools of us all," said Balen. "He's slapped our faces for us, damn it, and now we can like it or lump it. I reckon that your daughter knew he was a straight shooter all the time."

"She? How could she know? Agnes, I have half a mind. . . ."

I feel as though I'd go mad. My wits are turning. Agnes, what *do* you know about this fellow . . . this Reata . . . this sneak thief and juggler and . . . what do you know about him?"

"I haven't talked an hour with him in my entire life," said the girl. "How could I know anything about him?" But she began to laugh, and she kept on laughing from time to time, as though there were a ceaseless supply of bright happiness in her that could not be exhausted by words, or even by laughter itself.

There was a greater chance for the colonel to be outraged and infuriated when, late in the day, he left Jumping Creek, where all men were still vainly searching for Reata beyond the town. At his ranch, he sat beneath the trees, watching the sun burn lower in the west and begin to fill the sky with gold, with his daughter beside him, and Tom Wayland, also—big Tom Wayland pretending that he did not notice the looks of scorn that the girl freely gave him whenever he glanced her way— there, into the midst of the peaceful family circle, as it were, Reata suddenly appeared in their midst.

At one moment there had been nothing near, and suddenly Reata had stepped out from behind a tree and was saying: "Good evening, Colonel. I've come to speak to Miss Lester, with your permission."

"What permission?" exclaimed the colonel. "I've a good mind to. . . . My permission, you say, you impertinent young scoundrel? Speak to Agnes? Why, I'll have you. . . ."

Agnes Lester walked right by her father and stood between him and the other.

"What is it, Reata?" she said.

The colonel grew dizzy, and almost fainted when he saw how close she stood to this man and, with her head tilted back, smiled up at him.

This weakness prevented Lester from interrupting, and that was why he was able to hear Reata saying: "I've come to say good bye. I thought I could say something else, but I can't. The man who wants my scalp is pretty apt to get it, unless I move fast and keep on moving. I've been traveling in a pretty shifty way recently, for that matter, but he's made men and horses grow up in my way before and behind. So I've got to run and keep on running. He'll chase me still, the way he's chased me before. But maybe one day I'll shake clear of him and have a chance to see you again, far off, safely."

The colonel, having made out this speech, was even willing to be still, but he almost had an apoplectic stroke when he saw his daughter deliberately turn with Reata and walk away with him through the trees toward the front of the house. At this, Colonel Lester gasped, and he would have lurched in pursuit had not white-faced Tom Wayland gripped and held him.

"It's best to leave them alone," said Wayland. "Anything that speaks against him just now . . . anything that tries to come between them . . . why, it would make Agnes leave home and go barefoot after him around the world. Be quiet, please . . . she'll be back here soon enough."

While the colonel was still gasping and wheezing, she did, in fact, come slowly back through the trees, her head bowed, and so she went silently up into the house.

Even Colonel Lester, who could not see many things, could understand that Tom Wayland had been right.

As for Reata, he went over the first hill as swiftly as Sue could streak it in order to put one landmark between him and the girl. And in the hollow beneath that hill he was stopped by a rider with a raised arm.

It was the Overland Kid, who said to him tersely: "Reata, I'm busting away from Dickerman. I wanna quit the job with him, and there ain't a thing in the world that I'd rather do than go along with you, if you'll have me."

Bewilderment closed the lips of Reata.

"You're a better man, and a bigger man, and a righter man than me," said the Overland Kid, "but it seems to me I might be useful to you . . . I'd try to be square. Would you give me a chance?"

Reata swung the mare close to the Overland Kid and gripped his hand hard. He was still holding it as he said: "Partner, I'd rather have you along than any man I know in the world. But it's no good. You and I were two little rats trying to scamper away from the king of the rats. If we run together, we'll both sure be found. They say that no man ever gets away from Pop Dickerman, but I'm going to try. Later on you'll hear whether I'm dead or living. Then you can make your own try to get free. But the two of us together would be ten times as easy for him to catch as one man alone. But, if you ever get far enough away from him, come and find me, and I'll be mighty happy to be your partner, Overland."

"Do you mean it?"

"Aye."

"All right, then," said the Kid. "I can wait, then, and take my own turn."

Afterward, he sat his horse and watched the roan mare canter smoothly up the hollow, and then over the next rise, where the image showed for a moment like a little black morsel being drawn into a vast conflagration, for the sky was on fire.